Ruthless
HEIR

USA TODAY BESTSELLING AUTHOR
FAITH SUMMERS

Ruthless

HEIR

Chapter ONE

Harper

I'M NOT DRUNK ANYMORE. BUT I WISH I WERE.

Being drunk transported my mind away from this absolute disaster.

It's nearly 4 a.m. and here I am, sitting in a cell in the county jail.

Kudos to those who said I'd end up locked up one day for that temper of mine. *Congratulations, you were right.*

Sitting on a metal slab that's supposed to be a seat for several hours within the restraints of my jail cell has taught me a life lesson I'll never forget.

Apart from being numb from the waist down, the only thing I've been able to do is stare at the damning concrete wall before me.

The wall is no bigger than that of the walk-in closet I had when I was a little girl. But to me it feels just as foreboding as the Great Wall of China.

The only difference is my cell wall isn't centuries-old famous, and it has remnants of scratch marks and lewd graffiti scattered across it. Like silent testimonies left behind by desperate inmates confined within this small, sparse space.

"What's *your* name, sweet thing?" comes the rusty voice of the guy in the cell to my right.

The man stinks of alcohol and is covered in so much filth I can't tell how old he is. With his matted hair, bloodshot eyes, and missing teeth, he nails the homicidal maniac look big time.

I probably don't look, or smell, much different.

My honey-blonde hair is now a dirty blonde. My tank top and jeans are stained with beer and greasy bar food. I look and feel like hell from drinking too much. And honestly, that rank smell could be coming off me.

"I promise I can make all your dreams come true, *hot stuff*." He makes a smacking sound with his mouth as if he's calling a dog.

The crazy to my left has the same demented vibe as missing-teeth guy, but he doesn't say anything. All he does is watch me.

Watch me the way a stalker would when they've found a fresh victim, a college-aged girl like me.

Cursing my life for the millionth time, I ignore them both, the way I have for the last four mind-sucking hours.

Is this kick-my-ass karma?

This...

Me, being thrown in the county jail when I was trying to get my things back from my thieving landlord.

Okay. I'll be reasonable. I'll admit the jail part of my conundrum *is* my fault.

Yes, I was drunk, and no, there was no way I was going to get away with setting fire to my landlord's car. But even though I was plastered off my face, it was *his* fault.

That asshole kicked me out of my apartment without notice.

After a twelve-hour shift at the bar, and the stupid drinking contest I got suckered into, I went home only to find my things had been tossed outside.

I'd already let my landlord know I'd catch up with rent at the end of the month. But still the few belongings I'd brought with me from UCLA, including my violin, were in a heap on the curb like a pile of useless crap.

That was mean-spirited and terrible enough, but when I discovered he'd kept my laptop and my mother's wedding ring I saw blazing red.

My mom's ring may only be worth five grand but it's as priceless to me as a Ming vase.

I never sold it when I hit rock bottom and ate ramen for a couple of months.

I never sold it when I was in danger from the loan shark I'd never be able to repay.

I never even thought of selling it when I needed money to leave UCLA and get far, far away.

That ring is the only thing I have left from my mother and the last connection to my father. That's why I lost my mind and torched my lousy landlord's car after he refused to return my things.

And... that's how I ended up behind bars with a five-thousand-dollar bail bond hanging over my head.

Before I can leave, the bail money would need to be paid, along with the rent arrears and damages to my landlord's car. Knowing that asshole he'll also most likely press charges.

My heart tightens and twists when I think of how much trouble I'm in. I've always been strong but this is way too much, and I'm all tapped out.

I can't help feeling like this is some kind of punishment from the universe for screwing up my second chance at life.

A second chance that was given to me four years ago after a car accident that robbed me of six years' worth of memories. To this day ninety percent of those memories are still locked away in my mind.

Eight months after the accident my father died and my stepmother took all his money. She left my brother, Josh, and me with nothing. We went from riches to rags with my father's last breath.

I was still in physio and at high school when Dad died, but

I was given yet another chance in a hopeless situation when Josh stepped up to take care of me.

He got leave from the Navy and practically nursed me back to health. Then he made sure I was still able to go to college to pursue my dreams of studying music and playing the violin.

Things were good until I started my sophomore year and I made one mistake I can't take back.

I fell for a sweet-talking, manipulative, dangerous man.

A dangerous man who left me with a $100,000 debt to a loan shark while he serves a life sentence in prison for murder.

All the red flags were there with Nick but I chose not to see them.

So, this *could* be karma kicking my ass.

Now I sit here in jail waiting for the only person I never wanted to disappoint—*Josh*.

I could have called Beth, but the bail fee stopped me. She's the only one who would have understood and shoved tonight's disaster under the rug that covers all my other secrets.

I hated calling Josh and owning up to my lies, because he thought I was in Europe for my summer internship.

Josh went big-brother crazy when I told him where I was and what I did. He was so angry I thought he might reach through the phone and shake me until I shattered. And when he picks me up, he still might.

He must hate me so much right now.

No. Think positively.

It's Josh. He would do anything for me. And he has.

It's a shame he had to find out that I'm here in Nowheresville, Massachusetts. He didn't know I'd left UCLA over three months ago, and he still doesn't know about my huge, huge debt. *And I'll never tell him.*

My plan is to attend NYU for my last year of college. I came to this little town to get a job and make payments on that bleed-me-dry loan. But nothing has worked out the way I planned.

I never got paid for the first job I had here. Later I found out they were being investigated for scamming new workers.

My job at the bar just started but I'm sure I've lost that, too, because my asshole landlord's brother is my boss.

The door at the end of the cell block opens. I stand and pray that Josh is here and the guard is coming to get me out.

The big, burly guard walks in but my hopes flatline and my soul hits the floor when I see the tall, handsome man following behind him.

In absolute, utter disbelief, I stare at Asher Le Blanche. My brother's best friend. Aka the worst person I could ever see right now.

Dressed in a charcoal-gray Kiton suit that emphasizes his solid muscles, Asher walks with the intimidation of a black panther, radiating the kind of power that makes my lungs lock.

Despite the ungodly, middle-of-the-night hour, he maintains his Apollo looks and elegance even here in this grimy little county jail. An unfitting setting for the next heir to the Le Blanche Empire.

His thick dark brown hair is slicked back as if it was styled for a Tom Ford advert.

His sculpted jawline and cheekbones are enhanced by a five o'clock shadow and his glacier blue eyes are chef's knife sharp. Sharp and clear as a sheet of ice. And just as cold.

Asher Le Blanche is the kind of man who commands attention when he enters a room. Although he's a world class jerk-off who could chew you up and swallow you whole on a daily basis, the magazines call him one of the most desirable bachelors in America.

To me he was the guy I was obsessed with since I was ten.

Unfortunately, I was cursed to remember that. Along with how I snuck into his room on the night of my eighteenth birthday and waited for him, *naked* under his sheets. I wanted him to be my first.

I don't know what stroke of madness came over me to offer myself to him like a sacrificial virgin. But I did.

I'm brave that way. Here's my problem: I. Don't. Think.

On that night I was Persephone, Goddess of Spring, and I wanted him to be my Hades.

His rejection still echoes off the fragile walls of my heart.

The foolish mistake of throwing myself at my brother's best friend is what sent me fleeing into the accident.

My only reprieve is that he doesn't know I remember. I kept that secret to myself.

It's been three long years since I last saw him. No way could I imagine that our reunion would be this nightmare.

I'm mortified Asher knows the crazy thing I've done, that I'm in jail, and I have no job, nowhere to live, and he has to rescue me.

But the worst thing? Seeing him still sends ripples of desire racing through my body.

"You're free to go." The guard unlocks my cell. "You're lucky your friend here came when he did. Another five minutes and you would have spent the whole day with us."

I say nothing. It's best I don't.

I look up at Asher and his eyes lock on mine. His expression shifts from disgust to disapproval to disappointment.

My pride shrivels to nothing under the rocks clogging my throat.

Why does fate continue to be so cruel to me?

With my dignity in scraps, I step out of the cell and Asher moves closer.

He's six foot six but under the weight of his scrutiny he seems as colossal as a Titan rising from the depths of the ocean. Or the Underworld.

At five foot four I always feel like a gnat next to him. And he always treats me like one.

"Josh couldn't make it." That's all he says in a rich deep baritone laced with power and dominance. He always sounds like that when he's angry.

"Thank you for coming to get me." My voice sounds mechanical and forced, because it is. I don't *want* to speak to him but I know

I *have* to. He's here and he would have paid for everything. "It must have taken hours to drive from the Hamptons."

"Three hours. Thanks for that."

"I didn't mean for any of this to happen. I—"

"Let's just go."

The guard waves us forward, and we follow.

I walk past missing-teeth guy, who blows kisses at me, and stalker guy, who continues his creepy stare.

I'm considering whether I might have it easier if I stay in jail with them.

Being with the crazies would be less humiliating than going anywhere with Asher.

We're led to the front desk where Jethro, my asshole landlord, is waiting for us. I'm not surprised he's here.

The sight of him leaning against the wall with his mottled bald head and pot belly hanging out makes my stomach churn and burn. But I notice there's something different about his worn-down expression. It looks like fear.

Fear that doubles when his gaze flicks to Asher.

The guard heads behind the counter and Asher walks ahead of me toward Jethro.

"Did you box up Harper's things?" Asher uses his boardroom-stern voice.

"Over there." Jethro points to a large brown box on the floor by the visitor's chairs.

I look up at Asher. "You got him to pack my things?"

"Of course."

My heart softens and for a fleeting moment an unexpected comfort sparks in my soul. I haven't felt safe in such a long time it feels foreign to me.

"The laptop had better be there." Asher squares his shoulders and looks Jethro up and down.

"It's there."

"And the ring?"

Jethro hands Asher Mom's ring. I'm shocked he didn't already pawn it.

Asher turns to me. "Think you can hold on to it this time?"

I want to slap him hard, but I take the ring when he holds it out, grateful to have it back.

"They should've kept you locked up for what you did to my car." Jethro half-lunges at me. With his wide nostrils flaring he looks like a warthog.

"You should've been locked up too, you miserable thief," I snap back.

"I'm the thief? You little bit—"

Asher grips Jethro's shoulder and gets up in his face. "Don't finish that sentence. I already cut you a nice check. Now back the hell off and don't mess with me. You won't like it if you do."

Jethro shudders and his boss-man attitude dissolves into nothing.

Asher looks at me and cocks his head toward the door. "I'll take you to Josh's place."

"Okay."

The three-hour drive with him to New York will be excruciating but I don't have a choice, so I nod. He picks up the big box as if it weighs nothing, and we leave.

We step out into the cold, dark parking lot. I'm freezing in my tank top and jeans, though I act like I'm fine.

Asher's ritzy red Maybach stands out like a Rolls Royce in a sea of crappy cars. It looks as out of place as he does with me.

He puts my box into the trunk then opens the door on the passenger side.

I get in and the first thing I notice is that the car smells exactly like him. Like expensive cologne, European leather, and power.

While I wait for him to get in I do a mental check of all the things I owe him.

Payment for bail.

Payment for my rent.

Payment for the damage I stupidly did to Jethro's car.

When Asher slides into the driver's seat the tension between us feels like it might combust.

We pull out of the parking lot onto the road and he cuts me a hard glance.

"Did you seriously have to torch your landlord's car?" His voice rumbles like thunder around us.

"He took Mom's ring. He deserved worse."

"I'm aware. But you're insane. Arson is a felony." His voice rises and his face reddens, making me feel chastised. "You can't go around setting fire to people's cars. You're lucky that ingrate took my money to repair the car and drop the charges."

"I'll pay you back as soon as I can."

Asher whips me another scathing stare. "With what money?"

"I'll find a way. Rob a bank? Sell my eggs?" I hear my words and wish I could mop them up like beer spilled on the bar, but I act confident and volley a steely stare back at him.

"No egg selling. The world doesn't need any more brainless Harper St. Johns trying to right wrongs." His jaw clenches, making him look even meaner. "What the hell are you doing in this town anyway?"

A tremor of dread shoots through me. I have to lie to keep my secret from him. "I had to get away from L.A."

"Why didn't you go to New York? Aren't you transferring to NYU?"

I roll my eyes at him. "I almost forgot Josh tells you everything."

"Of course he does. We've been friends for over twenty years. So, why the small town?"

"I'm still on the waiting list for housing."

"You could have lived with Josh."

"I needed to be on my own."

"Josh is worried sick about you." Asher speeds along the dark shadowy road. "Everyone believes you're in Europe. Why would you lie like that?"

Because I had to. "I didn't want to bother Josh." That's the truth, too. A half-truth. "He's done enough for me. I wanted him to spend time with Lisa. She's only seen him once this year. He loves being in the Navy but since he made lieutenant his assignments have gotten longer."

I thought my answer was a reasonable one, but Asher's expression becomes stonier.

"When you called Josh from jail he was in Florida to propose to Lisa. He tried to be here for you, but he couldn't get a flight."

Icy fingers of guilt slide down my throat. "Oh my God. I feel so bad."

"Good. You should feel bad. Your brother was willing to trash his plans, postpone proposing, all because of your immature ass."

My ribs squeeze as if ropes are wrapped around them, and everything inside me feels tight and hot at the same time.

"You don't have to make me feel worse." I try to keep the quiver out of my voice but fail.

"I was the one who drove three hours to this grubby little town to bail you out of jail. So, yes, you should feel bad."

My blood heats, fueled by exhaustion, frustration and shame. "I'm sorry the town was unfitting for a billionaire like you with a silver spoon shoved up his ass."

I know I'm pissing him off and I don't care. I'm done being nice. He can take his kick-a-girl-while-she's-already-down attitude right back to hell.

The despicable look he gives me should make him appear monstrous in the moonlight. But damn it, he still looks like Apollo.

"Don't test me, Harper." He uses the same stern tone he took with Jethro. "You know you're wrong. After all you've been through in L.A. with your ex, you shouldn't have been so stupid."

I hate that he's right. And that he knows about Nick.

Since Josh tells Asher *everything*, I assume he knows Nick was a thief, a con artist, and a murderer.

"You need to be more careful. In the last three years you've made bad choice after bad choice."

The additional blow makes me think he's also talking about the past.

The past with him when I was eighteen, and all the reasons he didn't want me.

"Yeah, sure." I keep my answer short and emotionless, an attempt to show I'm over him and over this conversation, too.

"Any other bad choices I should know about?"

"No. None." I look away, hoping he doesn't ask me anything more.

I stare out the window, wondering what the hell I'm going to do.

I may not be in jail anymore, but I'm still trapped.

Chapter
TWO

Asher

WE'RE AT JOSH'S PLACE NOW. THE DRIVE HERE WAS horrendous. The last two and a half hours pure silence, pure hell.

"Good night." Harper tosses the words over her shoulder with a grudge in her tone. She makes her way up the stairs, her long ponytail bouncing with every step, and I try not to notice her shapely legs or her lush, round ass.

"Good night," I answer but she doesn't look back at me. I didn't expect her to.

Maybe we shouldn't talk tonight. Besides, I can't stand those jade-green eyes of hers staring back at me with so much hate.

I'm a bastard at the best of times. But even I have to admit that I ripped into her too hard.

I couldn't help it. What she did was insane. All of it—going to Massachusetts and lying about Europe, then getting in trouble with her landlord.

Harper's wild, ballsy streak has always fascinated me, but none of that sounds like her. Neither does getting involved with a murderer like her ex.

This isn't the first time I've felt that life went to hell for her after my rejection.

Her bad luck began with the accident. Not a day goes by when I don't think

about it or blame myself.

After I rejected her she ran from me and ended up in a head-on collision that took her memories and almost her life.

Honor stopped me from taking her in my bed that night. Honor to my best friend.

That night feels like a dirty secret between us. Except only I remember her offering herself to me.

Maybe it's better I'm left with the memory and she isn't. At least that's what I keep telling myself. Then I feel like a coward for thinking so.

I shouldn't feel thankful Harper doesn't remember what happened between us. And I'll always feel ashamed that I left out the real reason she was at my place when I told Josh what happened.

On top of that I'm an asshole for holding on to the memory of her naked body spread out against my satin sheets. That image never *ever* left my mind. It renewed itself tonight the moment I saw her in the jail cell.

It's still there now, along with the reminder that Harper St. John is Josh's little sister. She's still eight years younger than me and absolutely, positively, completely off limits.

Those things are still true even though I'm aware she's more beautiful now than ever. The few years we've spent apart have given her the face of a goddess and the sort of body that could rule a man.

Harper's long gone from the top of the stairs but I continue staring. The same odd feeling from earlier pulls at my gut, whispering to me that she was lying.

When she said there was nothing more to tell me something

felt off. The same something that feels off with her entire story about going to Massachusetts.

As a senior financial analyst it's my job to know when something is wrong.

The same wrong feeling I get when I know an investment is not worth my time is spiking my nerves now.

I'd bet my entire billion-dollar fortune and the damn silver spoon she thinks is shoved up my ass that her friend Beth knows what's going on.

I could go to Beth and try to get the intel from her, but it's not my place.

I also could have pushed Harper but I know she wouldn't have cracked.

I'll always help Josh whenever he needs me. However, there's a line I can't cross when it comes to Harper. The respect privacy line.

At least I know she's safe. Now I can get back to my own problems with my father and my waning future at Le Blanche Global, my family's multi-billion dollar investment and hedge fund company.

As great as my father is, I know if I don't find a wife in the next few months I won't have the future I deserve at the company.

Then it will be my life that will go straight to hell.

The following night Josh drops by looking like he's been through all the wars of this world.

His usually neat black hair is a ruffled mess, his beard looks like a bird's nest, and dark circles surround his eyes.

I was working out downstairs in my home gym when he arrived, so we headed back down there to talk.

We sit on the treadmill and I toss him a beer from the mini fridge. He catches it and glances at the bench press across from us with the weights stacked to a hundred and sixty pounds.

"Geez, are you sure you can manage all that?" He looks me over, sizing me up.

"Of course. Can't you?"

He laughs out loud as if my dig was the funniest thing he's ever heard. "I can lift that awake and asleep."

We've had this running joke about who's the strongest since high school, when we started to match each other in height and build.

"Need me to spot you?" Josh cocks his head toward the weights again then opens his beer and takes a swig.

"You look too wiped out to spot anyone. And I'm sure you didn't drop by to razz me about how much weight I can press."

"No. I owe you for picking up Harper last night."

"No worries. How is she?"

"Don't get me started. She pissed me the hell off, but I had to fly back to check on her."

"I knew you would."

"I owe you money, too, bro. I transferred the fee for her bail and the rent arrears to your account. I need to know how much more you spent."

"Don't worry about it." I grab a towel and wipe the sweat off my face. "It's cool."

"Come on, Asher, don't do that to me." He gives me a worn-out big-brother smile. "You must have paid a hell of a lot to get that guy to drop the charges and cover the damages on his car."

I know Josh is doing okay now, but he doesn't have an extra twenty-five thousand dollars to drop on me. "Consider it an early wedding present."

"That's one very expensive present, but thanks. I guess all I have to do now is propose to my girl."

"You didn't propose?"

His shoulders sag and he shakes his head. "I've rearranged it for this weekend. But the good news is Lisa has no idea what I'm up to, so I can still surprise her."

"I'm sure she'll say yes."

"Yeah. She's wanted to get married for a long time." He looks proud, but seconds later the haggard expression returns. "I have a huge favor to ask. One that I shouldn't."

That doesn't sound good. The last time he asked me for a favor like that I ended up babysitting a fucking pig. It was our high school rival football team's mascot. He and some of our other friends had stolen it. "What's going on?"

"Harper's timing for being rebellious couldn't be worse. I thought she'd be in Europe for the next two months, then she'd live on campus at NYU. But she's here now, my lease is up next week, and I just got confirmation of my new position. I'm being deployed on a submarine mission for the next nine months."

"*Nine months*? Whoa." That's the longest he's ever been away on a submarine mission.

"I know. But when I get back, I'll be in charge of a special unit in North Carolina, so I'll be working at the base most of the time. I'll still have to travel overseas, but not as often. It will be good for my marriage."

"That's a lot to digest, but good for you for getting a promotion."

"Thank you."

"Now, what's the favor?" I straighten and give him a thin gaze.

"Harper. Could she stay with you for a few months? She got turned down for housing and there's nothing near campus that won't cost my entire month's salary."

I'm still stuck on the first words he said and I'm sure I look dumbfounded.

"*Me*? You want her to stay with *me*?"

"I promise it will only be for a few months. Just until she gets campus housing. I swear she won't cause any trouble."

I toss him a look filled with so much skepticism he gives me a big grin.

"Okay. We both know my sister *is* trouble. But I really need your help, Asher. The shit from last year with her ex really messed her up. And I swear she's still not completely healed from the accident."

At the mention of the accident guilt tugs on my insides, melting my resolve.

"I need her to stay with someone I can trust." He keeps his gaze trained on me.

Trust. It's strange he should say that. I remember a time when I was *sure* he didn't trust me around Harper. I understood why.

I was the ultimate playboy and Josh was my partner in crime. Having a firsthand view of what I was like with women, he knew me.

Years ago, I foolishly slipped up when Josh caught me looking at Harper.

What followed next was a scathing warning to stay away from her that I'll *never* forget. The harsh words he spoke that day told me he would never approve of me being with her, much less trust me around her.

That was nearly six years ago. We never spoke about that incident again and as the years flew by it seemed he was satisfied I was no longer a threat he needed to worry about.

"I need her to stay with someone who will look after her the way I would." Worry fills Josh's eyes and I realize he's asking this favor because he's desperate.

It's clear he's more worried than ever about Harper and is in a situation where he can't help her without jeopardizing his job.

Any issues we might have had in the past no longer apply because it's better to treat with the devil you know than the one you don't. And my best friend knows that I'm the devil who will always have his back.

Allowing Harper to stay with me could be the worst idea ever. Not only because of the past or the fact that she and I will probably kill each other, but because there's too much shit going on in my life.

But Josh needs me. Which means she needs me too. Agreeing to help may also give me a chance to redeem myself for the part I felt I played in Harper's accident.

"Alright. She can stay with me."

Josh sighs with the relief of a man who's just had a ton of weight lifted off his back. "Thank you. Seriously, I owe you again."

"Have you spoken to her about this yet?" *There's no way he did.* "No."

"You know she won't agree to it, right? She's going to raise hell and then some."

"I know, but she doesn't really have a choice." Josh downs the rest of his beer. "Her life is a desperate mess."

The comment pushes my previous concerns back into my mind. "Did she explain why she didn't go to Europe?"

"She said she couldn't afford the living expenses. She didn't want to ask me to pay because I've always had to help her."

Harper said similar things to me, but I still have that off-key feeling. "Maybe she can have a fresh start now."

"Yes. And I know she'll be safe with you."

"She will." That's the one solid truth I know I can promise him.

I grab my beer and take a gulp, wondering what I'm getting myself into.

"What's happening with the company? Found the next Mrs. Le Blanche yet?" Josh grins.

"No. Not yet."

"Come on, Asher." He smirks. "You have so many women to choose from. Can't you just pick one?"

"It's not that easy."

He wouldn't understand. Not anymore. In fact, I have very few people left in my world who would understand that I'm absolutely not ready for marriage. Neither do I have the desire to get married.

My brother, Hunter, got married last year and he's head over heels in love with his wife. They have a baby on the way.

My cousin Luc is the same. Married to a woman he's obsessed with and now they have a baby on the way, too. Josh is the last bachelor in my circle, but he'll be marrying Lisa.

"Asher, you're a man of many talents. I'm sure you could make it easy if you wanted to."

"Sure, except I've never wanted to get married. All my life I knew I'd have to if I wanted to become CFO of the company, as per my grandfather's terms of inheritance. Unlike most people I even knew who my wife would be."

Annoyingly, my grandfather took care of that, too and signed my life away with a contract binding me to marry his friend's grand-daughter, Priscilla De Rosa.

It may have been a bid to secure wealth between the families, but it fucked with my choice.

I managed to escape the marriage a few months back when I discovered that Priscilla was not just having a secret affair but was pregnant with another man's child.

"At least you don't have to marry Priscilla."

"Yes, but I *still* have to get married."

His brows knit and he looks like he doesn't know what more to say to me. "Have you spoken to your father?"

"He's supposed to call me in a little while. I know it's not going to be a good call. I've been dodging him for days."

The change in the company occurred last year when my father decided to hand over the New York branch to Hunter and me while he'd look after the international division. That activated the need for a new leadership structure.

Hunter at the head as CEO and me as the CFO. At thirty years old I'd be the youngest Le Blanche in the family to have such a role. *If* I get married.

"Between the marriage thing and the shit with the Fairchilds, I'm not sure which I should be worried about more," I seethe.

My father's *dear* best friend, Nigel Fairchild, owns a brokerage company that has been in partnership with Le Blanche Global for over thirty years. Nigel wants seats on the board for himself and his son, Nolan.

My father is ecstatic about the idea, but I've always hated Nigel and Nolan, so I'm completely against it.

The position on the board opened with the restructure and the passing of Archie Blackstone, an old mentor of mine. Neither Nigel nor Nolan could ever hope to fill his shoes.

"I think the Fairchilds have shady-as-fuck ulterior motives. I just can't prove it." I bite the inside of my lip. "And I can't tell a guy like my father that I have a hunch his best friend is a shifty motherfucker."

Nolan has been my fucking nemesis for as long as I can remember. He's always coveted my achievements and status to the point where he'd go out of his way to sabotage me in my own family's company.

Like what he did to me last Saturday.

I hooked up with an actress at a party, not knowing she was tied up in a federal drug investigation. The next day a scandal broke when the feds raided her home and found all manner of drugs. Then a bunch of photos of us together *in her house* surfaced on the Internet that made it look like I was part of the scandal.

Hunter and I were able to do damage control to some degree. While doing so we found evidence that suggested Nolan could have paid my publicist to get dirt on me to make me look unfit to run the company.

"There must be something you can do." Josh furrows his dark brows. "You can't let that shit slide. I have no doubt that Nolan was involved."

"I'm working on it." I won't stop until I find whatever I need to eradicate Nolan *and* Nigel. It's better if they're out of the picture completely.

Hunter and I are the next generation of Le Blanche Global. I don't think it's wise to place people on the board who could mess with us or the company in the future.

My phone buzzes on the table and I check the screen. "That's my father."

"Good luck. I'll leave you to answer that." Josh stands, crushes the can and tosses it in the trash. "Let me know what happens."

"Sure. Catch you later."

He heads out the door and I grab my phone, hoping like hell my father gives me the news I want to hear.

"Hello, Father." I imbue my voice with my usual cool confidence.

"Asher Le Blanche, you're a hard man to reach. Considering we work in the same building, on the same floor, that seems rather odd to me."

I can almost see him, the great Preston Le Blanche, sitting in his office at home still dressed in one of his well-tailored black suits at this hour. In my mind's eye I imagine the disgruntled look he usually reserves for times like this when he's pissed at me and trying to control his rage.

"I've been busy."

"So I hear."

"What's going on?" I ask as if I don't know. It's just that there are so many things to choose from, I'm not sure which he wants to talk about first: *the search for a wife, the scandal, something else, or all of the above.*

"Seriously, Asher? I can't believe you can ask me that."

"I'm trying to get a handle on everything."

"I'd love to know what that means. There's the scandal we're still trying to do damage control on and the matter of you getting married. Hunter told me that you guys felt Nolan might have had something to do with your publicist's betrayal. Why on earth would you boys think that?"

Here we go. My father is the emperor of his empire and one of the most powerful men in America but he's completely blind when it comes to the Fairchilds.

"Father, I'm sure Hunter told you that we found an email conversation between Coraline and Nolan discussing my suitability to run the company." I can't keep the anger out of my voice. Saying those words outside my head makes me realize how bad and outrageous the situation is. "Nolan asked her to keep an eye on me. Then we found evidence that she was paid by someone to follow me, take pictures of anything suspicious and send them to the paparazzi."

"Hunter has told me all of that. But the problem is there's no evidence suggesting that Nolan paid her off."

"You've got to be kidding me. You don't think that's enough?"

"I think it's unacceptable for Nolan to have contacted Coraline with such a matter and question your leadership. But until I see facts I can't put the blame on him. Definitely not when he didn't set you up for a fall. Your taste in women did that."

He's making me sound like the playboy I used to be in my early twenties. I haven't been that guy in years.

At the same time what the hell can I say? Nolan didn't set me up with the actress. I picked her and fell right into his trap.

"Father—"

"No, Asher. You need to listen to me. I have faith in you, and I have no doubt you can run the company. That will never change, no matter what anyone says. However, I have to be realistic."

"What does that mean?"

"It means I have to go by your actions."

I stifle a groan. "Father, I've been working nonstop."

"I know, but you haven't tended to the most important aspect of your future. We severed the marriage contract with Priscilla almost six months ago, yet you've made no effort to find a suitable wife. I gave you the choice of using the time wisely to explore your options but time is no longer on our side."

Again, he's right. "I still have a little over six months. I'll sort it out."

"You said that months ago. Back then I agreed but now, I'm stepping up."

"You don't have to do that." *Shit.* I don't want him to meddle with my life.

"I have other things to worry about, Asher. It's time I move on. You're not taking this seriously, so I have a solution."

"What's that?" My breath catches in my lungs, turning to lead.

I hear him take a quick breath. "I want you to consider marrying Portia Fairchild."

A boulder drops into the pit of my stomach and plummets to the floor, then my ears burn, going from hot to cold to hot again. I stand and my heart kicks up a beat, pounding as fast as if I'd just finished a ninety-minute spin class.

"*Portia Fairchild*? As in Nigel's daughter?" The female fucked-up version of Nolan. My father has clearly lost his mind.

My free hand curls into a tight fist. I want to hit something and smash the hell out of it until there's nothing left.

"Nigel and I think it makes perfect sense for the two of you to marry. Nigel and I have been friends since we were children. And you grew up with Portia. You know her."

That's why this idea sounds just as bad as driving into an active volcano at full throttle.

People think I'm ruthless and callous but Portia has been the devil incarnate since she was little. If she wasn't stealing and lying, she was physically hurting people and blaming others for her cruelty. As she got older she became the woman who'd spread her legs for the man with the deepest pockets.

"No. I won't do it." My answer is as sharp as the tip of a knife. "I'm not marrying Portia."

Father is silent. My father loathes that word—no. Only a handful of people have uttered it to him in his lifetime and lived to see their next minute unscathed.

"This is beyond outrageous," I rant. "You know how I feel about the Fairchilds, yet you want me to marry Portia. Like fuck. I'm not doing it."

"Asher, control yourself." He sounds more like the domineering leader he is and less like the understanding father I know him to be.

"No. You're not going to sign my life away like grandfather. It's unfair to shove me in that position again. Even you must see that."

He's silent again and I hope I've appealed to his better senses.

"Asher, things have reached a stage where I have to be firm. You've known what you needed to do to get the CFO position. There's no way you can disagree that you've had sufficient time."

I exhale through gritted teeth. "No, I can't disagree." *And I can't explain why I couldn't pick one woman in the sea of choices I had to marry.* I just couldn't find the right one. "I can't agree that this is right, either."

"Alright..." He pauses for a beat and drags in a breath. "Here's what we're going to do: I'll give you two weeks to find a potential wife. Two weeks will place us at the six-month mark. If you find a girl, I'll allow you three months to date then prep for marriage for the following three months."

My entire body sighs with relief. "I'll find someone and sort it all out."

"I hope for your sake that you do. You do realize you'll essentially have three months to get to know this *unknown* woman."

"I know."

"If things don't work out with her you may choose another, but you won't get any more time. If you're not ready for marriage at the end of the term and you still want the position in the company, then you'll *have* to marry Portia. Is that understood?"

"Loud and clear." This is a fucking nightmare.

"Asher, I'm allowing this because I know how you felt being tied up in the previous contract. I want you to meet someone and have the kind of relationship I have with your mother."

That might be my only saving grace. Even though my father knew we'd have to have arranged marriages he wanted us to have the real thing, like he has. I'm not sure he understands though that it's not that easy.

"I get it, Father."

"Good. I hope you can get over this distrust you have for the Fairchilds, too. I'm moving forward with putting Nigel on the board, and I'm allowing Nolan the chance to trial for a seat. As such, he'll be working on the tech company with you."

Damn it all to hell. I saw this coming. That company is exactly what they were after. It belonged to Archie. "That company is supposed to be under my care. Archie wanted me to have it."

"Don't push me, Asher. Archie left the company to *Le Blanche Global*. That means it's under my care. I just gave you a chance. After that scandal you're lucky you still have a job. If you weren't my son things would be different."

Translation—*shut the hell up or get out.*

"Fine." The Fairchilds have won this battle. I'll allow them that but it's not fucking over yet.

"I sincerely hope you can make this work."

"Of course." I try to keep the sarcasm out of my voice but know I fail. My father knows I'm agreeing because he's pushed me against a wall.

"I'll see you tomorrow."

"See you."

He hangs up and my chest caves. I allow the phone to slip from my hand and fall to the floor. A surge of anger washes over me and I shove the exercise bike to the ground.

I usually have an answer for everything, but this is shit. And it's my fault.

I had time to find a wife. If I had found one, I wouldn't have hooked up with the actress. Now I have to deal with the consequences of my actions.

In the last hour I've agreed to let Harper move in with me and it feels like I'm caught in a war with my father.

I have to figure this out.

Chapter THREE

Harper

MOVE IN WITH ASHER?

"No. Absolutely not." I shake my head so hard I feel like it's going to snap off my body and smash on the floor.

Josh pushes off the kitchen door and glares at me. His face is military stern and the warmth that previously shone in his eyes has fizzled into the air. "Harper—"

"No, Josh." I throw the cleaning towel back on the rack and step away from the sink.

He has a dishwasher but I was doing the dishes by hand to take my mind off things. I've had such a shitty day dodging calls from the loan sharks. Now this.

"Listen to me. I've done my best to sort out this situation for you." He pushes his shoulders back and puffs out his chest like we're gonna fight. "I'm not going to be in New York. I'm gonna be gone for nine months, then I'm moving to North Carolina with Lisa."

"I know, but why can't we just extend the lease here?"

"Because the ship has sailed. The landlord has already put the place on the market and he'll have people viewing it in a few days. I'd have to reapply and pay the higher cost. Also, I doubt they're gonna just rent it to me for two months when they could get someone who wants it for longer."

"We could ask. You've been here for nearly ten years. I'm sure they'd be willing to come to some agreement for two months."

"No. Because you may need it for longer. We don't know if you'll get campus housing by the time college starts."

My pulse races, a drumbeat of dread. I can't believe this is happening. Or that Asher seems to be my only option.

I gaze at my brother, knowing I'm out of options but still wanting to resist.

Josh was away for most of the day. We spoke before he went out, and of course he raised hell about last night. He said he was going to check things out regarding a place for me. I never expected him to come back with *this* crazy solution.

Live with Asher. And Asher agreed.

I'm not sure how I should feel. The natural reaction most people would feel is gratitude. I do feel that on some level but that little part of me that's still stuck in my emotions from the past feels like shit.

Josh would only ask his best friend if I could live with him because he knows he won't touch me. And Asher would only agree for the same damn reason. It's like putting flowers next to a lion.

Josh walks up to me and rests his hands on my shoulders. "Sis, Asher has plenty of space in that big old house of his and he agreed to have you stay with him. Also, staying with Asher is *free.* It means I don't have to cough up more money I need to be putting aside for Lisa and me."

Of course. And now I feel like such a jerk. He's spent thousands on me just in the last year. I shouldn't even be asking him for more just because I don't want to stay with Asher.

His eyes soften again, becoming more like the version of him I'm used to.

"It's just for a few months, Harper. Unless you have another idea, this is your best option." He nods with conviction, as if to give his words more weight.

"Alright." Although I agree, I'm going to brainstorm with Beth again when I see her tomorrow.

Her doors would be open to me if her place were bigger. She has an already cramped one-bedroom apartment. Also, I'm not too keen on staying with her because of *all* the men who frequent her home on a nightly basis. We'd all drive each other insane.

Beth knows people. Not the good kind of people, but *people*. The kind who have contacts. One of them is bound to have someplace I can stay. So that may be an option. If not, then I'll have to suck up my pride and stay with Asher.

Josh looks more at ease after hearing my acceptance. "You'll be fine at Asher's place. This is a good chance for you to cool off before college starts. I've also put two grand in your account for living expenses. I'll put some more in at the end of the month."

"No, no. You shouldn't have done that. And you can't give me any more." Listen to me talking. As if I'm in a position to turn away money. "You're right. You need to save for you and Lisa. I need to get my shit together."

"Harper, I didn't mean that to sound like I wouldn't help you."

"I know, and it didn't sound that way. I'm just telling you that I know what I need to do. I'll get a job. Something I can do for the summer and continue when college starts." I do my best to make it sound like I just need something to cover my day-to-day expenses. If only Josh knew I need so much more than that.

"Okay. But I need you to tell me if you ever get stuck. You'll be able to contact me by email. I might be delayed in responding because of a bad signal, but you know the drill."

"Thanks. And thanks for the money." I won't even contemplate spending that money on trying to find some fleabag motel. This is

New York. Anything I find, no matter how fleabag-ish, will cost an arm and a leg.

"No worries. Let's call it a night. Tomorrow is going to be a busy day. I have to spend the next few days packing before I head out to Florida for the weekend. I think we should plan to move you into Asher's by Saturday. That way I can see you off."

I nod slowly, stifling the reluctance I feel curdling in my stomach like sour milk.

I survived Nick. How is it possible that I feel more helpless than ever? I'm twenty-two and can't take care of myself. That's terrible.

There's nothing physically wrong with me, and I can't even lean on the accident which happened over four years ago to explain why I'm in such a mess.

This is all happening to me because of bad decisions. I can blame Nick all I want but I need to take some responsibility, too.

I could have left him at any point. Instead, I chose to stay even when I felt there was something up with him. Now I have to fix this mess and hope I can get my life back on track.

"Is there anything you need me to do?" Josh's soft voice pulls me from the doom of my thoughts.

"No. What about me? Can I do anything else around the apartment?"

Josh releases me and smiles. "No. Not tonight. You've cleaned up the place well." He looks around the sparkly clean kitchen then back at me. "I don't think there will be much left for the cleaners to do."

"It's the least. You've done so much for me."

"That's what I'm here for. Get some sleep, Sis. I'm exhausted and you must be, too. We'll catch up in the morning."

"Alright."

We turn off the lights and head to our rooms. But I can't sleep yet. There's too much on my mind. The stress of everything is freaking me the fuck out.

I change into a pair of tattered PJs and prop myself against the stack of pillows on my old bed. As I rest my head the swirling patterns on the ceiling greet me and when I shuffle onto my side my gaze lands on my collection of classical literature and music books on the shelf.

This apartment holds the rest of my belongings and special memories. Memories I cherish for the simple fact that I *remember* them.

I lived here throughout my senior year at high school and six more months after. I was still in rehab at the start of freshman year at UCLA, so I started in the spring semester and caught up over the summer. I don't have any other breaks in my studies, but it feels like I'm a year behind everyone else, as I'll finish college when I'm twenty-three.

Josh got this place when he was eighteen. I don't remember, but he told me he couldn't wait to move out of our family home. Clarissa, our stepmother, had been a world-class bitch who made our lives hell.

I'm glad I don't remember those parts of my life or her getting married to my father. The few months I had to deal with her after Dad's death were more than enough.

The other painful thing I don't remember is my mother's passing. After the accident I woke up from my coma still believing she was alive, but I'd lost her when I was fourteen. Mom had a rare lung disease that was incurable.

When Dad told me she was gone the pain I felt was like pouring acid into an already festering wound. Then, in the same breath, I discovered he had chronic heart failure and only had months to live.

My chest tightens at the memory, and I grab the nearest pillow to press it against me in an attempt to hold in the pain that still feels fresh.

I guess I'm thinking about my parents and the past because the version of myself that existed back then hadn't fucked up her life yet.

The worst thing I'd ever done at that point was throw myself at Asher.

On that humiliating night I poured my heart out to him, hoping for something more than friendship, only to be met with a pitying look.

He said I was like a sister to him. A *sister*. The word echoes in my mind, sharp and cold. That was when I left.

It's funny I remember running toward my car and driving away but I don't remember the actual accident.

Maybe there's a reason for that. I was told it was a head-on collision. I don't think I'd ever be able to drive again if I remembered.

I know I'm lucky to be alive. The strong part of me is trying to give me the pep talk I've fueled my mind with for years.

In a *Wonder Woman* voice it says that if I can make it through so many nightmares, I can make it through anything, including my current disaster.

I just don't know how.

I've never had to dodge loan sharks before and I've never owed anyone money.

This is my first debt. I don't even have a credit card.

Foolishly I listened to stupid Nick when he wanted us to get a house together.

We got together at the start of my sophomore year. Nick was a music manager who managed big-label bands. He intrigued me from the get go because he was almost ten years older than me, was successful, and truly swept me off my feet.

After almost a year of dating we moved in together in his apartment. Six months later he suggested buying a house together. I was so excited to own a home with him I missed all the warning signs that something was wrong.

The first red flag reared its head when he asked if I could get a loan for a deposit in my name. He said he had bad credit and would be turned down.

I thought nothing of it. I'd always had good credit and at the time had secured a six-month internship with a theater. I was part of their orchestra and my work with them would go toward my college credits.

The next red flag was who we got the loan from. I still remember Nick taking me to this dimly lit office to meet Vito. The air smelled of cheap cigars and danger. It was the kind of place you just know you shouldn't be in. But Nick said we could get a low interest loan with a higher amount.

We got seventy thousand dollars. And that led to the next red flag. The money was deposited in Nick's account.

That was the turning point for us. He was different after, controlling and volatile.

Nick started using more hardcore drugs and became violent. Violent with me. It was like the old him had been a mask the entire time and he'd unleashed the real him.

"I'm sorry. I just get angry because things are hard. I'll never hit you again," he'd say. And I believed him.

I believed him to the point where we kept adding more money to the loan in an effort to make things better—less hard. That's how it got to be as big as it is.

But none of it was used for the original purpose of buying a house.

I kept hoping for him and our situation to change when he started doing business with these investment type people. But they turned out to be just as shady and disappointing as Nick.

I felt like such a fool when the lawyers revealed Nick had spent the money on drugs, booze, and high-end prostitutes.

He was a monster.

But nothing was as bad as watching Nick murder those people at that convenience store in cold blood like a wild animal starved for blood.

Nick was acting weird before we even left the house. He also seemed to be high on shit. I didn't want to get in the car with him, but I was too scared to say anything. Now I wish I had.

All I managed to do was prep a message to send to Beth in case I needed her.

Nick took me to the convenience store and used me as a decoy. While I was paying for snacks, he pulled a gun I didn't even know he had and shot the cashier and his wife. Just like that they were gone.

One minute they were talking about their upcoming family vacation and the next they were on the ground dead, laying in a pool of blood.

While I was screaming Nick simply stepped over their bodies as if they were never real living people, then filled up his rucksack with the cash in the register. After that he grabbed me, placed his gun to my head and forced me to go with him.

Beth was the only one who knew about Nick's turn to the dark side. We had made a pact that if I ever called her and didn't start talking straight away, she was to call the police and get them to track my number.

That's what I did. And that's how I saved myself.

As Nick carried me off and drove away in his car, I feared he'd kill me too, since I saw what he did. I also feared I'd be seen as an accomplice to the murder because Nick made me look like I was helping him.

The only thing that kept me alive until the cops caught up with us trying to cross the state line was Nick's twisted idea of love for me. It was even more twisted that that night was my only way out of our bad relationship.

Luckily the police had the surveillance footage from the convenience store, so they were able to see that I was being used.

I was asked to testify against Nick, which I happily did, and as I did it, I looked him in the eye from the witness stand so he'd know I helped put him behind bars.

My phone rings on the nightstand and I nearly jump out of my skin at the sound.

I don't need to look at it to know who's calling.

I already spoke to Beth and it's late, so the only person it could be is the man I've feared speaking to for the last few months.

Vito—the loan shark.

The knots in my stomach grow tighter and the air in my lungs stalls.

Deciding to be brave, I sit up. Dodging his calls will only make things worse.

I pick up the phone, confirm it's him, then drag in a deep breath and summon all the courage I've ever had so I can speak to him.

"Hello." My voice sounds child-soft, a cautious rasp.

"I was beginning to wonder if I was ever going to speak to you again." Vito's voice is smooth but filled with a precarious edge.

"I'm sorry I haven't been able to get to your calls. I've been working hard." A half-truth mixed with a lie.

"Be that as it may, you're late. Your last payment was made three months ago. You know I don't like waiting."

"I know. It's just that with everything that happened with Nick—"

"I want my money!" His voice sounds like thunder rumbling through the phone. It ripples through the line and shakes my soul.

I swallow hard, trying to control the tremor trembling through me. "I know, Vito, I'm sorry. I just... I don't have it right now."

"That's not my problem. I've been very *understanding* about Nick." His voice dips menacingly low, the tone cutting into my core. "But I have my limits. You've only paid back twenty thousand on the loan. You still owe me a hundred grand."

"I'll get it, I swear. I just need some more time." Oh God. I'm in no position to make any promises.

"You have one month, but I want twenty g's."

"Twenty grand?" I almost choke. "I'm not going to be able to get twenty thousand dollars in a month. I was planning on paying the five thousand dollars in arrears."

"Sweetheart, you've already broken the terms of our agreement with your late payments. And there's a thing called *interest*."

"But it's twenty grand." Tears sting the back of my eyes, and I shudder from deep within my core.

"My dear Harper, you know the rules, so I hope for your sake you find a way. If you don't pay things will get... *unpleasant.*"

Fear claws up the walls of my chest, making my insides feel raw. He means he'll hurt me.

"Do you understand me?" he checks.

I nod quickly although he can't see me. "Yes, I understand."

"I'll give you the courtesy and get the boys to check and call you every week to see if you're on track. Speak soon."

He hangs up before I can answer. I don't even know what I'd say.

The air burning my lungs whooshes out and I grab the bottle of water on the side. I open it and take a gulp to soothe my throat, but it doesn't work.

I'm fucked. How in the ever-loving fuck am I supposed to find all that money in a month's time?

The answer is: I can't.

The only thing I have going for me is that Vito doesn't know I left L.A.

I'm so stupid. Moving in with Asher is the very least of my problems.

As it stands now, I may have to run again.

Chapter
FOUR

Asher

HUNTER LEANS OVER THE POOL TABLE AND LINES UP HIS shot. Luc and I watch him closely.

Hunter's a real pro at pool. Always has been. We're good, too, but not like him when he's on a winning streak.

Tonight's game is a fierce one and Hunter near enough always wins when we play pool at his house. I sense tonight will be no different.

We gathered here to let off some steam.

The last five hours have been just like old times where the three of us would get lost in a game of pool and forget the world.

At times like these we're just three guys hanging out. Brothers.

Hunter and I took Luc for a brother when he came to live with us after his parents died. So, we've been close like this for the last twenty-one years.

After a tense day at work with my father, God knows I needed a break from reality that only Hunter and Luc could provide.

Although my father and I left the conversation the other night with a mutual agreement, his cold-shouldered, standoffish behavior today made me feel like the villain. I could only imagine he must have been pissed at me because of the scandal—which is pretty much under the rug now.

I've never had any problems with my father. I didn't think I would start now after thirty years.

Hunter pulls the cue back and that effortless confidence which has earned him the nickname of the Wall Street Shark starts to solidify on his face. I can almost feel the shot coming before he makes it, the kind of move he's always pulled off whether we're in a high-stakes game or making millions on a risky trade.

The next sound we hear is the cue meeting the ball. It echoes through the hall as the cue ball shoots forward and connects with the striped eleven, sending it on a perfect trajectory toward the corner pocket.

The eleven drops with a satisfying thud and the cue ball keeps moving, gliding powerfully across the table like it's got a mind of its own—just like Hunter.

He straightens with a satisfied smirk on his face and slicks his dark blond hair back, then he watches the rest of the scene play out with Luc and me.

Hunter doesn't have to say anything. He knows the game belongs to him.

All we hear next is *click, clack, clack, clack,* as each ball makes its way across the table and down into the waiting pockets.

Seconds later all we're looking at is the green felt on the table, cleared of all the balls.

Hunter wins again.

"Pay up, losers," he chimes, snapping his fingers like he's got a tune stuck in his head.

"Why do you always win when we play here?" Luc frowns, slapping down five hundred dollars on the table. He's allowed his dark curls to grow out, so he looks like he did back in high school.

"I win because I'm good and you suck."

"Are you kidding me? If there's one thing I'm supposed to be good at, it's anything that involves a ball and a stick."

I can't argue with Luc. He's right. He's an all-star NHL player and captain of the New York Hawks.

"Different game, different strokes, my man." Hunter laughs, throwing a punch into Luc's shoulder.

Luc rolls his eyes at him. I do, too. Sometimes my brother is too cocky for his own good. It's fine, though. Every dog has their day.

I'm just bitter because I'm in a rut. I can't escape the way I want to.

"What's your excuse, *little* brother? Why did you suck more than usual tonight?"

I hate it when he calls me *little* like that, and Luc always smirks. I'm barely three years younger than the two of them.

"I've got too much shit on my mind." I tap the side of my head and hand over my five hundred dollars.

Hunter counts the money like a bookie who's just been paid. From the conquering smile spread across his face you wouldn't think he's one of the richest men in the world and CEO of a renowned global company.

His thing is he likes winning, whether it's one dollar or a million. I swear he gets off on it. He's the same with everything.

Last year the two of us had a bet that Luc and his wife, Autumn, would be pregnant by the end of the year. He lost to me because I knew they'd want to enjoy each other a little more before they had kids. Sure, it was only for a few more months, but I was right. It was Hunter and Luna who got pregnant first.

Marriage and babies have been all the talk for over a year, so I stick out like a moldy, gangrene thumb. I can't even pretend to be interested in either topic because my family knows me too well.

"One more game?" Hunter beams, leaning against the table.

"Not me. I'm out. I'm taking Autumn to dinner." Luc puts his stick back in the rack and throws us a proud smile over his shoulder. "She has a new craving for French food."

"Really? Luna loves Mexican food even more."

"Yeah, Autumn likes that, too."

"Let's go on a couple of double dates next week and try a couple of different places."

"Perfect. Let's do that." Luc looks like it's the best idea in the world.

And this is where I get lost. They double date all the time and their wives are best friends even though they came into the family with their own best friends.

Outside of these meetups and work meetings I hardly see them anymore. I'm sure if Hunter and I didn't work at the same place weeks would go by when I wouldn't see him.

I'm cool with it. It's nice to see them so wrapped up in their wives and their lives, but I'm noticing it more now because I won't have what they have. Definitely not if I'm forced to marry Portia Fairchild.

"See you guys later," Luc says.

He leaves and Hunter points his cue at me. "Let's grab a beer and talk."

"Sure."

We grab some beers and Cohiba cigars then head out to the terrace, into the cool night air.

We sit on the wicker chairs, light up and drink.

"Alright, talk to me." Hunter takes a long drag on his cigar. "Obviously I know what's going on, but you seem extra stressed."

"Because I am." I pull in the woody smoke of the cigar and allow it to settle in my lungs for a few seconds before I exhale it. "Father is really pushing my buttons."

"It's because he likes things a certain way and his schedule is all messed up."

"Because of me. I'm not married yet, not CFO yet, and he thinks I'm not taking this seriously enough."

"I kind of expected this from you, to be honest. I mean the delay."

That surprises me. "Did you?"

"Yes. Of course, you'd be delayed in finding a wife if you'd been locked into a marriage contract all your life and you'd just been freed from it."

"I never planned it that way. It's not like I've gone wild. And the first woman I hooked up with in months just happened to be the one to draw the wrong attention to me."

"I didn't expect you to go wild. But I thought you'd take the time to think—which is what you've done. I'm sure Father saw this coming, too. That's why he's acting the way he is."

"That doesn't exactly help me. And he's made the situation worse with this shitty idea to marry Portia."

Hunter frowns and bites the inside of his bottom lip. "That's the part that worries me. That and his closeness with the Fairchilds."

"Hunter, you're CEO of the company. Can't you talk to him?"

"I've already spoken to him, but my power only lies with New York. Father still has the ruling decision over the company as a whole until he retires. I can tell you he's not happy with either of us for our *witch hunt*, as he called it, of the Fairchilds."

"It's not a fucking witch hunt."

"That's how he sees it. And you know how he gets when he's made up his mind about something."

"I just don't get why he's so adamant. I'm pissed as fuck that I have to work with Nolan on the tech company."

"Look Asher, take it from me. You have to focus on yourself. You have less than two weeks now to give Father a name. That's a big deal."

"I know, but something is up with Nigel and Nolan."

"Asher, other than the email with your publicist we got nothing but your hunch."

"I'm not some crazy person. Something just doesn't sit well with me when it comes to them."

"You checked them out. We even got Jericho to check them out and Knight did a full background investigation. Neither of them found anything."

Jericho and Knight Grayson are friends we went to high school with. Jericho is a tech genius who went to MIT. He has a penchant for finding dirt on anyone. I have a few tech skills like that but am not as adept as him. The fact the three of us found nothing says a lot. It also makes me look like a troublemaker.

"That doesn't mean there's nothing to find. And you can bet it was Nigel who suggested I marry Portia."

"That totally crossed my mind."

"Of course it crossed your mind. If she marries me the family gets a portion of Le Blanche Global." That's how it works. "We'd have her father and brother on the board, and as my fucking wife she'd have ownership rights of the company with me. When father retires that would extend to the entire empire. Please tell me you see the picture I'm painting, Hunter."

"I see it." His voice is quiet and reflective, the sound of deep contemplation.

"The fucked up thing about it is, I feel like my hands are tied behind my back."

"And if you marry Portia, it's for life."

That sounds like a death sentence.

Our grandfather wanted us to have real marriages, so the first thing he set out to do was exclude all avenues where we could fake it until we made it. That means no exit clauses or any of those terms. I can't even file a prenup and exclude her from my money because our marriage will be until death do us part.

Grandfather saw to that, too. If we got married and our wives died, to keep the position in the company we'd have a year to re-marry. *One year.*

That old man fucked us up big time.

Things played out exactly like how he thought they would. He would have known that Luc would choose to play hockey and not be part of the company leadership. And I'm sure he also knew that Luc would be the first to get married.

Hunter was a given because he's the leader of our pack. Everyone knew I'd be the one to struggle. Except I thought I'd be struggling for different reasons because I was supposed to be married to Priscilla De Rosa.

"Take your time and think and plan. You have a lot going on."

"Tell me about it."

"Also, don't you have Harper St. John moving in with you on Saturday?"

Something pulls on my insides at the mention of Harper's name. She hasn't strayed from my mind. It was two nights ago that I agreed to help my best friend, and his sister has ridden my mind like the devil.

"Don't remind me. Harper is the epitome of trouble. I've never met anyone like her. I don't have time to babysit her or the capacity for her shenanigans."

"I don't think you have to *babysit* her."

"Hunter, she ended up in jail for torching a man's car."

"Maybe so but she's a woman now."

"No kidding."

Hunter gives me a curious stare. "Does she still not remember what happened between you before the accident?"

He was the only person I told the truth. "No. And I haven't been around her on a one-on-one level in years. I wouldn't know what I'd do if she remembered. It will certainly make things even more awkward than they already are between us. I still feel guilty about her accident."

"You know that wasn't your fault. Come on, Asher, what was the alternative? Turn her down or…" He looks at me like he's waiting for me to finish the rest of the sentence.

"Fuck her."

"Exactly."

"It's not that simple." I shake my head.

"But it is. You were trying to do the right thing by not touching her. She was barely legal, and you were twenty-six. You can't blame yourself for an accident that followed because you were doing the honorable thing."

"Hunter, you'd blame yourself too."

"Yes, I would but there has to be a line of reasoning. I'm sure you know that."

"I know."

"Is that really what you're worried about?" Hunter gives me a narrowed gaze and his previous curiosity returns full force. "The *past*?"

"Why are you looking at me like that?"

"Nothing. Just remember she's not a child anymore and you don't have to do everything to please your best friend when it comes to his sister."

"Hunter... please. Now is not the time to be taunting me."

"I'm just saying."

"I *know* what you're saying." He's always thought I had a thing for Harper and won't acknowledge it. I'll never give him the pleasure of knowing he was right. "She's Josh's little sister and he trusts me to take care of her. That's all I'll be doing."

That's all I *need* to do. Nothing more.

"Okay, okay. I'm sure you'll figure it out. So, what's the plan for everything else? I kind of need to know."

I breathe out a ragged sigh. "I'm going to go through the list of potential wives you gave me one more time, then start dating."

I've had that list for nearly two months. There are twenty women on there with a full profile and pictures to match. When I got it all I did was flip through then file it away. At the time I thought I'd make my own arrangements. I also thought I had all the time in the world.

"Luna and I compiled a good list of potential women we knew you'd like. Layla helped too."

"I know."

Layla is Luna's sister. She became my assistant at Le Blanche Global a few months after my previous assistant retired. At the moment Layla is probably the only person there who keeps me sane.

We have a similar personality. I think it also helps that she's in the same age group as me. My previous assistant was great, but she worked for my father first and was so prim and proper it was difficult to get her to see things my way.

She certainly wouldn't have put a list of potential wives together for me.

Knowing Layla helped with the selection makes me feel more at ease. It means there may be one or two women that I can actually choose from.

"I'll get Layla to sort out my schedule so I can meet everyone on the list next week." I nod. "I need a couple of choices by next Sunday then I'll take the last two days to select one girl."

"Good plan. I think you should focus on that. You no longer have time on your side."

"Don't I know it."

The problem is time was never on my side. It's always screwed with me.

The sound of hearty feminine laughter fills the air, then Luna and Layla walk out onto the terrace. They've just come back from yoga.

The two look like twins even though Luna is younger. She also has waist-length black hair while Layla has a trendy bob.

Luna's belly looks bigger than when I saw her just last week, but she makes pregnancy look good. She's nearly seven months. It's strange to think that in a few more months the baby will be here. The first baby in the family. My parents are gonna go wild.

The excitement is even more heightened because Hunter and Luna decided they didn't want to know the gender until the baby is born. I could never do that. I'd be too anxious, and it would make me crazy.

Hunter instantly puts out his cigar and I do the same.

The rules are no smoke of any kind near his wife and unborn child.

"Now my night is complete." Hunter beams, standing so he can give Luna a quick hug and kiss.

"Mine too. We just came out to say hi." Luna smiles then she looks at me. "Hey Asher."

"Hey there." I nod at Luna and Layla. "How was class?"

"Absolutely fantastic."

"That's great."

"You have death-row-prisoner worried face, boss man." Layla frowns. "I hope that's not to do with work."

"I'll fill you in tomorrow."

"Oh Lord, that doesn't sound good. Maybe I should be sick tomorrow."

"Don't you dare." I chuckle.

She rolls her eyes at me and cocks her head toward Luna. "I need ice cream."

"Oh yes that sounds great."

"I got ten different flavors delivered earlier," Hunter announces.

"You are the best husband. That's why I love you."

"I love you more." He kisses Luna again then she and Layla saunter back inside.

"You need a woman like my wife." Hunter grins at me, glancing back at the path where Luna was.

"There's no chance of that happening. You got lucky."

"I know I did. But you will too. We just have to put a little more work into it."

Work... He's right. I wish he wasn't, but he is.

Everything that's going on around me will require work and keen focus. But first I have to take back control.

The Fairchilds threw me off and so did this thing with Father and his idea that I marry Portia.

My hunches have never been wrong, so I won't play their game.

I'll sort everything out and when I'm done, I'll make sure the Fairchilds don't get a goddamn thing.

That asshole Nolan will regret ever messing with me.

Chapter
FIVE

Harper

"ASHER LE BLANCHE, AGE THIRTY, NET WORTH $15 BILLION, *one of the heirs to Le Blanche Global, a multi-billion dollar investment and hedge fund company,*" Beth reads from the laptop screen using her best newsreader voice. "*Asher Le Blanche's keen insight and ability to anticipate market trends have consistently delivered outsized returns for his clients, earning him a reputation as a financial prodigy.* And this is the guy you don't want to ask for help?"

Beth tosses her long black hair over her shoulders and throws me an incredulous glare. She looks even more like a Disney princess with her blue eyes saucer-wide and her ruby-red lips pressed in displeasure. She could easily be a dark-haired Ariel or Rapunzel.

"We're not talking about this again." I shake my head at her and continue folding my clothes.

We're in my bedroom packing. She's been here for the last two hours trying to convince me to ask Asher for the money I need to pay off Vito.

"I'm trying to make you see sense." Beth stands and places her hands on her slender hips, assuming her Miss-know-it-all persona. "The man is a billionaire."

"I *know*. And I am seeing sense. My answer is still the same. No, I'm not going to ask him."

While the idea seems like a no-brainer if you know someone whose net worth is fifteen *freaking* billion dollars, it's not an option for me. There are some lines in life you don't cross. I already crossed one with Asher Le Blanche. I won't cross another.

That said, if Asher helped me pay the debt the worries of what Vito will do to me would cease to exist. I just can't bring myself to ask for that kind of help.

"It's bad enough I'm going to live at his place." I exhale slowly, trying to keep my nerves from taking over again.

"Why is that so bad?"

"You *know* why. Living with Asher is going to be awkward as hell."

"Yes, but at least you know him. It's not as bad as staying with someone you don't know."

"Sure, but given all that's happened I feel so uncomfortable. The money situation just makes it worse." The questions Asher asked the other night told me he knew I was still in trouble.

"What about his parents? I'm sure they'd lend you the money. Weren't all of your parents college besties?"

They were. That's how we all came to know each other. My mother was friends with Asher's mom and my father was friends with his father. So, I have the close family relationship from both sides.

"I haven't seen Asher's parents in years. I can't just show up on their doorstep and ask them for money. I would be so embarrassed, especially since I didn't exactly stay in touch with them as much as I could have."

Asher's parents were very supportive after my father died and my stepmother took everything. I know they helped out a lot financially and even got us a lawyer.

We lost touch when they started traveling more and I got wrapped up in my own world with its overwhelming problems.

"My life is a state of shit right now and I don't want to make anybody's impression of me worse than it already is," I add, feeling like a loser again.

I've been on edge since Vito's call the other night and I've barely been able to hold myself together.

Josh could tell something was wrong with me when he saw me the next day. Thankfully, he thought I was worrying about moving in with Asher. I made him none the wiser.

Beth walks toward me, takes the jumper I was folding out of my hands and places it on the desk. "Come, you need to sit."

She ushers me over to the chair by the window, sits me down and moves the curtains aside to let in some air.

"I have to sort this out myself, Beth." I lean forward, resting my elbows on my knees.

"How are you going to do that? You can't find twenty grand in four weeks." She lowers her voice. Josh is here and he's been checking on me almost every hour. "You know I'd help you if I could."

"You've helped me more than enough. I wouldn't want you to help me again. I still owe you." Beth gave me five thousand dollars to pay some of the loan repayments after Nick went to prison.

"I'd still help you out. And no, you don't owe me. It was a gift."

"Thanks. That means everything to me." I sigh, sounding like I haven't taken a breath in a hundred years. "I was thinking that maybe if I got a job, I could get a loan."

That's plan A. If that doesn't work the only option I'll have is plan B—*running*. I don't want to run because running means death. I don't have to wonder if Vito would kill me. I know he will.

"Getting a loan isn't that simple." Beth bites the inside of her lip and cocks her head. "Banks aren't always willing to give you a loan just because you have a job. You'd also need to have had the job for a certain length of time."

"Yes, but I can try. I *have* to try. And at least I have two grand from Josh. Maybe if I can make that up to ten Vito will allow me some more time to pay the rest."

"From what you told me that call didn't sound like he'd be willing to do anything of the sort."

"Beth, you're not helping."

"*Yes,* I am. You need to listen to me because this is serious shit."

"As if I don't know that." I glare back at her. She really is not helping by telling me things I already know or giving me bad options. "Telling me to ask Asher for the money is not my idea of finding a solution. He picked me up from jail, Beth. *Jail.* Do you know how embarrassed I was? And he paid my bail and everything else."

The determination on her face loosens. Thank God. She's like a dog with a bone when she gets one of her bright ideas.

"And he knew about Nick."

"Asher mentioned Nick?"

"Yes. It was only left for him to call me an idiot airhead. He thinks I'm completely incompetent because that's exactly how I look. Then there's Josh. I'm like a sponge soaking up all his reserves and a burden on him."

"Don't say that."

"It's true. I'm not being hard on myself. I'm being realistic. It's time I take my life in hand and straighten it out myself without begging people for help or draining my brother."

Josh shouldn't have to tell me the money he has is for him and Lisa. I know he didn't mean anything by what he said but I still feel bad for pushing him to put up that kind of boundary between us. He was right to say it.

"Okay, maybe we can figure something out. I can ask around and see what I come up with."

"Thanks, Beth."

"Don't thank me yet. Just remember most of the people I know are a little on the wild side. *I* wouldn't even get mixed up with some of them for certain things."

She gave me the same answer when I asked if I could stay with any of her friends. When she narrowed my options down to either stay with a drug dealer who had a spare room because his roommate was on the run, or a guy she thought might be a pimp I realized staying with Asher was *definitely* the better option.

"Anything you can do will be appreciated."

"Alright. Give me a few days."

"Thanks. And thank you for everything else. You've been there for me a lot."

She grabs a chair and pulls it closer so she can sit next to me. "You know I'll always be there when you need me."

Beth has always been a good friend to me. We met when we were five and have been friends ever since.

"I know. I'll always be there for you, too. I'm just not sure how useful I am. Only one of us has saved the other's life throughout our friendship."

She smirks. "That's not entirely true. Remember the waterpark trip in fifth grade? You came after me when I went on the adult slide and ended up in the deep end of the pool."

I roll my eyes at her. "That's not the same thing."

"I couldn't swim."

"Neither could I."

"But we were together. I would have been terrified if I'd been on my own. I still maintain that clinging together and flapping around in the water *together,* saved us from drowning."

I don't know how, but I burst out laughing. It's been so long since I laughed it feels strange to me. "You are so crazy."

"The point is we save each other when we need to." Beth nods.

"You have your head screwed on though. I don't."

"I beg to differ. I'm the one who didn't go to college, had the type of boyfriends you couldn't take home to meet *anyone,* and I'm the one who knows all the unsavory characters of this world, as my father put it."

"Yet you have a successful beauty salon, an apartment of your own, and the guys you date don't try to screw you over. Trust me, you have your head screwed on. I still remember being terrified that night when Nick killed those people."

Her smile fades. "Don't think about that."

"It's still fresh in my mind. It was only eight months ago. My entire world changed, and I don't know how to fix it. All I was supposed to worry about was playing my violin."

"You just hit a bump in life's road." Her smile returns but it's softer and sadder. "My grandma used to say when that happens it's because the universe wants to set you on the right path and that's the only way it can do it."

"Well, I hit one hell of a bump. I'm not sure how the universe is going to direct me to the right path."

"Wallowing in your sorrows is not going to help. Let's get you moved into Asher's and figure out everything else."

I nod, liking that idea. My brain can't handle anything more this week.

"How are you feeling about him? Asher. You haven't said anything about him." She speaks in a cautious tone.

"There's nothing to talk about."

"Are you still pretending you don't remember what happened between you?" She gives me a poignant, curious stare.

Beth is the only person who knows that secret of mine and I'm going to keep it that way. "Nothing happened between us. That was all on me."

"Yeah, but—"

"Beth, don't. I'm over it and I'm over him." Annoyingly, although I say that with ease, in my heart I don't fully believe it.

"I just wanted to check how you were feeling about him."

"I'm fine. I mean. I'm... fine with those parts. It is what it is and I'm okay with that."

"Okay. I guess there's enough to worry about. How about we finish packing and I take you out to dinner? It's been a while since we've hung out together in New York. We could go to that pizzeria you liked last time. The hot waiter we both used to ogle is now the owner." Mischief lights up her eyes.

"Good for him." Everyone seems to be doing better than me. "And yeah, let's go there."

"I think we could both do with some giant chocolate shakes and cheesecake."

"Sounds good." I could do with the break.

I guess I should make use of the comforts I have today because I'll be moving to Asher's house tomorrow. I can't imagine what it's going to be like living under the same roof as him, directly under his scrutiny.

My breath catches in my throat as I step out of the car and stare at the mansion before me.

It's unlike anything I've ever seen before. The Hamptons have a reputation, but this—this is beyond anything I imagined.

The beachfront mansion with its sleek, contemporary design features towering columns and expansive stone walls that seem to go on forever. Each detail is exquisite with the kind of luxury you'd see on a TV show showcasing the rich and the famous.

Josh walks around the car and leans into my shoulder. "The house is something else, isn't it?"

"I can't believe Asher lives here."

"Told you he had space." Josh smiles back at me.

I glance up at him. "Yeah, enough to fit a small country."

"Something like that."

The last place he had—*where I offered myself to him*—was an apartment. A penthouse near the city suitable for a bachelor pad.

This feels like a home.

"Come on, I'll take you in."

"Is he here?"

"No, he had to work. His assistant will show you around and take care of you. Asher will be back by dinnertime."

Well, at least I have a few hours to get used to the place without him.

I follow Josh through the massive double doors and into a foyer that looks like we just stepped into another world.

Cool marble covers the floor and hand-painted murals run along the walls. This place is a masterpiece. And I guess it shows just how grown Asher is.

We move further inside into the living room, where an elderly lady with a bouffant meets us. She has dark-rimmed glasses, and a Cruella De Vil look about her that makes it difficult to imagine her ever smiling.

"Hi, Olga," Josh greets her.

Olga. Yes, that name definitely suits her. I can't think of another that would.

"Hello, there," she responds in an accented voice that sounds Eastern European. Maybe Polish or Russian.

"This is my sister, Harper. Harper, this is Olga, Asher's assistant."

"Pleased to meet you." Olga extends her hand to me and I shake it.

"It's nice to meet you, too."

"I will get you something to eat then show you around when you're ready." Her tone is very professional. I can see why she's Asher's assistant. I imagine he must be extremely busy to be worth billions.

"Thank you. I'd love that," I tell her.

"Very well. I'll get Fred to unload your things and take them up to your room and leave you to say goodbye to your brother. Come find me in the kitchen when you're done." She points to a hallway to the left of us.

"I will."

"Thanks, Olga," Josh says with a curt tip of his head.

To my surprise she gives Josh a thin smile.

I watch her leave then I turn back to Josh, feeling my heart grow in my chest with the weight of saying goodbye to him. With the exception of the last few days, we haven't seen each other since before Christmas when the shit went down with Nick. Josh flew to L.A. and was with me for the entire month.

Saying goodbye to him now feels like back then but worse.

"You're going to be okay, kid." He gives me a playful punch on my shoulder.

Although I've been willing myself not to cry, a tear rolls down my cheek. "Thanks for everything. I'm so sorry I wrecked your plans with Lisa and—"

"It's okay. We're past that. I want to hear good things when I see you again."

I nod, hoping good things could really happen. It's been a while since I had anything of the sort and right now the forecast doesn't look good. "I'll be okay. Good luck for tomorrow but you know Lisa will say yes, right?"

"Believe me, if I didn't know I wouldn't be proposing." He laughs. "She'll be happy then I'll be gone for nine months and virtually uncontactable. That's not exactly how I planned to start our engagement."

"But it will be okay. Lisa will be even more excited to see you when you get back."

"I hope so."

I met Lisa a few times and she's exactly the kind of woman I hoped Josh would find.

"You can call her if you want." Josh smiles with hope in his eyes. "You know she'd love to hear from you."

"Sure. I'll call her. Be careful, Josh. I always worry about you."

"You know I'll be fine. I was born to be in the Navy. It sounds weird but I love going on the sub missions. It's like being in a whole other world."

"It *is* a whole other world." I chuckle.

His smile fades and his shoulders sag. "I gotta go now, Harper. Are you feeling okay?"

Bless his heart. He can see that I'm not okay. "Yes."

"Need anything else before I dash?"

"Just a hug from my big brother."

"I have plenty of those." He smiles wide and I take a mental picture of the way he looks so I can keep it in my heart.

We hug and I savor the safety I feel from being with my only family member who I know will always take care of me. I hope one day I can return the favor. And I hope like hell nothing bad happens to either of us and this isn't the last time we'll hug.

When we pull apart he plants a kiss on my forehead and ruffles the top of my hair like he used to when I was little.

He dips his head and leaves, and I stand there until I hear the front door close and the car driving away.

I'm alone now, thrust into a new situation. And from the looks of it a whole new world.

I gaze around the living room and take in the French Provençal décor and wrought iron chandeliers hanging above me. Everything is so beautiful and elegant I feel out of place just being here.

This is the first time I've been to the Hamptons, and I never thought I would be living in the home of one of its top-tier billionaires.

Asher only just turned thirty. Who knows where he'll be in a few years? I guess that's what happens when you're born with the right kind of wealth.

Pulling in a deep breath, I steel my mind and prep it to venture down this new path. Then, like Alice going down the rabbit hole, I follow the marbled hallway to a state-of-the-art kitchen that's bigger than my last apartment.

Olga is in there talking to a younger woman who looks to be the same age as me. The woman gives me a welcoming smile that makes me feel more at ease.

Olga introduces her as Kimberley, the head chef. Again, I'm impressed and I wonder who and what else I'll come across today.

After I eat a delicious meal of gourmet sandwiches on the terrace, Olga gives me the tour. By the end of it I decide it doesn't feel right to call this place a mere house.

With its eight bedrooms, three living rooms, function halls, dining room, *Beauty and the Beast* style library, and garages, this place feels more like a palace. Or a manor at least. Like one of those English countryside manors with a moor and a lake.

The only real difference here is that Asher has private beach access and the woodlands. He has the best of both worlds, and I feel like I'm in a dream.

My bedroom is certainly the finest room I've ever stayed in in my life, and I'm almost too afraid I'll mess it up.

There's a queen-size bed that looks like something designed for a princess, a walk-in wardrobe, shelves galore, and a boudoir dressing table.

Nick made me feel like I was less than human. No wonder I feel like I don't belong here. Because I don't.

As nice as this all is, when I sort out the loan I have to get my own place. Campus housing or not—and I have a feeling it will be the latter.

I don't know how life is at NYU but back at UCLA those who get turned down for campus housing don't often get placed later, so they have to find somewhere near campus.

My problem is I applied way too late, so I'm not at all surprised.

The day wears on. I don't have that many things to unpack so I'm set up within an hour.

Beth comes by to see me, and she's as besotted with the place as I am. We spend the rest of the day on the beach, then she leaves at nightfall.

At eight thirty I make my way down to the dining room with butterflies flapping around in my stomach.

Asher is home. Olga told me to come down for dinner at this time and I heard his car when he arrived.

When I reach the dining room door I breathe deeply to calm myself, then I take that step inside as if I'm about to start the first day of the rest of my life.

My breath catches when I see him. He's standing at the head of the table talking to Olga.

Dressed in a suit like last time, he looks as handsome as ever. Except today he has a five o'clock shadow that gives him a sexier, rugged edge.

Still, he looks like his net worth—powerful, important, wealthy.

And here's me in my yoga pants and off-the-shoulder jumper looking completely underdressed for something as simple as dinner.

Oh, well. I can't do anything about that now.

What was that mantra I saw on *America's Next Top Model*?

Walk like you own the world even if you're wearing a paper bag.

I try and do my best.

As I walk in, he looks my way with those bright blue eyes and God help me, those old feelings resurface. Then I realize they never actually left.

Chapter SIX

Harper

PRIDE IS A TAUNTING DEVIL TO THOSE WHO ARE HELPLESS. It sits on your shoulders laughing at you when you fall on your face and realize you need help from the one person you shunned.

Nights ago, when I last saw Asher, I cursed him to hell and back in my mind. To me he was another asshole in my world and I hoped I'd never see him again.

Now here I am in his home, a step away from being a hobo on the street with no place to go.

When I get closer Asher pastes a smile on his handsome face, revealing sinful dimples that look even more alluring with his fuller beard.

"Hi," I say first, because I should be gracious and grateful.

"Hey."

"We'll start bringing the food out now," Olga says, giving me a once-over.

Throughout the day I've tried to figure her out. She hasn't got a wide range of emotions so it's hard. It does, however, seem like she's not sure about me. Regardless of being Josh's sister, maybe she thinks I'm a gold digger.

I can assure her I'm not. As long as I can play my music, I'd be quite happy just to pay off my debt and live a comfortable life.

Olga leaves us and Asher returns his focus to me.

"Sit." He points to the chair next to him on his right.

I sit and he does, too. There's enough space between us but I feel like he's too close. Like when we were in the car and he seemed to take up all the air and space.

"Thanks for letting me stay with you." I bring my hands nervously together.

"No worries."

"I'll try not to overstay my time."

"Stay as long as you need to."

Again, I feel that pang of indifference and that he's doing this for me because of his loyalty to Josh. But of course he is. They're like brothers and he's just doing Josh a favor. "Thanks again."

"Have you settled in okay?"

"Yes. Your house is impressive."

"Glad you like it."

"I do. It suits you."

"It's a good place to come home to after a long day."

"Did you have a good day at work?" My God, we sound like a pair of strangers who just met on the subway. Not like two people who've known each other nearly twenty years.

"The best."

I don't miss the sarcasm in his tone which implies he didn't have a good day, but I won't ask for details.

I'm momentarily thrown and that awkward silence I hate sneaks between us.

Thankfully I'm saved when the door opens, and Olga and the kitchen staff bring in the food.

They carry in several delicious dishes of chicken, beef, and fish, along with an assortment of garnished vegetables. It looks like they prepped for a banquet. I almost ask them if they're going to join us. There's no way all this food is just for Asher and me.

When they finish laying out the food on the table and depart, I think of all the times I was starving in the past and couldn't even afford a pot of ramen.

I'm not overly hungry now because I ate throughout the day, but I feel like I should eat to make up for all those bad times. And because the staff went through the trouble of making it.

"Wow. The food looks amazing." I smile, scanning the spread on the table. "It's like I'm in a *Harry Potter* movie."

Asher chuckles. "My staff tend to go all out."

"They certainly do. The food looks great, but sadly I'll pass on the shrimp and fish. As delicious as it looks, I don't eat seafood."

A dull look washes over his face. It's so distinct I consider whether I offended him, but I don't think it's that. There's something in his eyes that looks like guilt. It throws me off again because I'm not used to seeing him look that way.

"Did I say something wrong?" I search his eyes, and he straightens.

"You love seafood."

My eyes widen with complete surprise because he's totally wrong. "No way. You must have me confused with someone else."

He gives me a sidelong stare. "Harper, you think I have *you* confused with someone else?"

"Clearly. I would never eat fish because it's gross and shrimp looks like—"

"Worms with beady eyes."

He took the words right out of my mind, and I realize that I must have said that before but can't remember.

"Please don't tell me I've had shrimp in the past." I wrinkle my nose, narrow my eyes and grimace, knowing I look completely disgusted.

"You *love* shrimp and *all* seafood. You're an all-you-can-eat-shrimp at the crab shack kind of girl."

"*Crab!*" My voice raises by several octaves. I can't help my re-action. I'm shocked and grossed out in equal parts.

"Yes. You love that, too."

My stomach turns and bile rises into my throat, but I set aside my disgust and think of the bigger issue here. "I don't remember."

I bite the inside of my lip and Asher looks even more guilty. Suddenly I realize why. I'm surprised it never occurred to me before that perhaps he feels guilty because the accident happened after he turned me down. I didn't think he would care that much.

No... that's wrong of me to say. I'm just being a bitter bitch.

I heard Asher came to visit me every day in the hospital when I was in a coma. Then when I came out of it, he was always there with Josh and Dad. They were there every day, every chance they could get.

"Why don't you try a piece of shrimp?" He nods at the platter of grilled shrimp dipped in lemon and garlic.

"Oh no." I wrinkle my nose. "I don't think I could."

He grabs a fork and spears one of the shrimp, then holds it out to me. "Try it."

I want to say no again but the thought of him feeding me has me hooked in place like an idiot schoolgirl who'd agree to go to the ends of the earth with the boy she likes.

"Come on, you know me. I'm not going to give you some-thing you don't like." He nods, biting the inside of his lip.

I release a heavy sigh and decide to brave it. "Okay. Just a lit-tle bite, though."

He moves the fork closer. When I open my mouth, his eyes drop to my lips and, just for an instant, the blue of his irises dark-ens. If I didn't know better, I'd think that was desire in his eyes.

I lean in and take a bite of the shrimp, no longer thinking *it's shrimp*. Instead, I'm transfixed with trying to figure out what that look is.

Then the burst of flavors hits me and my eyes snap wide. I lean in again and take the rest of the shrimp and, oh my God, how the hell could I have possibly thought *this* was gross?

"See, told you." Asher smiles.

"Oh my God. This is divine."

"That's exactly what you said last time, too."

"Did you get me to eat it?"

"I did."

"How? And when?" I'm completely curious.

"You were fifteen. I went on vacation with you and your family to Cancun. Josh and I had just graduated so your dad wanted to do something special. Anyway, you and I made a bet. I won. That's how you ended up eating shrimp."

I've seen pictures of us at Cancun and that's all they were to me—pictures. It's nice to get some more context.

"What was the bet?"

"We played chess. I bet that I'd put you in checkmate within the first five minutes."

"Well, no wonder I lost because I don't play chess." I shake my head and giggle.

"Yes... you do. You won the championship at school the year before."

The smile falls off my face. "*Me?*"

"Yes, you."

"Who taught me to play chess?"

"I did." A spark of pride comes into his eyes.

I stare back at him, feeling dazed. I never knew we spent so much time together. Or rather, I don't remember. The only memory I have of Asher and me is the worst one. The one from that night.

Josh, Dad, and Beth did so much work with me after the accident to help me remember certain things about my life but there were so many more memories I lost. Most of them with Asher it seems.

I guess I might have tried harder to reacquaint myself with more memories we shared, but because I remembered his rejection, I thought it was best to stay away. Then Dad died and my world changed forever.

"I guess there's a lot I still don't remember," I state with an awkward smile.

"Don't worry about it. I'm sure we'll get the chance to talk about some of those things while you're here." There's a warmth in his eyes that reaches out to me with that safe feeling again.

"That would be nice."

"Eat, don't let the food get cold." He lifts his chin, motioning to the shrimp platter. "Continue with those."

"Thank you."

At least it seems Asher and I are getting off to a good start.

We tuck back into the food, and I devour the shrimp and fish.

Everything is so delicious I'm now grateful there's so much of it.

I remember Mom cautioning me to never eat as much as the guys. *Sorry, Mom, this food is too good to resist.*

I eat like a little pig and then some.

"This is all so good," I state when I decide to take a break. My sides have only just started aching.

"You look like you enjoyed it."

"Thoroughly. Did Kimberly make all of this?"

"She did. She's a world-class chef."

"I can't believe you have a world-class chef in your home."

"I don't have time to cook, and I hate junk food."

And it shows. You can't maintain a body like his on junk. "I need to eat better."

"You will here."

I guzzle the last of my wine and he watches me with a curious look crinkling his eyes.

"How are things since Massachusetts?" he asks, studying my face.

I was waiting for him to ask me about that. "They're fine," I lie, hoping he doesn't see through the fakeness in my words and *me*.

"Really?"

"Yes. I sorted everything out." I've done nothing but panic. He doesn't need to know that though.

"*Everything* like what?"

"I'll be looking for a job Monday and going to lessons with my old violin teacher. Then there's are a few things I have to do at NYU."

"How are you otherwise? Massachusetts was kind of a big deal."

I get the feeling he knows things aren't right with me. If he didn't, he wouldn't be asking.

"I'm okay. And I swear I won't be any trouble or torch your car if you piss me off. I'm sure it's worth more than me so I wouldn't be able to compensate you."

He sits back against the chair and levels me a hard stare. "The car isn't worth more than you. However, I think we should go over some house rules, so you aren't tempted to torch my cars."

Cars... most people own one. How many does he have? I saw the two garages on my tour ,but Olga didn't let me inside either of them.

"What are your house rules?" I raise a brow and keep my gaze fixed on him.

Asher assumes his business persona and the lightheartedness he previously displayed is gone. Gone as if he's been split in two and the evil twin version of himself has taken over.

"I'd like to know where you are if you're out after ten."

What the hell? I've never had a curfew. "Do I get to know where you are if you're not in by ten?"

"Yes," he replies in a stiff tone. "You're also welcome to go wherever you like in the house except my office, my bedroom and the bigger garage. I'll get you a car so you're not taking public transport."

"I can get an Uber if I need to go out." I don't want him to spend any money on me.

"Ubers cost money, especially around here. It's also a long way into the city. In traffic, the price can go up. Having a car will be cheaper and you can go wherever you want."

"But you don't have to—"

"I'm getting you a car." His voice is firmer and the look in his eyes tells me not to fight him.

"Okay, thank you. I'll pay you back as soon as I can."

"You don't have to pay me back. I'm a busy man. I promised Josh I'd take care of you. I don't have time for extra worries so knowing you have a car is a benefit to me as much as it is for you."

I don't know how to respond to that. Or how to feel. Yes, a car would be great, but it definitely sounds like it's more for his benefit, so I don't burden him the way a child would with *extra worries*.

"Okay." I'm starting to sound like a mindless robot now, programmed to answer with one to three words. "Anything else?"

"I'm sure I don't have to ask you to keep the place tidy. I have a good team of maids here, but I've always prided myself on not giving them more than their fair share of work."

I won't remind him that he and Josh shared a room at Princeton, and I remember the place looked like they were raising livestock.

"I'm a very tidy person so you don't have to worry about that."

"Just making sure you know how I treat my staff."

"Anything *else*?"

"There will be weeks when I'll be away on business. I still expect you to let me know where you are whether I'm in or out of the country." His expression turns stonier, like a statue. "I'd also like to know who you bring in the house at all times. Of course, I don't mean Beth. She can come whenever she wants. I mean *any-one* else."

"Like men?" I throw back because I don't know why he doesn't just say what he means when it's obvious that's what he's talking about.

"Yes, like men."

"I'm not a child, Asher. I haven't been one in a very long time. I know how to behave in someone else's home."

"I'm sure you do but your choice in men is questionable. This is a hoodlum-free zone."

Great. We're back to square one. And he's right back in the asshole crew again.

It serves me right for thinking we'd gotten off to a good start and that he could be nice to me.

Chapter
SEVEN

Asher

H ARPER LOOKS LIKE SHE WANTS TO RIP MY EYES OUT.
I know I pulled another asshole move by being out-right rude to her and spoiling the good rapport we had going. But what I said needed to be said.

I never met Nick, but Josh told me enough about him from before the guy even went rogue.

I understood Josh would be worried because he's Harper's brother but there never seemed to be anything likable about Nick from the beginning. The first thing I thought about him was that he was shady as fuck with his contacts in the music world and the underground. I turned out to be right.

Surprisingly, that was the one time I desperately wanted to be wrong.

Someone needs to set Harper straight so she doesn't end up with the same kind of fucked-up loser jerk ever again.

As I can't imagine Beth or Josh having that serious

down-to-earth talk with Harper, that someone needs to be me. Even if she's glaring at me like she hates me.

"Don't worry. If I want to hook up with a *hoodlum* I definitely won't do it here," Harper sneers. "There are plenty of hotels around. Or to save expenses I'll just do it in a club or get fucked against some wall in a back alley. Those are always free."

The vein in my head pulses, feeling like it's going to pop.

And so does my dick when the vivid image of her naked body drifts into my head like alluring smoke. Then the very vivid image of her being taken against the wall of some dark alley follows next, infuriating me even more.

I'm not supposed to be imagining her with some guy. And judging from the instant reaction from my dick, I'm still annoyingly attracted to her and interested in her in all the wrong ways.

It was bad enough when I gave her the shrimp and imagined her plump lips sliding up and down my cock. Then she made things worse when she reminded me she wasn't a child anymore.

Of all the people she knows in her world, I'm the only one who doesn't need that reminder.

I can see she's not a fucking child just by looking at her in that flimsy off-the-shoulder jumper that draws all my attention to her round breasts and the tight yoga pants that fit her body like a second skin.

Fuck. This whole off-limits thing is messing with me already. Nothing has ever been off limits to me except her. I'm a man who always get whatever and whoever I want. But *not* her.

So, back to plan A.

I meet her vicious gaze and harden my own, so she knows I'm serious as fuck. "Clearly, you've learned nothing if you can say that to me."

"What do you mean by that? That I've learned nothing?"

"You *know* what I mean. And obviously you're not gonna find anybody good if you're planning to hook up with a random guy in a club or some fucking back alley. Surely you have better sense than that."

Harper stands and I almost expect her to slap me. She's close enough and ballsy enough to do it.

"You are so fucking out of line." She sets her hands on her hips and stares at me with blazing eyes that almost look feral. "How could you sit there like you're some kind of saint? As if *you've* never hooked up in a club or a *back alley.*"

I hold my tongue, remembering the scandal that broke only last week. Harper would have a field day with that. I'm not going to act like a saint or lie, because there's a chance she could still find details floating around on the net.

"We're not talking about me." I clench my jaw and my fist at the same time. "We're talking about you."

"You're treating me like I'm an idiot. Like what happened to me with Nick was my fault." That's the first time she's said Nick's name to me, and she actually looks drained for hearing it outside her head.

"I didn't say that." I tone my voice down on seeing the shift in her mood.

"You don't need to. Before you say anything more try to remember it's not always easy to walk away from someone you love. Nick wasn't always a monster."

Her jade eyes glaze with tears and the sight grips my insides.

Instantly I feel like shit for making her remember what Nick did to her.

I know *everything.* If he weren't in prison, I'd find him and kill him. I mean that.

I don't think she's an idiot. I'm just being protective. Sure, I know I'm being *overprotective,* but I don't want her in any danger. How the fuck do I explain that without sounding like an asshole?

"Harper—"

"Don't. Don't talk to me, Asher. You are such a fucking asshole. So don't talk to me."

With her hands balled at her sides she walks away, leaving a cloud of tension filling the room.

Damn it. This is the second conversation we've had this week, and both have ended with her storming away from me.

What the hell am I going to do if I can't talk to Harper without us ending up at each other's throats?

Olga walks back into the living room with a pensive expression. I know she heard everything. The whole house would have heard us.

"Is everything okay?" she asks.

"Yes. It's fine."

"Is there anything I can do?"

I shake my head. Olga is great because she keeps things professional. That's why I hired her. At the same time I know there's a side of her that cares. That's come from our eight years of working together. But she'll only push as far as I allow.

"There's some stuff I have to figure out when it comes to my little house guest."

"I see. Well, if you need me for anything let me know."

"Sure."

With that Olga leaves me to my thoughts.

No one can help me with Harper. This is all on me.

Harper is going to be with me for the next... *however* long. And that's just the thing. I don't know.

Earlier I realized there was a very real possibility that she might not get campus housing for a while, if at all.

College starts in seven weeks. Most people would have applied for housing well in advance. Harper's transfer was short notice. That means I'm stuck with her and stuck with whatever is going on inside me when it comes to her.

I haven't even told my father about her staying here. It's fine for now but there'll come a point when things will go to hell.

If they haven't already.

Harper avoids me the next day.

It's one of the rare Sundays that I'm home. I originally hoped to spend the day with her, but she's acting like a ghost living in my house.

The only signs of life that come from her are the occasional shuffle in the kitchen, the tap of the keys on her laptop I hear when I stand outside her door contemplating whether I should check on her, and then I hear her playing her violin later in the night.

I placed her on the other side of the house because I knew she'd need to practice. I didn't want her feeling cautious about making noise.

Even if the whole house could hear her, it would be fine. Harper is one of the most talented violinists I've ever heard. My parents are obsessed with classical music, so we were always going to the opera and theater for one event or another.

They loved violin music in particular. That's how I know Harper is talented. I've listened to some of the finest violinists the world has ever seen.

Harper has been playing since she was five. Thankfully those memories stayed with her after the accident. But she still had to spend a year relearning skills she'd developed in the years in between she can't remember.

As I listen to one of her signature pieces the notes soothe me. I want to go in and talk to her, but I hold off.

I know her. The best way to deal with her silent treatment is to ride it out until she needs me. If that doesn't work, I'll find a way to make her talk to me.

She stays in my mind all night and as I head out to work early the next morning.

Monday morning meetings can be a bitch at best. But a Monday morning meeting with my father, Hunter, Nigel, and Nolan is not the kind of meeting I want to have with my head all over the place.

I've known about this meeting since last week, but I still feel as worked up as when I first found out Nigel and Nolan would be in the building today.

However, when I arrive at Le Blanche Global, I put my game face on then head to the boardroom where they're already waiting for me.

I'm not late. They're just early.

Father sits at the head of the sleek, glass conference table as usual, but I notice Nigel and Nolan have strategically placed themselves on my father's left.

Nolan is in my seat. Father always has Hunter and me on either side of him. That's okay. I'll let that slide.

"Morning, all," I say only for my father's sake. I've realized that he's the one I need to keep things sweet with.

I don't have to worry about Hunter because he'll always be on my side. As for the other two, I don't care. Nigel and Nolan can fuck themselves.

"Morning, son," Father replies, seeming more like his usual self even though I detect a hint of reservation in his tone.

Nigel and Nolan nod at me. The two—*and Portia*—remind me of the Lannisters in *Game of Thrones*. Both father and son are as twisted as the TV show characters and even have a similar appearance with their light blond hair and lean build.

I look away from them and move to sit next to Hunter, who seems pleased with my pleasantries. He knows I'm just playing the game.

Layla rushes through the door after me. She's taking the minutes for the meeting.

"Morning, everyone. I hope I'm not late." She beams, cutting me a glance to which I shake my head.

"Not at all, dear. Take a seat." Father points to the chair next to Nolan.

He's fond of her because she can multitask with pretty much everything. I also think he considered her as an option for me right up until she started dating the son of one of his top clients and we all saw how well suited they were.

Her freshly-cut dark bob bounces as she makes her way over to sit with her little notepad. Unfortunately, the moment she sits Nolan's eyes move straight to her tits.

Layla is not a woman you mess with, so she spots his ass straight away then checks him with a tight-lipped smile that says *I'll rip your face off if you look at me again.*

The fool gets the message and looks away, then focuses back on me.

That's fine, too. We can do this silent war dance all he wants. Let him think he has me where he wants me in my own company.

What he doesn't realize is people like me observe, then plan for those who think they can fuck with them and obliterate everything in their path.

"Okay, now that we're all present let's start," Father begins, and all eyes go to him. "The transfer of ownership of Vivitron was finalized this morning. I'm proud to say Le Blanche Global now owns Vivitron as intended by my dear friend Archie Blackstone. We are always expanding but owning Vivitron carries substantial weight because of the success it already enjoys. With that said we need to talk about logistics and who will be responsible for what."

"Are we bringing them into our development pipeline or keeping them separate?" Hunter asks.

"We need to integrate them. But within a timeframe that allows all of us to get used to the new changes. We need their talent, and I don't want to change too much about their processes, but they need to adapt to our culture. That's why I think Asher would be best placed working with Nolan. You both have the financial analytical skills to make sure everything runs smoothly with no hiccups."

I want to remind him I don't need Nolan for anything because

I've managed larger projects on my own but I hold back and dip my head in agreement.

"I'm sure we can work together. Can't we, Nolan?" I level him a hard stare.

"Certainly." He smiles back but I see straight through his fakeness.

"Wonderful. I think we should spend the rest of the meeting discussing the implementation plans."

I half listen for the rest of the meeting, my mind splitting between what my father is saying and my own plans.

The only thing I can do right now is watch Nolan. If shit is going to happen it will start with him. Nigel is too careful to slip up. He also has more years on him to have perfected the art of manipulation.

That said, he doesn't have to do much when it comes to my father. They grew up together so my father has that extra layer of trust he wouldn't show any old person.

The meeting ends after two hours and my father closes it on a positive note.

He and Nigel head out first but Nolan hangs back, looking like he wants to speak to me.

"A quick word, Asher," he says, keeping his hawk eyes fixed on me as I stand.

"Sure."

Hunter and Layla stand together by the head of the table and watch us. Nolan appears to want to speak in private, but I stay right where I am.

Whatever he has to say to me can be said in front of Hunter and Layla. I'm not allowing him the chance to piss with me then lie about it later.

"What's up?" I give him a crude smile.

"I understand you have a problem with me."

"The way I heard it it's *you* who has the problem with me."

"Who did you hear that from?"

Clever answer but very stupid. "I saw something with my own eyes."

"I can assure you that whatever you *saw* wasn't done with any ill will toward you."

"I'm not so sure about that."

"I'm looking forward to working together. This is a big break for my family's company. I wouldn't like any disagreements between us to mess it up."

"Let's cut the shit, Nolan. I know you were behind the scandal."

"What makes you say—"

"Don't do that." My voice is a notch lower than a shout.

That shuts him up. He knows I wouldn't call him out on something like that if I didn't have evidence. His problem is he doesn't know what I have. At the same fucking time the asshole also knows I don't have anything solid to prove the extent of his guilt, or his ass wouldn't be allowed in the building.

I lean forward, aware Hunter is giving me one of his warning stares. He's worried I'm going to snap and go for Nolan's jugular.

"We can work together just fine, and life will be good for your family's company and mine. But don't fuck with me."

Nolan grins as if I just told a joke. "I think you fuck with yourself enough, don't you? There's no way *I* would screw around with women the way you do and tarnish my family name."

"Hey," Hunter cuts in.

"It's okay, Hunter." I give him a brief glance then look back at Nolan. "Perhaps you should worry about yourself instead of me, *Nolan*. I would if I were you."

"And I will."

"Good. It looks like *Nolan* and I have an understanding now. So in the future, if he thinks it's a good idea to hire people to watch me again, he knows I'll fuck him up."

I didn't come here to play nice today. I came to play smart and Nolan landed in my trap by wanting to *speak* to me. What an idiot.

If I were him, I would have laid low. Not confronted the beast when he's all fired up.

Now he can run home to his mommy and daddy and tell them what I said.

"Let's meet during the week and discuss the next steps," he says, ignoring my threat.

"Of course. Either Layla or I will be in touch."

"Wonderful." With a stiff smile he walks out, trying to keep his head up.

I don't know what the hell he thought I was going to say to him, but I can tell the conversation didn't go as he expected.

People make the mistake of thinking I'm passive because Hunter usually takes the lead, but that's one mistake Nolan will never make again.

"Asher, you need to be more careful." Hunter speaks in a low warning tone.

"Are you kidding, Hunter?" Layla cuts in. "That guy is a major asshole."

"I agree but he's also manipulative and conniving. So we *all* need to be careful."

"Don't worry. I will be." I glance back at the door, wondering what Nolan will come up with next.

I can still see him through the glass door, walking down the corridor. Just before he reaches the end Portia and Nigel emerge from one of the rooms with my father.

My skin crawls at the sight of Portia. She's got the same light blonde hair as her father and brother and looks like the female version of them.

"I have to go to my next meeting." Hunter comes up to me and follows my gaze. "Please don't get in any trouble."

"Like I said, don't worry about me."

Hunter sighs and heads out.

I look back at Layla as she gathers up her notebook and pen.

She walks up to me and gives me a concerned stare. "I've never seen you get so worked up before."

"Nolan really gets under my skin. Now more than ever."

"I don't trust him at all, so I understand." It was Layla who first suspected that my publicist had gone rogue. "That meeting your father is heading into is about Nolan and Nigel getting on the board."

I grit my teeth. "I don't know what I can do to stop that from happening."

"Nothing, apparently. At least not right now. You need to worry about yourself, Mister. Things just got worse. We have brand-new Monday morning problems to deal with."

"God, what now?" I bring a hand to my head and stare back at her.

"You need a new publicist or someone who can manage the PR diary. There is a backlog of people and organizations wanting to meet with you. I've tried to fit most of them in as best as possible but it's cutting into my work time. You're gonna need someone soon."

"Damn it."

"Maybe I can get a temp in. Or *two*. Truthfully you do need two people. One on a full-time contract and an assistant. I can do all the training for both positions." She smiles, seeming to like the idea of using her skills. Apart from yoga, her background is PR and business management. She just enjoys the business side of things more.

"We can get two people, but I don't want a temp for either of those positions. We need to hold interviews as quickly as possible. I need people I can trust."

"You're right. Nolan may pull the same stunt again or do some other shit despite your warning."

"Exactly, so I need someone here who can't be swayed. Tell everyone waiting on me that I'm booked out for a month. I need to prioritize the most important things."

"Which is your dates with the potentials?"

"Yeah." Thank goodness I can be real with her and she can be discreet. The papers would have another field day with this story. I can see it now.

Billionaire heir seeks wife to secure position in company.

"All the women have signed new NDAs, and I've made arrangements for you to meet them by Saturday. Starting tonight at six."

"Thanks. That's perfect timing." And in line with my plans. Hopefully I'll be able to pick a couple of options by Saturday.

Layla's eyes light up with the spark of an idea. "I think you'll *love* my friend Alexis. She's your final date on Sunday. Let's just say I saved the best for last."

"Well, if you think she's the best then that's a good sign. Why am I not meeting her first?" I give her a narrowed stare.

"She's in Bali teaching yoga on a retreat. I met her through Zack. He introduced her to me after our first date. She's super fun and beautiful."

"She sounds great."

"She is. Zack has known her since they were kids. He knew I would like her because I'm obsessed with yoga. And I knew you'd like her because she seems to be your type."

My type.

Right now I'm not even sure what my type is but I smile back at her just to be polite. Like everyone else, she's just helping me.

I already know I won't like anybody on that list any more now than I did when I first looked at it.

Meeting these women is just a matter of dotting my i's and crossing my t's.

Chapter
EIGHT

Asher

DATE NUMBER ONE: COMPLETED.
Status: Negative.

It was a complete no-go. Along with nearly two hours of my life I'll never get back.

At least it's not too late. It's just past eight so the night isn't completely wasted. I head into the living room and take off my jacket, relieved I cut my date short.

Jennifer Paxton was a smart, beautiful, successful lawyer. She had all the qualities I love in a woman, but our entire date was like a role play of a fictional court case. Seriously, I don't even think I could make that shit up.

From the moment she suggested the role play I checked out.

She was to be the prosecuting attorney and me the defense.

The fictional case she made up was of a man who'd stolen his friend's intellectual property and claimed it as his own.

I stuck around for an hour only because she was Hunter's top recommendation. The extra forty minutes came about because our food was late. I made my escape by telling her that I had an international business call to make that I couldn't reschedule.

I've never been so bored on a date in my life. Or angrier at my brother.

How the fuck Hunter thought I'd like *that* woman is beyond me. There was a point where I wondered if I was being too picky. Then I imagined myself with her and realized I was being the right amount of *selective*.

If all my dates are like tonight, I don't know what the fuck I'm going to do.

Nineteen more dates to go.

Tomorrow has to be better. I suppose if the worst-case scenario were to happen and I don't like any of them by Sunday, I'll still have two days before Father's deadline to figure something else out.

I hope it doesn't come to that but it's the backup plan. As to what I'll do during that time is anyone's guess.

I look around for Harper. The house is quieter than usual.

Olga works a half day on Monday and most of the house staff have an easy day where they finish early, too. It's because they know I'm likely to get back late.

It looks like I'm by myself.

I head to Harper's room and confirm she's not there. I don't like not knowing where she is.

Deciding I've had enough of the silent treatment, I grab my phone and call her.

To my absolute annoyance the phone goes straight to voicemail. "Harper, where are you? I'm home. Call me when you get this." I try to keep the irritation out of my tone but my voice is swimming with it.

She probably won't call back, and when she sees me—if she decides to talk to me—she may say it wasn't ten yet.

I decide to grab a beer and head out to the balcony of my room to smoke and drink. I need some downtime.

Today felt like it was several lifetimes rolled into one.

I loosen my tie and kick back on the chair with my beer in one hand and a cigar in the other.

As I smoke and drink I mull over my plans for the week I'm not looking forward to. When I get past this finding a wife thing my focus needs to be on Nolan.

I need to get him out of the picture completely. Once I get rid of him it should become easier to remove his father, too. Finding dirt on Nolan will lead to Nigel because that shit will have been orchestrated by him.

Nolan is Nigel's puppet. Nolan isn't clever enough to think of his own accord. But Nigel is. Nigel is the mastermind behind all of this.

It's clear they want to push me out of the company. The fucked-up thing is it would be easy. Nolan and I have the same skill set and our fathers are friends. That's a deadly cocktail by itself.

On top of that, my father is bound by all these terms and conditions set out by my grandfather for the company that prevent him from intervening even if he wanted to.

Grandfather saw the company as a living person, never a thing or a simple entity. He set the kind of rules you would with a child, to make sure it's taken care of if you're no longer around.

The rumble of a motorcycle engine cuts into my thoughts.

It gets louder and I realize it's actually on my property.

But who could that be? I have motorcycles. I'm used to hearing my own. Hunter has a motorcycle, too. So do a couple of our friends but I'm not expecting any of them.

The sound gets closer, and I swivel my head to the left just in time to see a black motorcycle blazing up the driveway. Riding it is a guy dressed in full black leather with visor-style sunglasses and long black hair. A blonde woman is glued to his back, wearing his helmet.

A blonde woman who looks like *Harper*.

The sudden realization that it's *her* makes me drop my cigar and I push to my feet, staring at them open-mouthed.

They careen around the path and stop in front of the house. Where I'm standing they should be able to see me but they don't.

The bike rolls to a stop and Harper gets off.

My eyes unashamedly move straight to her hot little body dressed in a pair of short-short denim shorts and a tank top that shows off way, way too much cleavage.

She pulls off the helmet, unleashing her long blonde hair that makes her look like an erotic mermaid.

She hands the helmet to the guy, and he gets off the bike and looks her up and down like he wants to eat her.

He's as tall as me and built like a wrestler. Or a Viking warrior. A full beard covers his chin, and tattoos cover his neck and the parts of his arms and fingers that I can see outside his biker jacket.

I swear some of those tattoos look like Russian Mafia prison tattoos but I'm too far away to confirm that.

He looks like the kind of guy who would be in the mafia or into extreme sports. I know guys like that. They're all dangerous but the difference here is that I

know them. I don't know this guy.

He says something that makes Harper laugh. Any second now I expect her to twirl her hair and do that annoying fake flirty laugh women sometimes do to sound sexy.

She laughs again but it sounds real. I don't know why but it gets to me.

Maybe because I haven't seen her look so happy or laugh like that in years. She barely cracked a smile with me the other day when we were eating dinner.

She cocks her head and the two start joking around.

My blood heats when he reaches out and touches her face then traces a line from her cheek down to her neck and wraps a lock of her hair around his finger.

Who the fuck is he?

I'm aware that Harper has plenty of friends from the past here in New York, but seeing this guy jars me. This is no ordinary guy. And he's not a *friend*.

He's touching her like he wants to fuck her. But...maybe he already has.

Was he who she was talking about the other day?

When she said there were plenty of hotels to hook up in? Or clubs and fucking back alleys. He certainly looks like the type who would do all the above.

Okay, like she said the other day, I'm no saint. I've done all the above too, but this isn't about me. And I don't want her to do any of that shit.

Is that where they've come from?

My stomach twists with a foreign feeling when I think of that guy with his hands all over her body.

The feeling and the image boil my blood like lava in an active volcano and my body temperature rises like it's gonna blow.

When he leans in to kiss her cheek and tug on her top, my wild imagination takes over.

I skip past the sex and think of him hurting her. Hurting her the way Nick did. That's enough to move me.

Rage fuels my steps and I race down the stairs.

"I promise Harper won't be any trouble," says Josh in my head.

No, Josh. Your sister is the fucking goddess of trouble.

Just like there are the goddesses of spring, love, war, happiness, death. Harper is right up there with them.

My mythology is a little rusty, but I think the goddess of trouble was called Eris. The one who played a key role in the Trojan War. Harper is the incarnate of her.

That would certainly explain the dark-haired saber-toothed *X-Men*-looking dude on my drive talking to her.

I fling the door open, hoping like hell they're still just *talking*.

I'm thankful when I see that they are. The sound of the door smashing into the wall makes them jump apart.

Harper's eyes widen when she sees me and the guy gives me a curious stare.

Now that I'm close and can see him better, I think I'm right. This is exactly the kind of freak she shouldn't be talking to.

"Who the hell is this?" I stare him down, knowing I've embarrassed Harper and not caring.

I look at her and see I'm right. Her cheeks are red.

The guy extends his hand toward me and gives me a pleasant smile. "I'm Jack. I was just making sure Harper got home safe."

He sounds decent enough but I don't care. All psychos sound like that when you first meet them.

"She's safe now so you can leave."

Jack looks taken aback, and Harper looks like she might wither away. She steps between us and frowns at me with a claw-your-eyes-out look on her face.

She looks back at Jack with a nervous smile. "Sorry, Jack. My brother's *best friend* hasn't taken his meds today."

What the fuck?

Suddenly I'm *just* her brother's best friend and I no longer have a name.

"Don't want to cause any trouble between you and your *brother's best friend*." He looks back at me, assessing me like he wants a fight.

That's fine. I'll give him one. He has a little more muscle than me but I've handled bigger guys. I'd take him down in a heartbeat. God knows I need to work off some steam.

"There's no trouble at all." Harper moves closer to him, breaking the demented stare he's giving me. "How about I see you next week at the party?"

At the mention of this party, he looks away from me. It's like she said magical words that have him back under her spell.

"Sure thing, baby girl."

Baby girl?

My hand balls at my side and my knuckles crack.

"Call me," Harper says in a sweet voice.

"Of course." Jack winks at her and gives her a quick kiss on her forehead.

The asshole ignores me until he gets back on his bike, then he throws me a

vicious look before he guns the engine and rides away, tearing down the drive in the same manner he came in—*wild*.

As soon as he turns the corner and we can't see him anymore Harper snaps her gaze back to me and summons the filthiest look I've ever seen.

"What the hell is the matter with you? Did you have to be so damn rude to him?"

"Where did you meet that guy?" I cut to the chase.

She stares back at me as if I've just sprouted fur all over my face. "What the hell are you asking me?"

"You heard me. Where did you meet him?"

"You are unbelievable. He's a friend of mine."

"That is not a friend. That guy wants to fuck you."

"Oh my God. I'm not talking to you right now." She marches past me, dashing up the wide steps and into the house.

I follow. I'm not done with her yet. "That's the kind of guy you shouldn't be with."

"Why? What's wrong with him?"

"Are you serious? Apart from the attitude, just look at him. Covered in tats with that long hair like a pirate. Everything is wrong with him."

She stops and whirls around to face me. "You are being completely ridiculous. You have tons of tattoos and there was a time when you had long hair, too."

"I was in college and my hair was never that fucking long. How old is he?"

"Thirty-four."

Hearing that fucks with me even more. No wonder he called her baby girl. "Harper. He's too old for you."

"No, he's not. He's perfect for me.

"So he isn't just a friend, then? You two are fucking around?"

"Guess what? I'm not having this conversation with you." She turns and continues her pursuit down the hallway. But I still follow.

"You're not going to that party next week."

To my surprise she laughs.

"I'm serious. You're *not* going." I raise my voice.

"Really? I'd love to see you try and stop me. Jack also happens to have an extra room and I'm more than welcome to stay with him. I've decided I'm going to take him up on the offer."

I grab her arm and pull her back so hard she crashes into my chest. "Like fuck are you staying with him. Josh asked me to look after you, not *Jack*. You're staying here. There is no way I'm going to let him down and allow you to move in with some asshole."

"Asher, Josh is in a submarine hundreds and hundreds of miles away. Deep, deep, deep under the sea. If I choose to leave neither of you can stop me. You are a ridiculous nightmare and I can't live with you. You're the one who's an asshole. Not Jack. Now let me go."

Her words sting worse than I imagined they would. I stare back at her, realizing I'm not going to win here. Not tonight. So I release her.

Harper rolls her eyes at me and storms away.

I watch her until I can no longer see her and when the haze of rage clears from my mind, the second layer of realization dawns on me that she's right.

My behavior just now was…

Not like me at all.

This girl is making me act fucking crazy.

I bring a weary hand to my head and breathe out a haggard sigh, sounding like a man who's fallen into a deep dark hole he can't get himself out of.

Just now I was rude and ridiculous, enraged and furious, volatile and ruthless.

My temper went from zero to one hundred in a matter of seconds just because Jack was with Harper.

Because he was *touching* her.

Something wicked slithers down my insides and something more hits me that sums up my behavior with one simple annoying word—*jealousy.*

I wasn't acting crazy for no reason.

I behaved that way because...

I'm jealous.

Chapter
NINE

Harper

GOD IN HEAVEN. WHAT AM I GOING TO DO?

  I march into my temporary room and slam the door behind me. The impact makes the bookshelves rattle.

Feeling my blood still heating, I slump against the wall and allow the coolness from the satin wallpaper to seep into my skin and calm me.

Asher is an absolute nightmare.

The other day at dinner was bad enough but what happened just now with Jack was utterly outrageous.

Sure, I'll admit that I told two little white lies that definitely fanned the flames of Asher's rage.

I lied when I said Jack was perfect for me. And I lied when I said I was thinking of moving in with him.

Jack *does* have a spare room that I'm welcome to stay in, but I'd be an idiot if I didn't know he wants to fuck me.

He was the gorgeous waiter Beth and I met years ago who now

owns our favorite restaurant. It turns out he became more gorgeous and more interested in me.

We went to the restaurant today and I got talking with him. Beth had to leave early and I ended up spending more time than I should have with Jack.

He's a nice guy and maybe I liked the attention.

But Nick was *nice*, too. In the beginning.

I saw Nick as the guy the universe sent to make up for what happened between Asher and me. Or rather what *didn't* happen.

I didn't just have a silly girly crush on Asher. I was head over heels.

Memories of us may still be trapped in my mind, but I know myself. I may come across as having this big ballsy personality, but I wouldn't have simply thrown myself at him without good reasoning. Or the emotions behind it.

It took a lot of courage to do what I did, but more than anything I know I would have allowed my heart to guide me.

I think that's why I remember the incident and the sting of Asher's rejection. My heart never forgot it even if my mind did.

It was just my bad luck that Nick was the devil and the answer to nothing but disaster. So, I'm not about to hop into bed with a guy I don't really know.

Neither am I in a hurry to start a relationship with a guy I'm sure just wants me for sex. Asher can take a damn hike for thinking I am.

The one true thing I said to him is that he's a nightmare and I can't live with him. I can't. It's already driving me insane.

I already lived with a control freak and it was awful. I feel terrible comparing Asher to Nick because Nick was a monster, but they're both controlling.

At least I could figure Nick out. But when it comes to Asher I don't know where to begin deciphering him.

On one hand he seems to be acting out of loyalty to Josh, but then I look at him and his eyes tell a different story.

In his eyes I see the kind of possession a man feels when he's claimed a woman and decided she's his. But of course, I'm wrong. He doesn't feel that way about me at all. And I think I'm just seeing what I want to see.

You're like a sister to me…

I'll never, ever forget those words.

I straighten and make my way to the bed where I sit and stare at my violin on the desk.

I was supposed to get back two hours ago to practice, but I needed the break. Not from music—*never from music.* It was everything else.

I got a text from Vito first thing this morning and it jarred me for the entire day.

Quickly I pull my phone out of my pocket to check if there are any other messages from him. When I lived in L.A. he'd message several times a day.

Thankfully there are no more messages. Just the one from this morning.

Checking in on you. Just want to make sure you're on track to pay the money,

Vito.

I can almost hear his gravelly voice laced beneath every word.

I messaged back to tell him everything was fine, but nothing was further from the truth.

Within ten minutes I got rejection emails from two of the jobs I'd applied for that I thought I would get.

They were the ones I felt most confident about. One was in a bar in a hotel, the other a swanky restaurant on the river. The pay was really good and the hours flexible.

The money wouldn't have been enough to pay Vito the arrears but getting a good job is supposed to be the vehicle to getting a possible loan and also to sustain me.

I'm still waiting to hear back from the other sixty jobs I applied for. Beth might come through with something, too.

As for everything else, all I have to worry about is practicing. For that I enlisted the help of my old violin teacher, Daniela Moretti. I have my first lesson with her tomorrow morning at ten.

Since she's now retired and I was one of her favorite students, she's offered me free lessons which I gladly accepted.

It will be great to see her. Daniela has been my teacher since I was five.

We haven't seen each other since before I started college. It will also be good to step back into the music world and be the version of myself I've longed to be, if only for a few hours.

People say it's good to do something every day that makes you happy. These days I find that the little things I always took for granted are my happy things.

The past has taught me you need to enjoy what you have when you have it because you don't know what dangers lurk in the shadows.

Violin lessons might be the last thing I should be thinking about with the trouble I'm in, but every week is so different for me. Nothing is the same even from one day to the next let alone one week.

I pick up the violin and play the first piece that comes to my mind—*Bach's Concerto No.2 Adagio*.

As the notes flow from my fingers and ripple into the air I allow myself to get lost in the melodious sound. I release my worries with it.

The money, the problems, Asher.

Asher... No, he lingers like always, clinging to the corners of my mind and my heart, confusing the hell out of me.

No matter who I meet he's the only man who's ever had such a hold on me.

I wish he didn't. My life would be so much easier if he meant nothing to me and were simply my brother's best friend.

"Thank you, universe. Please kick me some more while I'm already flat on my face in the dirt." I scowl at my phone, glaring at the Uber app which is still telling me that there are no drivers available.

Ugh. This would have to happen today of all the days, wouldn't it? When I'm doing the one *little* thing I was looking forward to.

I have two hours to get to Daniella's apartment in Lower Manhattan. There are no Ubers, Beth is at work, and all the other taxi companies are either booked up or backed up because of the intense morning rush hour traffic.

My car is being delivered in the next few days, but Daniela can only do Tuesdays at ten. I didn't want to miss my first lesson or re-schedule for next week.

Maybe Olga can drive me. I'm supposed to ask her for whatever I need. Since I've been here I've asked for very little.

Granted that's because Olga hasn't exactly been friendly toward me. But to be honest, I've kept my distance.

She seems to be the type to judge and I don't know what Asher might have told her about me. That aside, if I want to get to my lesson today, she's my best chance.

With that in mind I leave the room and make my way toward the kitchen where I know she usually is at this hour. When I turn down the hallway I spot Rachel walking toward me. She's one of the nicer maids.

"Morning, Rachel," I greet her with a slight wave of my hand. "Is Olga around?"

"No. She's gone to the market. She won't be back until later."

Darn it. I'm too late. I stare back at Rachel and wonder if she can help. "Is there any chance you could do me a huge favor and drop me off in the city?"

Rachel's shoulders slump. "Oh, I'm so sorry. I would say yes but I have a few deliveries to wait for. Asher is here, though. I'm sure he'd love to take you."

My eyes instinctively widen. "Asher is here at this hour? I thought he would've left for work already." Yesterday I swore he left at the crack of dawn.

Rachel chuckles. "His schedule changes like the wind, my love. He's out by the pool. Go on. Go ask him for a ride. I'm sure it'll be fine." She gives me a little smile then saunters away.

After yesterday's drama I don't want to ask Asher for anything. I was planning on not speaking to him again for a long, *long* time. But as it stands, either I swallow my pride and my annoyance at him and ask for a lift, or I cancel my lesson with Daniela.

Thinking of the latter depresses me. But so does asking Asher for a ride.

The longer I wait, the more time I waste.

Damn it. I'll just ask him. If he agrees I'll only have to be in the car with him for a little over an hour tops. That's definitely not as bad as the hellish ride from Massachusetts.

Dragging in a deep breath, I force my legs to move and head down to the pool.

When I step through the sliding glass doors the fresh morning air greets me, along with the rhythmic swishing sound of someone swimming.

I walk along the concrete path leading to the pool and realize it's him.

When Rachel said Asher was by the pool, I thought he'd be reading the papers and drinking coffee, not *inside* it doing the backstroke with the strength and skill of an Olympic swimmer.

His arms cut through the water like blades, and I find myself staring at him, utterly fascinated.

As he glides effortlessly through the water, a hazy memory comes back to me of him and Josh hanging out in the pool at my parent's old house. I was ten, so that made them eighteen.

I used to watch Asher *all* the time but as I stared at his abs with all those chiseled muscles, that was the first time I truly felt attracted to him.

Moments later he swims over to the poolside and pulls himself out. Then I feel it again—*attraction*.

My eyes glue to his body and I notice how every part of him exudes a magnetic pull that's impossible to ignore.

The water cascades off his muscular frame in shimmering rivulets highlighting the defined lines of his torso, where intricate tattoos weave across his chest and down his sides.

I'd forgotten he had so many.

There's a hawk, a spider, Japanese characters and other cool things. Each design adds to the allure of his rugged yet refined appearance.

Of course, Asher's body is the type you'd expect to see on a magazine cover but there's something more—an effortless confidence in the way he moves.

A man like him knows the effect he has like the back of his hand.

His gaze meets mine and my breath catches. There's an intensity in his eyes. The same as yesterday. But there's something more there, too, that I can't put my finger on.

With his eyes fixed on me he picks up a towel and casually runs it over his hair then drapes it over his shoulders. Then he shifts his weight from one foot to the other and stares at me, a silent invitation to go to him.

I bite the inside of my lip and will myself to move once more, wondering if we'll argue again.

He might even tell me to ask Jack for the lift.

No, Asher wouldn't do that after practically forbidding me to see Jack.

I walk toward him and he straightens.

"Morning." I keep my tone cool and calm.

He raises his brows. "So, she's talking to me again."

"I need something from you."

He grins and I hate the way those stupid dimples in his cheeks make him look that much sexier. "What do you need from me?"

"A ride into the city. I have a violin lesson."

"Are you sure you want *me* to give you a ride?"

"There are no Ubers and Olga is at the market. I'll just need a ride there. I can make my way back."

He stares back silently for a few moments, and I think he's going to throw back another snarky comment, but instead he gives me a curt nod. "I'll be ready in fifteen minutes. Wait for me in the living room."

"Thank you." I turn and walk away but feel his gaze on me. I look over my shoulder and confirm he's watching me.

I head back to my room and grab my violin then I go to the living room where I wait for him.

True to his word, Asher is ready to go fifteen minutes later.

I thought he would be suited and booted as usual for the office but instead, he's wearing a pair of black jeans and a long-sleeved navy T-shirt that shows off his muscles. Seeing him look so casual takes me by surprise.

"What?" He quirks a brow.

"I didn't think you owned clothes like that anymore."

"I guess I'm always ready for the office. Come on, let's go."

Okay. He's being nice again. If I could get him to keep this up we just might make it through the journey.

I follow him outside and he surprises me again when we go into the *forbidden garage* where he keeps his cars that are off-limits to me.

I imagined him with all sorts of cars but when he opens the door I'm blown away. Nothing I imagined compares to the cascade of luxury cars he has stored away in here. I feel like I just walked onto the set of a Bond film.

There's the Maybach he drove to pick me up in Massachusetts next to three others—one in each color. Blue, red, black and white.

Lined up next to them are two Bugattis, a few Porsches, Lamborghinis, some other cars I don't know the names of and several motorcycles. There are at least twenty-five different vehicles here.

"Wow," I rasp "You have enough cars in here to start your own showroom."

Asher gives me a thin smile. "Collecting cars is a hobby of mine."

"Most people collect stamps or coins."

"I'm not like most people." He gives me a cocky wink and leads me to the black Bugatti.

He opens the door for me to get in before he slides into the driver's seat.

"Got the address?"

"Sure."

I take out my notebook and show him Daniela's address. He taps it into the GPS then starts the car and we drive away.

Silence fills the space between us once we're on the road but it's fine. It's better this way.

We get to Daniela's an hour later. I expect Asher to leave me, but he pulls into the parking lot for her apartment building.

"I can take it from here," I tell him.

"I have some time. I can wait with you and drop you back home."

That gives me pause because I thought he was blocked-out busy. "How come you have time for this?"

"Some days I have to work past midnight. Especially when I have international meetings. On those days I prefer to spend my mornings at home."

I think back to last week when he picked me up in Massachusetts. He would've just been coming back from work. That explains why he was still in his suit. I thought maybe he had an event or something.

"I'm surprised you work that late. I never imagined that you'd need to."

He grins back at me with a spark in his eyes. "You'd be surprised. Go on, lead the way."

I walk ahead and he falls in step with me. "I haven't had anyone sit in on a lesson in a long time."

"Don't worry. I'll stay in a different room or something, so I won't distract you."

"Okay, thanks."

No one would imagine that we had such a big blow-up yesterday.

We go up to Daniela's apartment and as soon as I see her, I feel like I could be eighteen again. Or better yet, a child with both her parents alive and well in the world.

Asher waits in her living room to go through his emails while we head to her private hall where the acoustics are amazing.

Then for two hours I allow myself the reprieve of playing my music.

"You play so much more with your heart now," Daniela says once the lesson ends. Her eyes are filled with pride and adoration, making the pale gray color look more alive.

"Thank you so much. That means a lot to me." I smile back at her.

"It is the truth."

"I guess my heart has always been the one thing that has remained true to me." All my memories and emotions are stored in my heart. Along with my zest for life. "It's where the music comes from."

"Me too, dear. In all my eighty years I have always played with my heart. I do hope you'll be staying in New York. It would be great to see you."

"New York is the long term plan. I'm hoping to get an internship in one of the bigger orchestras. I'll know if I stand a chance once I'm back at NYU." It's strange talking about my dreams when they seem further than they've ever been.

For as long as I can remember I've always wanted to be part of an orchestra like that of the New York City Ballet.

Mom loved going to the ballet. Whenever she took me to see a show I'd always imagine myself being part of the music that made the performance come alive.

Daniela rests a hand on my shoulder. "I have faith in you. I have no doubt that the best is yet to come from you."

"Thank you. And thanks for today."

"It was my pleasure, dear. I can't wait for next week." A kind smile brightens her face once more.

"Me too. See you next week."

"See you."

We say goodbye and I walk out feeling lighter than when I first went in.

It's like I have two different lives.

People look at me and mostly see the rebellious woman who seems to keep landing herself in trouble, but I swear I never purposely set out to be that way.

Sure, I have a thrill for adventure and I'm definitely the wild child. But *this* is the real me. The softer side where music is my world.

I've just had to toughen up over the years because life cut me a raw deal more times than I've had strength. That doesn't mean I love trouble.

The glossy floorboards creak as I make my way down the hallway and follow the path back to Asher. He gives me a small smile when he sees me.

"You look like you had fun," he states, standing.

"It was perfect."

"I have an hour or so. Do you want to get lunch at the diner?"

A smile twitches my lips. "The billionaire still goes to diners for lunch?"

"All the time." He grins back at me. "Let's go to that place you used to love on the Bowery. I think we need to talk."

Talk...

Yes, we do need to talk. But I hope that's not code for more arguments. "Sure."

Asher takes me to Penny's Diner, a place I remember us all going to when we were kids.

We sit in one of the booths at the back and order burgers, super-size fries and giant milkshakes.

When the food arrives, it looks so delicious we both dive in. I'm not starving by any means but it's the kind of food that makes you grow an extra stomach to fit it all in and still leave room for dessert.

I'm halfway through the meal when I glance at Asher and find him watching me.

"What? The food is great here." I chuckle.

"I know. I was just thinking."

"About the talk we need to have?"

"Yes."

At least I've had enough food so that if we argue and I need to walk out, I won't feel bad leaving a whole meal behind.

"I don't think you're an idiot," he says as if we're continuing a conversation, but I'm following. We're back to the other night at dinner.

"Don't you?"

"I don't, but I also don't like Jack." His voice drops when he says Jack's name.

I roll my eyes at him. "We're not going to argue again, are we?"

"No."

I sit straighter and stare back at him, trying for the millionth time to figure him out. "Are you sure? Because this is how it always starts. At first, you seem nice then you turn into a raging asshole."

"I promise." He holds up his hand and waves it back and forth like a peaceful white flag. "No arguments."

That's one hell of a thing to promise given the fact that arguing is all we've done, but I'll play. "Why do we keep arguing, Asher? I seem to piss you off no matter what I do, even when I do nothing."

"We argue because you don't like me being protective over you." he gives me a pensive stare.

"That's not protective. You're acting crazy. You can't tell me what to do or stop me from doing shit. Especially when I'm not doing anything wrong. You also can't stop me from seeing whoever I want to see." He doesn't want me, so I can't allow him to ruin my life even if I'm not interested in Jack.

Asher's jaw clenches, marring his pristine attempt to look calm and reasonable. Those piercing eyes of his bore into me and I know he wants to be as forthright as he was the other day. He's holding back, though.

"Let's call a truce," he suggests. "I'll tone it down if you agree to stay with me."

"Are you afraid Josh will be mad at you if I leave?" I fold my arms under my breasts and his gaze flicks down to my cleavage for a few heartbeats, making my stomach squeeze.

For a fleeting moment his eyes swell with what seems like desire. The kind of desirous look I'm used to from men. But the look disappears seconds later, leaving me wondering if I imagined it.

Did I?

I don't know and it doesn't matter. All I do is torture myself when I think like that.

Asher's face resumes that mask of confidence, so I push the thought out of my mind, promising myself that I'll stop trying to read between the lines.

"If you actually believe that scares me then you don't know me as well as you think." He sets his shoulders back and levels me a hard stare.

"Okay, so if you're not worried about Josh then why do you want me to stay?"

He holds my gaze, and his eyes become more open, less guarded, more vulnerable. "Maybe I just want to take care of you for as long as you need me to."

As the words fall from his lips, warmth blooms deep inside me, spreading through my chest like a slow, gentle wave.

Asher's gaze becomes steady and sincere, and it feels like he's staring right into my soul.

The world around us seems to fade, leaving only the sound of his voice lingering in the air. It wraps around me like a soft, invisible embrace and soothes me, breaking down the walls I've constructed between us.

"Does that answer work for you?" He cocks his head and continues looking at me with the same potent stare.

"It works."

"So, you'll stay?"

"Okay. I'll stay."

He smiles on hearing my confirmation. "Good. Is there anything else you want to talk about? Anything else worrying you?"

Yes, Asher. I owe a loan shark a hundred thousand dollars and I think he might kill me if I don't pay up. "No... There's nothing more."

Chapter
TEN

Harper

BETH SITS ACROSS FROM ME ON THE PARK BENCH AND places the bag of sandwiches between us.

Today is Thursday. We decided to come to Central Park for a change of scenery.

Beth wanted to meet up to talk about my job prospects. I chose the park because it's less stifling.

Things have been better between Asher and I since we agreed to a truce at the diner, but my anxiety is through the roof. I'm no further along in my plans than I was last week.

I also already know this is not going to be a good meeting. The moment Beth ordered extra-large cups of hot chocolate for us with triple shots of hazelnut syrup I knew a difficult discussion lay ahead.

Either she came up with nothing and wants to brainstorm potential jobs. Or she's come up with something and it's not going to be something I'm going to like.

Regardless I appreciate the time she's taken to help me. She didn't need to do any of it.

"Go on, tell me," I say. "Whatever it is can't be worse than the twenty job rejections I've received over the last few days. They have been pouring in like the rain."

"Oh, sweetie, I'm so sorry." She winces.

"It's okay. It is what it is."

Beth sighs and takes a sip of her hot chocolate before she sets the cup down between us and shuffles to face me. "I have good news and bad news depending on how you look at it."

Oh God. The last time Beth said something like that to me she wanted me to go on a blind date. I ended up being stuck with a guy who sold cockroaches for a living. I'd never even heard of that before. Usually, people try to get rid of things like that, not supply them.

"Can I have the good news first?" I tame my hair as a gust of wind lifts the ends about my face.

"Sure." She nods. "The good news is I found you two jobs."

My eyes widen. "But that's great news. What could be the bad news?"

"Wait until you hear it." The shadow of worry washes over her face. "But first I want you to consider doing both if that's an option."

"*Both*?"

"Yes. I'm extremely worried about you, Harper."

She knows Vito messaged me the other day. "I know you are."

"Seriously, it feels like your situation is getting worse."

"Because it is," I reply. "The clock is ticking, and I have nothing. Tell me what the jobs are."

"Job number one is at Le Blanche Global. Asher is looking for a PR assistant and a full-time publicist."

My shoulders sink and I breathe out a tension-riddled sigh. "A job with Asher, Beth? He'd never give me a job at his precious company."

"You don't know that."

"Yes, I do." The truce between Asher and me seems to be

working so far but it's early days. "I'm still lying to him. As long as those lies exist all hell will break loose between us if he finds out."

"He might not need to. Just hear me out. You learned a lot from Nick and helped him with stuff for his big music bands. This wouldn't be that much different."

"I learned some stuff from Nick, but my PR skills are well below what someone like Asher would need."

"Remember how you helped me with marketing and brand ideas when I started the salon?" Beth sounds enthusiastic.

"Yeah, but that's a small business. Le Blanche Global is a multi-international whatever company. I can't do anything there."

"Maybe Asher might give you a chance. At least for the assistant position. Assistants always pick up things on the job. More importantly, the pay is insanely good for an assistant's post and the listing said there was room for flexibility."

"That doesn't sound too bad. How much is the pay?"

"Five grand a month because you might have to work out of town at a whim's notice."

I gape at her in shock. "Five grand a month? Are you serious?"

Beth nods thoughtfully. "See, that's why I think you should at least ask him. It couldn't hurt to ask, right?"

"No, it couldn't. A job like that would be really good for me. It also sounds like a job where I wouldn't need to think too much."

"It would be exactly like that."

I've been worried about getting a job where I'd have to be more involved than I'd like. Jobs like that can overpower your studies.

I could handle PR. When I did it before it came second nature to me because I know how to talk to people.

"I'm going to ask him about it."

"I'm so glad you'll ask. I think it's a great idea. You also get paid weekly, and you get a travel and food allowance."

"That's even better."

"I thought so, too, but the downside is it won't pay the debt, will it?"

The little bubble of hope inside me sinks and I'm reminded of how much I owe Vito. "No, it won't pay the debt. I'm scared, Beth. We're running into week two and I'm not sure what more I can do."

"Well, maybe I may have the answer for that."

My interest piques once more. "What is it?"

"Please don't be mad at me."

"Starting a sentence like that doesn't exactly sound good, Beth."

"I know but I have my reasons and I don't want you to get mad at me. A friend of mine can get you a job at the Dark Odyssey. You know it's a—"

"Sex club." All the blood drains from my body as I stare back at her.

"I don't want you to think I'm insulting you by even bringing it up, so before you turn me down and end our lifetime friendship, continue listening."

"I would never end our friendship over something like that."

"I'm glad to know."

"What's the job?" This was the plot twist to her earlier comment.

"It's a waitressing position for high-profile clientele. It's five hundred a night with tips. You could be looking at anything from earning a grand a night to... well, at that place anything can happen. A guy could tip you ten grand just because he likes the look of you."

"I'd just have to sell my soul," I fill in.

She bites the inside of her lip. "Kind of. But you get your soul back once you're free of the debt. You'd definitely be able to pay the arrears with no problem by the end of the month. And if you stayed a little longer, like two to three months, you could pay off everything."

Everything.

The word echoes in my mind and I imagine myself debt free. But what is the cost of freedom? "It's not going to just be serving drinks, is it?"

"No. You'd have to do it topless and um... give lap dances. You'd get more money depending on what you'd be willing to do."

I groan. "So, I'd become a slut?"

"Harper, it's not like that."

"It sounds like it."

I look away from her and gaze out to The Gill, watching the swans swim past. My heart sinks with every second that passes, and I think of how low I've fallen.

"You have the job if you want it," Beth says in a reflective tone. "The hours are eight until midnight and you pick the days you want to work. If you want the job you'd just need to drop by and fill in some paperwork, then do the training when they schedule you."

Slowly, I look back at her. "Would you do it if you were me?"

She frowns. "You can't ask me that, Harper. We're so different from each other. Hence, it's me who's telling you about this job and not the other way around. Also, if something like this never crossed your mind before I think it's testament to how *different* we are, but to answer your question, yes. I would do it in a heartbeat. I *did* do it."

I suck in a breath. "When?"

"A few years back when you left for UCLA. My mom was sick. She needed brain surgery. We didn't have the money, and the insurance wouldn't cover the cost."

My insides squeeze and I look at her, hoping she'll tell me it's not true. Except why would she lie about something like that?

"Why didn't you tell me? I never knew your mom was sick like that."

"I didn't want you to know. You had a lot going on. *Too* much. You were just getting back on track after the accident. So I did what I had to do."

"You saved your mom." I bring my hands together on my lap and lean closer.

"I did. And I have no regrets because I *saved* my mom. She gave up a lot to raise me when my father walked out on us. So, I saw it as my turn to take care of her."

I nod in understanding. Now that she's laid out her story, taking a job at a sex club feels like a no-brainer if I want to save myself. "I'm sorry I wasn't there for you."

"You were. You just didn't know in what way. It was great just speaking to you when you called."

"That's not enough. I'll make it up to you."

"Let's get rid of your debt first."

"Yes." Clearing that debt would free me from Nick, too. I could even be out of Asher's place and in my own apartment near campus where I could stay for as long as I wanted to.

"I'll take the job." *One more thing to hide from Asher.* What lie am I going to tell him now? I'll have to think about it. "Thank you for getting it for me."

"No worries. I'll send over my friend's details, and you can make contact."

"Sure. This seems like the way, doesn't it?"

Beth nods. "Yeah. You could spend the next six to eight weeks at the club just to get the money you need quickly. Then do Asher's job during the day to get you through college."

"Sounds like a plan."

"Maybe in six weeks you'll be sitting here debt free."

"That would be a dream." And a relief on my soul. I don't know how much more I can take of the mental and emotional impact worrying is having on me. It's making me sick.

"I think you could make it happen."

If I don't want to ask Asher for help this is my only option.

Chapter ELEVEN

Harper

"HOLY HELL."

My heart stops at the sight of the beautiful gun-metal color Porsche parked on the driveway, gleaming under the morning sunlight.

The plan for today was to get to Le Blanche Global by ten and ask Asher for the job.

I was getting myself ready and about to call an Uber when Olga knocked on my door to let me know my car had arrived.

I rushed out, driven by excitement to finally have my own wheels, but I expected a small standard car. Not *this*.

I can't believe what I'm seeing. This car is no different from the luxury ones in Asher's garage.

I walk toward it, my fingers almost trembling as they reach out to touch the smooth, polished surface.

"It's gorgeous, isn't it?" Olga says in a warm voice.

I didn't even remember she was standing on the steps. "It's beautiful. Is this seriously for me?" I'm in complete shock.

"It certainly is." She walks up to me and we both admire the car's sleek, flawless body.

"I've never had such a good car before. The last car I owned was so old the wheels fell off." I laugh although it's not funny. That was the car I left in L.A. It gave out on me just before I decided to flee to Massachusetts.

"I think Asher wanted you to have something nice. It suits you." Olga smiles and I gaze at her, fascinated. It's the first time she's smiled at me since I've been here. It's like she's decided that I'm not a gold digger and I've passed a test.

"Thank you."

She reaches into her pocket and pulls out a set of keys. "These are yours. Want to take it for a spin? I assure you the wheels won't fall off this one, no matter how old it gets."

I laugh. "Absolutely. I was actually just..." I stop myself from giving away my plan. I don't want Asher to know I'm on my way to see him. I want to go for the element of surprise. "I was going to see my friend," I quickly add.

"Well, now you can travel in style." She hands me the keys.

"I'm so excited."

"Good. What time will you be back?"

"I think by one." Or much sooner if Asher turns me down as soon as he finds out why I'm there.

"Alright, I'll have lunch ready for you then."

"Great, thanks. See you then."

"Have fun."

If only she knew.

I practically skip into the car. When I sit inside I take a moment to admire the leather interior and all the mechanics on the dash. Everything looks so good I hardly dare to touch it.

I start the car and marvel at how smooth it sounds and so un-like the rickety, cracking noise my old car used to make.

This is amazing. And such a nice, unexpected surprise.

My soul needed something like this today. I'm nervous as hell about how the day will play out.

I'll be going to see Asher now, then later tonight I'll be heading to the Dark Odyssey to do the paperwork. I'm also supposed to get a tour of the club. The manager specifically wants me there to see the club in *action*.

I'm not overly fond of watching people have sex in real life but I couldn't exactly tell him that when that's what the club is all about.

I breeze down the driveway with a smile on my face and once I get on the road I speed up, loving the thrill of freedom surging through my veins.

I have to take photos later and send them to Josh. He'll be happy about this. He was always nagging me to get a new car.

It takes me an hour and a half to get into the city. Once I'm on Wall Street the view changes, immersing me in skyscrapers and other important buildings. This is the hub of ambition, success and unimaginable dreams that only the men who work here make possible.

And I'm like a little fish who just got lost in the ocean.

I find Le Blanche Global and my breath falters, caught in my chest.

The building looms into the sky like a gleaming pillar of glass and steel, its sleek surface reflecting the vibrant sun.

"Wow," I breathe, awed by the powerful presence of the building. I am definitely not in Kansas anymore. If I get the job this is where I'll be working.

I follow the cars going into the parking lot, then follow the people entering the triple height lobby and act like one of them.

I'm still going for the element of surprise, so the mission is to find Asher's office and…surprise him.

I know him better than he thinks. If he has time to prepare, he'll shoot me down faster than I can blink.

The entrance is framed by polished marble columns that give it a European feel. The lobby stretches before me, an expanse of

marble flooring and soaring ceilings with glittering chandeliers sparkling like daytime stars.

Golden accents line the walls, guiding my eyes toward the reception desk, where well-dressed professionals sign visitors in.

This is the perfect illustration of luxury. And by far the fanciest
place I've ever been in.

I take a deep breath, feeling the supremacy of the place settle
over me.

I can do this.

I can do this.

I can do this.

Mom used to tell me I could do anything if I made myself believe I could. So here I am, summoning her wisdom.

I also feel that if I get this job, I won't have to feel too bad about
the other one.

I head to the reception desk and sign in without saying a word,
like the woman before me. She obviously either works here or has
come for a meeting.

Once I'm done, I get a visitor's pass and am on my way to the
elevator.

So far, so good.

Thankfully the elevator is labeled by department. The management suite is at the top on the fortieth floor. That's where I head.

I imagine Asher's office will have his name on it, so I just have
to find that.

However, when I get out of the elevator and start looking for
his office, I realize the place is no different to a labyrinth. And the
floor is huge.

I feel silly for not factoring in the size.

It's definitely not going to be as simple as finding an office with
Asher's name on it. That might actually take hours.

And damn it, I'm lost. So lost I don't know where I came from.
There are two corridors that look similar.

I take the left one and end up in a waiting area that I hadn't seen before, then

suddenly I hear a familiar voice. One I haven't heard in years.

I turn to see Hunter, Asher's brother and CEO of this company. He's walking down the corridor with Luc, their cousin. The two walk like they're the gods of Olympus, strong and powerful with untamed male beauty and dominance.

My mind stalls for a moment and I wonder if I should ask for directions.

Yes, of course I should. This is perfect. They know me.

"Hi, guys." I wave at them and act like we just saw each other the other day.

They both stop and look surprised when they see me.

"Harper St. John," Hunter says, glancing at Luc with mischief in his eyes.

"Hey, there."

"We haven't seen you in years," Luc says.

"I know, it's been a while." I chuckle.

"Come to see Asher?" Hunter asks.

"Yes. Is he around?" This couldn't have been planned or timed better.

"He is. Do you know where his office is?"

"No. That's where I'm lost." I laugh as if I didn't just practically sneak into their building.

"We'll show you."

"Thank you so much." I flash him a grateful smile.

They lead me down one of the corridors I would never have seen and I hear Asher's voice coming from the office at the end with the door half open.

"That's him down there. Have fun." Hunter grins at me and points to the office door.

"Thanks for showing me the way."

"No problem. See you later."

He and Luc give me one last smile then head off.

Now for the next part of the plan. The part I have *no plan* for. I'm literally going to wing it.

I take measured steps and listen out as I hear Asher's voice again. He's talking to someone. It's a woman.

"I need someone who can use common sense, Layla. You can't teach a person common sense. And I don't have time for this shit," Asher is saying in that gruff voice that shows his rage.

"Two more interviews, then I'll get a temp," Layla replies. "We just need someone who can handle basic PR stuff."

They're talking about a job.

"I need someone who can deal with the press when they ask them shit about whatever scandal they heard about me. I don't want someone who needs to *clear* it with me first."

What idiot did that? Saying something like that just makes him sound guilty. More importantly, I'd know exactly what to say.

I reach the door but they don't see me. So I use the opportunity to get a better look at them.

Asher is standing by his desk looking stressed and Layla is gorgeous—of course, she is.

Sitting with her legs crossed, she looks like a glamorous 1920's painting, with her fashionable bob, vibrant red business dress, heels, and lips to match.

Asher looks my way and shock registers on his face when he sees me. Layla notices me next.

"*Harper?*" Asher says my name as if he's checking it's really me.

"Hi." I do my best to summon confidence by pasting a smile on my face. Then an idea comes to me that will be my make-or-break moment. "I would have said *no comment.*"

"What?" His gaze narrows.

"If the press asked me shit about whatever scandal they heard about you and you hadn't provided me an agreed answer, I would say I can neither confirm nor deny any allegations." I try to remember some of the on-the-go tips I learned when I had to work for Nick's company. "You're not legally obliged to answer any press-related questions if you don't want to. If they pushed back I would politely repeat the same answer. If they became overly aggressive or insistent I would *politely* end the call. Of course, there's also the threat of reporting them to the authorities for harassment if they continued to call."

The surprise on Asher's face morphs into full-blown shock while Layla smiles at me.

"Asher, who is this gem of a girl and where have you been hiding her?" Layla beams.

I walk into the office and over to her. "I'm Harper St. John."

I extend my hand to shake hers and she stands to give me a firm handshake. "Your Josh's sister?"

"Yes. That's me."

"I'm Layla Bianchi, Asher's assistant. *And* his sister in law's sister." Her eyes gleam with warm approval of me.

"Great to meet you."

"What are you doing here, Harper?" Asher asks in that gruff voice again, returning my attention to him.

"I wanted to thank you for my car. It's beautiful. I absolutely love it." I give him a grateful smile. Talking about the car first should smooth things over.

"You're welcome, but somehow I don't think that's all you came here for." He raises his dark brows.

"No." I bring my hands together and lace my fingers. "I also wanted to apply for the assistant PR position."

The sullenness that settles in Asher's expression is enough to make me turn around and walk back out the door. I would do just that if I weren't desperate.

That desperation roots me to the spot, encouraging me to stick around and argue my case.

Asshole. Now he's looking at me as if I couldn't be worse for the job.

"You have PR experience? It sounds like you do." Layla steps in, saving me from Asher's death glare.

"Yes. I helped out a company who managed rock bands. I didn't actually have a role, but I picked up a lot of stuff. There was a summer where I had to fill in for one of the publicists. It was when Red Viper took off. I'm a quick study, so I can learn whatever I need to learn." That's all I got. It's not a lot, but it's something. And I think I just might have Layla on my side.

"Red Viper! I love them," she gasps. "They're one of my favorite rock bands."

"Working here would not be like that." Asher cuts in, his arctic tone stealing the momentary warmth I felt from Layla's excitement.

"But they're a huge rock band. Imagine the phone calls she had to take."

Thanks, Layla. We just met and I like her already.

"Harper St. John, is that you?" comes a distinguished voice from behind me.

I look around and find Preston Le Blanche, Asher's father, standing in the doorway.

When he sees me the biggest smile spreads across his face.

The last time I saw him was at my father's funeral, and he was so kind to me, like always.

When I was a child he and his wife used to spoil me rotten because they never had a daughter. I owned dresses from every country they visited, and candies and cakes galore.

"Mr. Le Blanche." I rush over to meet him and he gives me a quick hug.

"Oh, please, call me Preston." He smirks. "We're practically family."

What a nice thing to say. "Thank you. It's so great to see you."

"And you. How are you, my dear?"

"Good. I just moved back to New York. I'm finishing up my studies at NYU. I came by to see Asher before he gets sucked into his busy schedule."

For some reason his eyes brighten on hearing that. "Oh, I see."

The vibrant look in his eyes increases when he looks across at Asher.

It doesn't seem as if Preston knows I'm staying with Asher, so I don't make him any wiser.

"Well, I'll let you guys catch up. Come to family dinner when you're free. Our doors are always open to you. My wife would love to see you. I believe she picked up a few things for you at Fashion Week."

"Oh my God. Thanks, I'll definitely be there."

"We look forward to seeing you." He dips his head for a curt nod then gives Asher an approving stare. "We'll speak later."

"Yes, Father."

I don't know why but I get the feeling there's something going on here. Something I'm not privy to but I feel like I've just become a part of it.

Preston casts me another warm grin before he departs.

"Layla, I need to speak to Harper alone," Asher says in a stiff tone.

"Of course." She nods then looks at me. "I hope I see you again soon."

"Me too. I guess that's up to boss man."

Her eyes brighten and she giggles. "*Boss man*. Girl after my own heart. I call him that, too."

She casts a look back at Asher then saunters away, leaving us. Leaving me.

When I look back at Asher, I feel like I'm in trouble again. Although I've done very little.

"Harper, why on earth do you want to work here? Please tell me it's not to irritate the hell out of me, because you do that enough at home."

"*I* irritate you at home?" I'm not supposed to argue with him if I want the job, but I can't help it. "Didn't we just call a truce the other day?"

"We did, but now you're here at my workplace."

"Asking for a job I need."

"A job you're not qualified for. Doing the few shifts you did at Nick's old company doesn't qualify you to do PR *here*."

"I learn fast. It wouldn't be that hard." I sound like I'm begging. I hate begging.

"Josh wanted you to focus on getting ready for college."

"That's nice of him but I need to earn a living."

"I want someone who's going to stay in the position, not looking for summer work."

"I'll be flexible, and I don't plan on leaving when college starts. That's why I want the *assistant* position."

He cocks his head and regards me with scrutinizing eyes.

"At least think about it. Right now, I'm in the house just practicing music. It would be nice to have my own money coming in." That's the best pitch I can give him without revealing too much more.

"Sure you don't need the money for something else?" He raises his brows again.

"No." Every time I lie to him, I feel like a jerk.

"Okay, I'll think about it."

The tension leaves my shoulders and the tightness in my lungs loosens. "Thank you. I guess I'll see you at home then."

"Sure."

That actually went well. Now I just have to hope he agrees.

It's late when I get back from the Dark Odyssey.

I was hoping to be home sooner, but the club tour took longer than I thought. And my God, did I see everything.

Literally *everything* in someone's idea of a dark fantasy came alive before me.

They have a regular dance floor and a bar like other clubs, but on the sidelines were sofas where people were having real live sex.

That was just the main section. Beyond that were fantasy and themed rooms. Rooms where people ate food off each other and other rooms where they were having orgies.

I can't even believe I'm thinking *those* words, much less that I saw it all with my own two eyes. I understood why the manager wanted me there during that time—so I wouldn't be shocked on my first day of work—but I'm completely overwhelmed.

It was *a lot* to process and my mind is still reeling from it.

I get out of my beautiful fairytale car and head into the house feeling like shit.

The day started out so full of hope and is ending with me questioning my sanity and feeling like a failure again.

Despite the gravity of the situation and the talk I had with Beth, knowing I have to lower myself by working in a sex club aches my soul.

I walk into the hallway and see that the light in the kitchen is on. It's normally off at this time.

Asher walks past the cupboard with his phone pressed to his ear. He's home.

This is the first night I've been out after ten, so I messaged to say I'd be late.

I stop in my tracks and stare at him. Whatever he's talking about has him so engrossed he's completely oblivious to me.

I wonder if he's come to a decision about the job yet. It would be so great to stop my job search. It would also be good to have a decent job. Something that will definitely cushion the blow of working at the Dark Odyssey.

Better yet... what if I took Beth's advice and asked Asher for the money I need?

Could I?

This is the first time I've truly contemplated asking him. I guess going to the club did a number on me and opened my eyes to all the things I'd have to do to get the money I need if I worked there.

Maybe it would be okay to ask Asher for a loan, and I could

just owe him the money instead of Vito. I could work it off and he wouldn't have to pay me for the PR job. That's if he picks me.

I walk closer but stop again when I think of what he'd say.

"Irresponsible troublemaker. I thought you'd have better sense than that."

Those are all things he's called me.

God, I can't imagine what he'd say if I told him I didn't properly check things out on the loan when I signed up for it. I didn't even look at the interest rate.

Of course, at the time, I didn't know that Nick was going to be laid off from the music company. Nick knew full well how screwed I would be and that's why he got the damn loan in my name. And he didn't care about me.

How do I explain to Asher that love made me blind?

I was so happy I found someone I could trust who wasn't Asher Le Blanche. Then love made me foolish.

"I need to figure this out, Hunter." Asher balances the phone on his shoulder while he grabs a beer from the fridge and pops it open. "I want this shit resolved before I get married."

His tone is so soft I almost miss what he said, but the word that caught my attention pushes to the forefront of my mind.

Married.

Is that what he really said?

Yes. He said *before I get married.*

That's what I heard. *I think…*

Surely if Asher were getting married I'd know. *Right?*

Josh would have said something. Or Asher. I've been living with him long enough.

"Father wants the wedding done and dusted by the end of the year so we can start next year fresh."

Oh God. It's true.

Asher *is* getting married.

Married.

The world suddenly feels like it's spinning around and around in my head.

My heart squeezes then it breaks silently in my chest.

I force myself to breathe, to steady the trembling in my hands.

And to wake up and come back to reality.

Asher is getting *married*, so now the dream is over. All those years of fantasizing about him have come to an end.

What a way to find out.

And no... I can't ask him for any more help.

I turn and walk away with a heaviness in my heart.

It's so stupid. These feelings I have of disappointment and regret.

Because he was never mine.

Chapter
TWELVE

Asher

MY LIFE IS ABSOLUTE HELL.

I sink into my chair, set my coffee down and stare at the swirling patterns on the ceiling. I just need a moment to think before I dive into work.

I hate working weekends, but I knew I'd have to go into the office today because I had to fit in all those dates during the week.

All those dates that were *all* for nothing.

Yes, ladies and gentlemen, it's official. I, Asher Le Blanche, am a world-class idiot. I must be the one guy in this world with a host of women at his fucking beck and call who can't pick one to marry.

Several friends of mine—and family members like Hunter—have had arranged marriages. Some of them never even met their wives prior to the wedding day. They were happy with photos. Heck, they were happy being betrothed before birth like I was.

But me...

What the fuck is wrong with me?

I was fine and ready to go along with this plan to find a wife with a no-holds-barred mindset. Then something happened.

What?

Was it really *her*?

Harper.

I can't even believe I'm going there. But in my line of work, when you've looked at all the variables that you think caused a problem and you still can't find a solution, you start looking outside the box.

You look for the thing you least expected to throw a spanner in the works.

Harper is the answer that comes to my mind. I can't actually think of anything else.

My mind started screwing with me that day I realized I was jealous of Jack.

I tried to push it out of my head. I even tried to deny it and lie to myself, but every time I saw Harper after that night the jealousy came back as I wondered if she'd been spending her time with him.

When she came to the office yesterday it was the weirdest thing seeing her in my work world. Deep down I even considered giving her the job because it meant I could keep an eye on her.

That uncontrollable demented feeling of jealousy mixed with possession made me think about the other thing I've had in the back of my mind to do with her. About when my arrangement to marry Priscilla was severed.

The first person I thought about was Harper. At the time she would have just come out of all the shit with Nick.

Because she was single and I was single, and I no longer had a marriage contract hanging over my head she stuck in my mind.

I think I fucked myself over from then. And it could be the reason I haven't been myself in *months*. That could also explain my despondency about getting married.

I'm not as irresponsible as my behavior might imply when it

comes to the company. You can't exceed your limits one moment then fall off the path the next with no reason.

Shit. I can't believe I'm sitting here entertaining this idea that Harper St. John is my problem when I know what's at stake.

Marriage to Portia if I don't find a woman on my own.

Marriage to Portia and the Fairchilds getting their greedy bastard hands on what I don't want them to have.

I have four days—including today—to figure this out.

I straighten, grab the coffee and take a swig. It's no longer as hot as I would like, so it tastes bitter.

I set it back down deciding not to have it, and Harper returns to my mind.

She's going to want an answer about the job.

She's not as qualified as I would like but she knows enough for the assistant post, which she would essentially perform alongside Layla. She also has one thing that no one else who has applied for the position has—*my trust.*

That answer she gave in her rendition of an interview was exactly what I would have wanted her to tell the press. She gave that answer because she knew I'd be okay with it.

So, as it stands, she's perfect for the position. But now that I know she affects me it might not be the best idea to spend even more time with her. It's hard enough having her in the house.

More importantly, I don't want to do anything to jeopardize my friendship with Josh.

I've always known that the one thing that would break us is if I crossed the line with his sister.

He's been more like a father to her than a brother even though their eight-years age difference isn't that significant.

Several incidents in the past made it clear Josh would be furious if I ever touched his sister. The most significant was when he gave me that warning, after he caught me looking at her as she got out of the pool at their old house.

She was seventeen, and I was twenty-five, so I knew I had no right.

He told me his sister could do better than a womanizer like me. But the worse thing he did was remind me of my bad breakup with Natalia, my high school ex.

He brought her up because she spiraled into drugs after I broke up with her. Then she killed herself eight months later, on the same night she saw me with someone else at a party.

I never stopped blaming myself for her death, and neither did people like Josh.

He thought of me as the perpetual playboy who was biding time before the marriage contract kicked in. So, I understood why he warned me away from Harper, but he specifically said he didn't want me to hurt her like I hurt Natalia.

Those words cut deep because I often wondered if Natalia would still be alive if I hadn't gotten involved with her.

What Josh never knew was I always saw Harper as off-limits. She was his sister, and the one girl I knew I couldn't pursue without destroying myself. The marriage contract stood as a barrier between us, even the night she tried to throw herself at me.

Now, there's no contract. Only the sting of Josh's warning haunting me.

"You really are here," comes Layla's voice from the door.

I look up and see her leaning against the doorframe, smiling back at me. The warmth in her eyes pulls me back from the dark memories of the past.

Dressed in an *Aerosmith* T-shirt and a pair of jeans, she looks quite the opposite to her usual professional business wear.

"What are you doing here?" I give her a little smile, although I feel mentally exhausted.

"Just catching up on some work for an hour or so. Luna and I are going to spend some time together later. It's our mom's birthday. Well, it *was*." The sadness of grief fills her eyes.

Last year she and Luna went through one hell of an ordeal

finding out the truth about how their mother died. In the same breath, they also discovered that their father wasn't the man they thought he was.

It was the type of dark and gritty story you'd see in a horror movie. Sometimes I wonder how Layla can be so positive and strong given what she's been through. It's admirable.

"You shouldn't be here, Layla. I would have understood if you needed more time to do your work."

She walks in, pulls up a chair, and sits in front of me. "I know, but I imagined coming here on Monday and having all that work from last week flowing into the usual Monday morning load. Admittedly I also needed a distraction. This day is always hard. But this year it's harder because we know what really happened to my mother."

Not many people can make me feel sympathy, but she does. "Are you okay?"

She nods slowly. "Yeah. I'll be fine. I have to be for Luna, and I guess myself, too. I'm the big sister."

"Doesn't mean you always have to be strong."

"I know, but I try. And I try to focus on good things, like Zack taking me away next weekend." She smiles and the radiance comes back to her eyes. "It's my first away trip with him so I'm looking forward to that."

"That's good. You two are getting very close."

"It looks that way. Also, pot calling the kettle black." She throws me an accusatory stare. "You're telling me I shouldn't be here when you're *here*."

"I have to be here."

"No, you don't. I know where you *could* be, but I won't say."

"What is that supposed to mean?" I narrow my eyes at her.

"Nothing at all." She smirks.

I have a feeling she's talking about Harper. Or rather not talking but hinting. Harper's little meeting stirred trouble for me.

"Layla." I shake my head at her.

"Anyway, I knew you'd be here, so I thought I'd check in on you. Especially because you'll be seeing Alexis tomorrow. I'm rooting for her, but I'm biased because she's my friend. Do you have a list of the final contestants yet?"

I sit back and allow my body to sink into the soft leather. "I got nothing."

Her eyes widen. "Nothing at all? You've been on eighteen dates with gorgeous women and—"

"I know. I haven't selected anyone. Not one of them appealed to me."

"What the hell happened? They couldn't have all been bad. Okay, the lawyer was something else. But the others would have been fine." She actually looks shocked.

"They were fine. I just can't see myself getting married to any of them. Maybe if it was just for a short time I could do it, but it's not, so it's a bigger deal."

"*Soooo, Portia then…*" Layla makes a show of biting the inside of her lip in an exaggerated way.

"Don't even mention that woman's name to me." My shoulders drop.

"But if you don't have anyone else lined up, your father is going to make you marry her."

"Yes. *I know.* Fuck… I need more time, Layla. My head isn't in the right place, and this isn't the kind of thing you can settle on in two weeks. And yes, I know I had months before. I guess my head wasn't in the right place then either."

She bites the inside of her lip again and gazes at me with curiosity dancing in her eyes. "I have an idea but you're going to hate it and probably hate me, too. Just remember there's a reason you hired me, and it wasn't for my good looks."

I smirk when she laughs and lean forward, placing my elbows on my desk. "What's this idea of yours?"

"Harper."

Here we go. I knew this was coming. "What about her?"

"I didn't know she was staying with you."

"Who told you?"

"I was eavesdropping and heard you and Hunter on the phone."

"Okay, fine. What does Harper have to do with your idea?"

"First of all, I think you should hire Harper for the PR role. She has your trust. Realistically, that's all you need. Secondly, because she has your trust, I think you should pick her for a temporary solution to your wife problem."

My blood stills in my veins. "What do you mean by that?"

"I mean fake date."

I clench my jaw and glare at her. "*Layla*..."

"Just listen to me. Your father just needs a name, right?"

"That is correct."

"He also said that you would have three months to date but if things went wrong, you could find someone else within the same time frame. What if Harper could buy you that time?"

My God ...

Why am I considering this?

Because it's a fucking good idea. But I can't do it. It would cross the line I've tried so hard to keep up and... *tempt* me.

Josh would also skin me alive. It would be a disaster.

"No. I can't do it." My voice sounds fragile, like glass about to shatter.

"Asher. You need to think about it. For a start, she would be perfect for several reasons."

"Name one reason, Layla."

"Did you see your father's face yesterday? I don't know if you realized that he thought she was one of your potentials."

"Yes, I did." Of course I knew that. When we met later in the evening my father wouldn't stop talking about her. It was like he was trying to sell me the idea of her.

"There you go. Who better to pick than a woman he adores? He even hugged her. *Your father* does not hug."

"My parents have always adored her."

"Great, but what about you?"

"What about me?"

"You like her." She gives me a sincere smile. The kind that stops me from telling her she's wrong.

"She's my best friend's little sister. Of course I like her."

"You know what I mean, Asher. You *like her* like her. I saw the way you looked at her. In any event, even if you don't want to go that way, I feel like she would be perfect to help you in the interim."

"Josh would kill me."

"From all the way over yonder deep in the sea? Come on now, Asher. The man is in a submarine. He won't know."

"But the press. They'll run wild with a story about me dating."

"The press, my ass. Of course they're going to run wild with the story. They always do."

"What would I say to Josh?"

"Josh is away for nine months. He left his sister with you, the guy who's always in the press for one thing or another. All you have to say if he sees any of the articles is that the press was being the press. By then you'd be married, and you wouldn't have to care. The stories would be old news."

Jesus… she *is* good. "Layla, that's a really good idea but I … this is a tough one for me. It's not that simple." I don't know if I can cross that line even if it is fake.

"Think about it. Go on your date with Alexis, tomorrow. Of course I'm still rooting for her, but this idea is better. It means you don't have to rush."

"Okay. I'll think about it." Although I say that, I know my answer.

There's no point complicating things that are already complicated.

Still, I can't deny that the idea is top notch. If only Harper were someone else.

Layla smiles and stands. "That's my good deed for the day done."

"Thanks."

"I'm gonna hit the office. I'll see you later."

"Sure. Don't work too hard."

"And you, boss man."

When she leaves her idea floats around in my head like a ghost haunting and tempting me in equal parts.

The thing that worries me is how badly I want to do it.

I get back from my date feeling more conflicted than ever.

Tonight's date was with Lucia, a pianist from Michigan who's just moved to New York.

She was nice but would have been a no-go because we had way too many awkward silences. It was clear within the first half hour that we couldn't even talk to each other.

I can't remember the last time I had a date like that. Maybe junior high.

I tried to make an extra effort tonight, so I know the problem wasn't me. I also stayed for the entire dinner and a movie.

At dinner I thought of every topic we could talk about and even initiated the conversation. Things like her hobbies, her career, her future plans. All she gave was one-sentence answers and never asked about me.

The only good thing about tonight was the movie. We saw the latest *Mission Impossible.*

I'm worried about tomorrow. Tomorrow will be my last date, and I'm screwed if I come home feeling like this.

I head to the kitchen to get a beer but notice that someone is in there.

It's nearly one in the morning. The only person I can think it could be is Harper. You'd never catch any of my staff in the kitchen at this hour. Not even for a late-night snack.

My stomach squeezes at the thought of seeing Harper, and Layla's plan resurfaces in my mind.

I should avoid her for a little longer, if only until after tomorrow's date, but against my better judgment I keep going. Because I want to see her.

Seeing her feels like some small compensation for the shitty, waste-of-time evening I had.

When I walk into the kitchen, I find Harper sitting on one of the bar stools at the island and all the blood rushes to my dick when I see what she's wearing.

A blue bikini top barely holds in her massive breasts and a towel is wrapped around her bottom half, but I can see the smooth golden skin of her stomach with the little metal bar in her navel. That's new. I didn't know she had a piercing there.

My fucking mind short-circuits and I curse myself for coming in here.

It's only after I perform a full scan of her body that I notice her hair is wet and pulled back into a ponytail. She was reading a thick encyclopedic book until I walked in. But did she go swimming?

Harper gazes at me and smiles. "Hey, there."

"Hello yourself. What are you doing up at this hour dressed like that?"

"Well, according to this book, if you swim in the sea after midnight on a full moon it brings you good luck."

I glare back at her, wondering if she's screwing with me. "Did you seriously go swimming in the sea at this hour?"

"Yeah." She giggles. "It's actually quite refreshing. You should try it."

And she thinks she doesn't purposely go looking for trouble?

She is going to be the death of me. If she keeps on like this, I'll have a full head of gray hair by Christmas. Between the craziness and the constant arousal it's going to do me in.

"Why do you need luck? Can't you just buy a rabbit foot like everyone else? Or a horseshoe?"

She looks more serious, as if she's going to tell me something important. "I think I'm going to need a little more than that to get the PR job."

I intensify my stare. "You did that for the job?"

"I did. Now I just have to see if it worked." She gives me a coy smile and lifts her shoulders into a sassy shrug.

I breathe out a haggard sigh, feeling as worn as the air expelling from my lungs. After talking to Layla earlier I thought about the job a little more and decided to give Harper a chance. It would be silly not to. I also thought it would be selfish to stop her from getting a job simply because I was worried about seeing her at work.

"You can have the job."

Her face brightens instantly and her eyes become more alive with hope. "Oh my gosh! Thank you so much. I swear I won't let you down. When can I start?"

"Come by the office Thursday and Layla will walk you through everything."

"Thank you and wow, I'm going to be working at Le Blanche Global."

I smile back at her. "Looks that way. And now that you have a job does that help solve some of your worries?"

She looks serious again but nods. "It does. It means I can… get my own place soon."

My heartbeat slows and something inside me twists from the thought of her leaving. "We agreed you could stay."

"Yes, but I can't exactly stick around if you're getting married."

One thing about Harper, she's not the kind to beat around the bush when she either wants something or finds out a secret. I guess it's not really a secret, though.

"I heard you on the phone last night," she explains. "Why didn't you tell me?"

Because I don't even know who I'm getting married to yet. "There was a lot going on. I wanted you to settle in first. I also didn't want you to feel like this—like you had to move out." *Nice save, Asher.* Thank God my mind never fails me.

"I understand but you still should have told me. Am I the reason your fiancée hasn't been by to see you? And I guess that's why Olga used to look at me like I was here to cause trouble."

"No, you're not the reason my fiancée hasn't been here." It feels so weird and wrong saying that word. Probably because I'm lying. "And Olga is always like that. She just takes some getting used to."

Shit, this is a fucking disaster. Harper thinks I have an actual fiancée, my father thinks Harper would be a great option for a potential wife, and Layla wants me to fake date Harper. How did things get more complicated than they already were?

"I'm glad I'm not the reason. I would have felt worse for the upheaval I've caused in your life. But… I'm happy for you. Congratulations." Although she smiles her eyes carry a wealth of dullness and regret.

I want to say something—even thanks—but all I can do is stare at her as everything rushes back to me.

I think of all the years I've known her and that disastrous night when I nearly lost her. That night I rejected what I desperately wanted—*her.*

Now, like some cruel twist of fate, she's here congratulating me because she thinks I'm getting married. And she can't remember how she feels about me.

"Thanks." I finally speak. Saying *thanks* is the best thing I can think of because it's what you say when someone congratulates you.

It's also best that I don't make her any the wiser that I *don't* have a fiancée so that when I do get one, I won't have to give any unnecessary explanations.

Harper gives me a small smile, picks up her book and walks around to me. Then she stands on the tips of her toes and plants a little kiss on my cheek.

The simple, sincere kiss sends a shiver through my hard exterior and is the most emotive thing I've felt in years. The last time I felt anything close was that night I rejected her. And back then she never even touched me.

Instinctively I reach out and cup the side of her face, allowing myself the few seconds to feel her. Feel her smooth silky skin beneath my fingertips.

Our eyes lock for a moment and I immerse myself in that moment, pretending that there is no Josh to worry about and she's not just my best friend's sister, or even his little sister. She's just Harper.

Zany Harper, who can sweep you out of this world with her musical talent one moment, then drive you batshit crazy with her insane antics the next.

"Good night, Asher." Her voice breaks the spell, and I drop my hand to my side, checking myself.

"Good night, Harper." I drag in a slow breath, my gaze still riveted to hers.

She steps away, dipping her head, then I watch her go. I stare after her like always. Except this time, I feel worse than ever, and numb.

Because I'm the one who's stirring trouble.

I still want her.

I never stopped.

Chapter
THIRTEEN

Harper

"ARE YOU OKAY?" BETH ASKS, LOOKING ACROSS AT ME. We've just pulled up in the parking lot of the Dark Odyssey and my heart is heavier than lead.

Am I okay?

That's a good question. I just don't know how to truly answer it.

I guess the simple answer would be no. Because I'm far, far, far from okay. But there's so much going on with me that I don't know which parts are worse.

Being here at the Dark Odyssey about to start my first night at this job?

Or Asher?

I was grateful that he gave me the PR job. We also seemed to connect when I told him about my crazy good luck ritual—which I actually did to calm myself after I got a check-in call from one of Vito's lackey's. If only good luck were as simple as swimming around the sea at night. I'd be immersed in it every night.

Aside from that everything else Asher and I spoke about felt strange.

He was strange and I saw that confusing desire in his eyes again that caused conflict in my soul.

At one point when he touched me, I almost thought he was going to kiss me. Then I realized how ridiculous that thought was and how ridiculous *I* was.

He's getting married. Which brings me to the main reason I felt he was acting strange.

He never told me his fiancée's name or anything about her. He never mentioned a wedding date, even though it seemed like it was soonish when I heard him on the phone talking to Hunter. He also never spoke about any of the usual stuff people talk about when they're getting married.

Maybe he didn't want me to know. But that would be strange too.

"Let's just go in," I say, trying not to sound as despondent as I feel.

Beth is playing my support system. Like a mother taking her child to school on its first day. She's going to see me off and make sure I'm okay then head home.

"Harper, you're going to be fine."

I nod slowly and force a smile. "Thanks for being here."

"Of course. Come on, Diane said she'd meet us in the dressing room."

Diane has been great and compassionate toward me. She's Beth's friend who's responsible for the recruitment at the club. It was she who gave me the job.

"Okay." I nod again, feeling like a robot. "Let's go."

We step out of the car and head toward the towering building, which seems to loom over me tonight like a mountain. This place prides itself on being high end, sophisticated and elegant. It's not the back-door seedy kind of place you would imagine when you think of a sex club. But my heart pounds inside my chest as if I'm march-ing toward my fate. Like I'm walking to the gallows

The automatic doors to the staff entrance whoosh open as we approach and a cold gust of air-conditioned wind brushes against my face.

It's cool and should feel soothing but instead it feels like an in-visible hand pushing me forward.

It can't be good if I'm already thinking like this.

We step onto the polished marble floor, our heels clicking against the surface.

I nod at the guard and the receptionist, offering a weak smile when they acknowledge me. Then I swallow hard, forcing down the bile that rises with every step I take.

By the time I reach the dressing room I feel like invisible chains are dragging me down and I can barely breathe.

We walk into the room, which looks like it came from the Moulin Rouge.

Diane steps out from one of the rows of boudoir dressing ta-bles with a vibrant smile on her red glossy lips. Her hair is red, too. She wears a wig so she can change her hair color, style and length as many times as she wants in any week.

"Girls," she beams in her soft French accent. "I'm so glad you're here."

"Hey, Diane." I smile. "Thanks for meeting me."

"No worries at all."

"You're a gem, Diane." Beth gives her a hug. "Thanks for taking such great care of Harper. As you can imagine, she's very nervous."

Thank God for Beth. She's the friend who will talk on your be-half even when you don't want her to but need her to.

"Don't be nervous." Diane looks at me and takes both my hands into hers. "Yes, things can get a little crazy and I understand this job would probably never be an option for you under normal circum-stances, but the best advice I can give you is to think of the money.

The money is what brings people here. People who have money and people who need it."

I don't think she could have said it any better. *Think of the money.* I need to because that check-in call from Vito's henchman last night truly jarred me.

"Thank you. That helps," I say, trying to look more enthusiastic. The worst thing I could do right now is sabotage myself with the job prospect that's going to save me.

To their credit, the Dark Odyssey knows that most of the staff who work here would never work here if they had the choice, so they pay them accordingly. In just my few training days one girl did a night's work and got snapped up for a million dollars just to accompany some guy to his private island for a week.

I heard she screamed like she'd won the lottery.

"Come this way. I've got your outfit for tonight. I've put you with a group of bankers. They're regulars. They're celebrating one of their birthdays, so they wanted a few extra girls. I'm hoping the tips will be good for you."

"Thanks, that would be great." In my heart I pray the tips could be good enough I never have to come back. But that's all reliant on what I'm willing to do.

Diane leads us to my section and when I see the blue glittery thong and barely-there bra I'm supposed to wear I almost cry. But I think of the money.

"This is it. You can get dressed here and when you step out into the club, you smile and become part of the fantasy. You're in the blue suite. And just remember, if the guys get violent call the guard. You don't have to do anything you're not contracted to do."

No, because being contracted to take your top off and give lap dances is quite enough. Isn't it? Maybe not.

"I'll be fine."

"Come and find me if you need me. I'll be around." She turns back to Beth and smiles. "I'll take care of her for you."

"I know you will," Beth replies.

"See you during the week."

Diane leaves us and Beth and I look at each other. Beth places her hands on my shoulders and offers me an encouraging smile.

"I know you have a million things on your mind and Asher is just one of them. But please think of the money."

"Believe me, I am."

"Those banker parties are where the money is at. Who knows, you could have the money for the loan arrears tonight."

"That would be nice."

"It would. When I worked here one guy paid me ten grand a night just to listen to him read the songs he wrote."

I smirk. "Really?"

"Yes. Of course, I'm forbidden to tell you who he is but let's just say he's super famous." Her eyes light up.

"Oh my gosh, you have to tell me. Now I'm definitely going to want to know who he is."

"No. There are some secrets you keep in your heart forever. And now you know you can trust me."

"I guess you're right. How come he wanted you to listen to his songs?"

"He was going solo from his band and didn't trust the people around him, so he came here for three nights and paid me handsomely."

"That is insane. Wow. And all you had to do was listen to him?"

She nods and smiles widely. "That was all I had to do even though he was gorgeous. I hope you find someone like that. A decent guy who just needs a listening ear."

"I hope so, too."

"And don't worry about Asher. I guess… some things are just not meant to be. He's one of them."

Nothing feels truer than that right now. For the last few days I've kept imagining him and his nameless fiancée.

All sorts of questions drifted through my mind, from *what does she look like* to how did he propose to her.

I'm sure she's prettier than me and if I know Asher he would have gotten down on one knee.

He's an alpha through and through but he also has those masculine qualities that women love. They're not for me. They're for her now. Whoever she is.

I guess I'll meet her soon.

"You're right. It wasn't meant to be." I can't help the sadness in my tone any more than what I feel in my heart.

"Get ready. Call me later when it's over. Or if you need to just talk on your break."

"I will."

"Cool. Remember, think of the money."

I dip my head and she leaves.

I turn back to look at the outfit I'm supposed to wear tonight and take it off the hanger.

"Well, at least I start out wearing clothes." I study the beautiful sequins on the bra and thong as they sparkle against the light.

Pulling in a deep breath, I set it down, take my clothes off and put on the bra and thong.

I look in the full-length mirror and my heart twists when I see myself. I'm practically naked.

Think of the money, Harper. Think of the money.

I force the thought into my mind and do my makeup. Minutes later I'm ready. The party starts in ten minutes. I have to join the other girls setting up drinks.

I take the route where I can avoid the sex and head up to the room.

The three other girls I'm supposed to work with are already there setting

up. I met them the other day when I came in to do my paperwork.

The two blondes are Clara and Denise, and the redhead is Amelie. They're wearing the same get-up as me.

"Hey, girl, happy first night on the job," Amelia says, raising a champagne glass.

The others join her and wave me in.

"Hi." I smile back.

"Don't worry, you'll get used to things when we get started. The guys are already here. They're making their way up."

"Oh, good."

"Come on, have some champagne. You look like you need a buzz," Clara says, holding out a glass to me.

She's right. I need something. I take the champagne and down it. I drink so fast I hardly taste it.

The three of them giggle.

"Have another one." Clara pours me another drink and I knock that back, too.

The buzz I was hoping for comes, so I nod.

"You good?"

"Yes, better."

The door opens and four men walk in carrying more drinks. They holler and hoot when they see us. They look like they're in their early—to mid-thirties.

"Thank God for fucking hot women," the tallest one cheers.

"Tops off now," the blond guy who looks like an oil tycoon in the making orders and I hate it when he sets his sights right on me.

The girls take their tops off, but I hesitate. Then I remember Vito with his threatening voice, threatening messages, threatening everything.

So, I think of the money and undo the hook of my bra.

Chapter
FOURTEEN

Asher

"I LOVE SAILING." ALEXIS GIGGLES. "I CAN ACTUALLY SAIL A boat myself."

"That's impressive. I've never met a woman who could sail." I stare back at her sitting across the table, and I realize why Layla picked her for me.

She is my type and she's beautiful, full of zest for life and energy.

From the moment we met we've talked nonstop. Our date started at an art gallery, then we came to this Italian bistro on the riverside.

Of all the women I've met she best fits the bill, and I think that just maybe she might be the one.

I'm trying here. *Really trying.* If I pick her the problem is solved. At least to some degree. I'd just need to wrap my head around the idea of being married to her.

"My father taught me to sail," Alexis says with excitement, her voice pulling me back to our date. "Our family is Greek so nearly everyone can sail. We meet in the summer in Mykonos and sail to every island in the Cyclades."

"That is fantastic. My brother and I do something similar but he's more into sailing than I am. I swear he'd live in the water if he could."

"I guess I'm like that, too. I spend most of my time near water. Maybe I can entice you to leave the office more often." The look of seduction she gives me is unmistakable.

At least I know she likes me. I never had a problem with that, though, with any of the women. It was everything else.

"I'm sure you could." I genuinely mean that.

"I see why Layla thought we'd be a good match." She dips her head. "I know the circumstances of your arrangement, but it was important for me to like you, too."

"And do you?"

"I do. No pun intended." Her smile widens and her eyes sparkle. "And me? Do you like me?"

"I do," I reply but... it doesn't feel right to give her hope.

"That's good to hear."

"I think so." I nod.

"How about one last drink for the road? And to celebrate liking each other."

"Sure. Sounds like a great idea."

We order two more cocktails. I'm driving her home, so I've kept an eye on my drinks.

There was a night when I was so drunk I had to call a taxi. I drank too much that night because I had another boring date. But that was my fault. I hadn't tried to have fun.

Tonight was what I'd call a success.

An hour later I drop Alexis at home and make my way back to mine.

On the drive back I reflect on everything.

If tonight was a success it means I found a girl. On Tuesday morning I can go back to my father with a name.

I won't have to worry about marrying Portia as I have a feeling that Alexis and I could work.

So why am I not more enthusiastic?

Maybe I just need the idea to sink in and be grateful I have a choice now.

Or rather a name.

Picking Alexis would also wipe out the plan to get Harper involved with something I know could be a disaster. It's too risky.

And, if Josh found out and there is nothing I can do to absolve myself, I don't know what would happen to us.

All those reasons make sense, yet when I think of introducing Alexis to Harper as my fiancée a knot tightens within me.

A knot that tells me that maybe I'm still not ready to make that choice yet.

When I reach home, I discover Harper isn't back. She'd sent a message letting me know she'd be home late.

It's only ten so it's not exactly late but I wonder where she is.

Is she with Jack?

Maybe at his place. In his bed?

Shit. There I go again. I need to stop that. I really do. If she's with him she's with him and I need to be okay with it.

I need to see it as none of my business and respect her privacy.

Of course, I can be there to beat the shit out of him if he hurts her but that's it. I can act the way a big brother would.

Serves me right. Didn't I tell her that I see her as a sister?

Absolute bullshit. It's come back to bite me in the ass now.

I grab one of those Belgian cakes Olga gets from the market. Harper likes them, too. As there's only one left, I put it on a plate and take it to her room.

The door is ajar, so I walk in and leave the cake next to her violin case. I move the stack of paperwork aside so nothing falls on the cake.

As I do something catches my eye in the drawer. It's only

slightly open but I can see a document inside with the Dark Odyssey logo on the header.

What in the hell is she doing with this?

The Dark Odyssey is a sex club.

That respect privacy line fades to nothing and I open the drawer and take out the... contract.

It's a fucking contract. As in a *work* contract.

Harper has agreed to work there as a topless waitress for a minimum fee of five hundred dollars a night with tips.

And she starts tonight. At nine.

Fuck. No.

I kick the bin, sending it flying into the wall, then I'm walking, then I'm running to my car.

Jesus. When I first thought the woman was a trouble magnet I hadn't seen anything yet.

This takes the fucking cake.

Topless waitress at the fucking Dark Odyssey.

Why?

Why would she need to do this?

One guess is that it's Beth who got her that job. But why?

I just gave her a job.

Maybe I got this wrong and she would only have taken the job if she didn't get the one from me.

Maybe she *is* with Jack and I'm losing my shit again.

You know what? I hope it's the latter.

But I don't think she's with him. I think she's at the club.

I tear out of my property and down the road, going way faster than the speed limit.

The question of why keeps hitting me like the rough waves of the sea in a tempest.

Something whispers to me that there's more at work here. The same fucked-up thing I sensed when I picked her up in Massachusetts.

This is about that, or the same thing as that. Because it doesn't make sense.

Why would Harper leave UCLA before the end of the semester with just enough credits to transfer to NYU when she'd already suffered a disruption in her studies?

Why would she go to Massachusetts instead of heading straight to New York?

Josh was here for weeks. Possibly the longest he's been around for a while. Granted, he spent most of the time with Lisa, but I know what he's like when it comes to Harper. He would have taken care of her if she needed a place. Chances are he would have kept his place for a little longer until she got campus housing.

Harper came and asked me for a job. And now there's this.

Why?

Money.

She needs money. Girls like her only work at the Dark Odyssey if they need money. A fuck of a lot of it.

What does Harper need the money for?

I'm like a madman ready to breathe fire when I burst through the club doors.

I walk past reception and straight to the manager's office. I've been here for a few private parties that some of my crazier friends have hosted, so I know my way around.

Security tries to stop me, but they take one look at me, recognize me as Asher Le Blanche and back the hell off.

I don't knock when I reach the manager's office; I just push the door open. I find a little woman inside with flaming red hair.

At first she looks at me like she's about to argue but then she recognizes me, too.

"Harper St. John. Where is she?" The words come out like a growl.

"I'm sorry, Mr. Le Blanche, I'm not at liberty—"

I hold up the contract and show it to her. "So help me God if you don't tell me where she is right the fuck now, I'll shut you down and destroy this place."

I might have a hard time shutting the place down because it's mafia owned, but that doesn't stop me from burning it right the fuck to the ground and starting a war with the mafia.

"Where is she?"

"She's hosting one of the parties," she explains with a slight hint of a French accent.

"Take me there."

She gives me a hard glare then reluctantly gets up from behind her desk.

I follow her out the door and she leads me up the wide steps where you can see all the people on the dance floor and on the sidelines fucking.

The place is crazier than when I was last here and that was only two years ago.

"In there." She points to a blue door.

I walk ahead of her now and open the door.

Inside are four guys and four girls. Including Harper. And the girls are topless.

She is topless.

I focus on Harper, at her full, round tits and perky dusky pink nipples.

She's staring back at me now with shock stealing the color from her face.

She was pouring a drink for the guy sitting in front of her. But now she's rooted to the spot, her eyes glued to me.

Even in my rage-fueled state I notice that beautiful body of hers. It's not like the eighteen-year-old version I saw years ago. Harper St. John looks like a goddess now.

And she's here at the Dark Odyssey showing it off to the cretin gawking at her.

He hasn't seen me yet. Neither have the other guys. They look wasted and too zonked out from gawking at the women to notice me.

When the cretin smacks Harper's ass my brain snaps back into focus. Hers does, too and she seems to realize in that moment that I'm here and looking at her—topless.

She covers her breasts and the guy snarls at her.

"Hey, come here and suck my dick." He grabs her arm and pulls her toward him.

"Let go of me. I already told you no." Harper tries to wrench her arm away from him but he's too strong for her. "Let me go."

I'm over there before he can take his next breath but now he's got her wrapped in his arms and struggling against him.

In one move I grab her from him and throw a punch straight into his face, so hard the chair tips over with him in it.

He jumps up enraged and glares at me. "Who the fuck are you?"

The fool comes at me. Big. Mistake.

One more punch goes to the center of his face, cracking his nose and sending the motherfucker back to the floor.

This time I grab him by his neck and lift him off the ground.

"She told you no," I snarl in his face, feeling nothing for punching him. "The club rules are that you can't force the girls to do anything they don't want to do."

I'm glad I came when I did because this fool didn't seem to get the memo.

I tighten my grip around his throat and he starts spluttering.

"Asher, stop." Harper grabs my arm, tugging me.

I glance at her. She's half trying to save this guy from being strangled and half trying to cover herself up.

"Asher." Her voice comes out strangled.

I release him and he drops back to the floor in a mess of coughing fits and splutters.

At that moment the door bursts open and the guards rush in. They can see it's me who's caused the problem, but they know better than to put their hands on me.

"That piece of shit there doesn't know what the word *no* means."

I point at the guy on the floor who scrambles away from me in fear that I'll come after him again.

I don't wait for an answer from the guards. I don't expect one. And I don't care for one.

I'm not here for them.

I take off my jacket and throw it around Harper's shoulders, covering her nakedness, then I take her hand and lead her out of the room with everyone's eyes on us.

I don't stop walking until we reach the corner by the stairs where there are fewer people.

I turn around to face Harper and release her hand. Her eyes are filled with tears, but I don't let the sight throw me off.

"What the fuck are you doing here?" I slam a fist into the wall beside her. Really, I just want to grab her and shake her.

"I…"

"You what? How the fuck could this be a good idea? What do you need the money for?" I come right out and say it. No point waiting for her to tell me.

"I'm in trouble." Her breath catches and the tears stream down her cheeks.

That… that gets me. Along with those words.

"What kind of trouble?"

"I owe a very dangerous man a hundred thousand dollars."

All I can do is glare back at her as the truth comes out and charges the air with menacing danger.

I shake my head at her. "Why didn't you come to me?"

"So you could behave like this? And call me out on my stupid decisions when I already know I fucked up?"

I clench my jaw and continue glaring back at her. She's right. I would have behaved *just* like this if I'd known before. But that's no excuse.

"Go get your clothes on. Let's go home." It's best I don't say anything more.

The drive back home is worse than the journey we took from Massachusetts.

It's worse in so many ways because now I know the truth.

I wait until we step inside, and Harper is about to escape to her room before I stop her, just as she's about to take off down the corridor.

"Did Nick get the loan?"

She faces me, her eyes red from crying. "Yes."

"In your name?"

"Yes. We were going to get a place together, but I didn't realize he was about to lose his job."

That motherfucker played her good. "What's this dangerous guy's name?"

"Vito Morales."

"Does he know where you are?"

"No. He thinks I'm still in L.A."

"Give me his number."

"Asher—"

"Don't. Just give me the number, Harper."

With trembling hands, she pulls her phone out of her bag and finds the number. She shows it to me. Since numbers are my thing I memorize it with one look and nod.

"Asher—"

"Not now, Harper. If you don't want to argue, don't talk to me now."

"I'm sorry." Her voice is so soft it feels like a caress on my skin.

"I'll see you in the morning."

"Okay… Thanks for saving me," she mumbles then with her head bowed she continues down the hallway.

When she turns the corner, I head to the living room. There I sit for a while before I decide to make the call to this Vito Morales.

I'm sure men like him accept calls at any time of the day.

I'm right. He answers on the third ring.

"Vito Morales here. This better be good." He has a gravel voice that sounds like he chain-smokes a hundred packs of cigarettes a day.

"I'm calling to settle a debt for Harper St. John."

"Who am I speaking to?" His voice fills with interest, becoming almost friendlier.

"A friend of hers." I never give my name for anything. The past has taught me to be cautious and careful.

"Must be a very good friend."

"Just message this number the payment details and I'll send the money over."

This phone is untraceable and the number unlisted so he can't use it to track me down to see where I am. It's perfect for dealing with people like him.

"Sure thing. Pleasure doing business with you, *Harper's friend.*"

"I need to know you won't bother her again after this."

"There will be no need to. You have my word."

"Then I look forward to hearing from you."

I hang up first and wait for the details to come through.

While I wait my mind buzzes with an idea.

Harper owes me now. And something wicked whispers to me telling me

exactly how she can pay me back.

Time to choose again. This time I'm choosing something that benefits me—*Layla's idea.*

If Harper agrees I'll do it. She can be my fake girlfriend and take the pressure off my wife situation.

It's fake so it can work.

This arrangement will also free up my mind and give me some time to focus on finding out what Nigel and Nolan are up to. I couldn't do that before because I knew I had to focus on finding a wife.

The more I think about this wild idea for Harper to be my fake girlfriend the better it sounds. Like a miracle answer that just fell right into my lap.

Josh doesn't need to find out. And if he or Lisa sees anything about us in the papers, I can tell them exactly what Layla said. The press is the press. Having the Le Blanche surname almost guarantees you a spot in the tabloids, and the press will run with whatever story suits them.

By the time Josh gets home I'll be married. Problem solved.

As long as Harper and I don't have any damning pictures—which we won't—it could work. It *will* work.

The only person who needs to believe we're real is my father.

We can put on a show just for him. And I suppose the other members of my family who need to believe we're real. People like my mother and Hunter and Luc's wives. No one else matters.

All we need are a few fake kisses here and there and some hand holding. We'll be no different to actors playing a part in a movie.

As for me and my obvious *real* attraction to Harper...

She's still off limits to me. Outside of the few fake kisses here and there and the hand holding I can still maintain that line between us because now she owes me.

This can be our business arrangement.

As long as I remember that it can only be a temporary solution.

And I must never allow my real feelings to push me too far over the line.

Because then I'll be in trouble.

Chapter
FIFTEEN

Harper

I SHOULDN'T HAVE DONE IT.

I should never have worked at the Dark Odyssey.

My heart is still racing and humiliation still heats my skin. I can't get Asher's face out of my head, with his eyes looking at me with disgust and disappointment.

Shit. I'm so embarrassed.

I didn't think I could ever feel like this again.

How cruel fate is that the most humiliating things in my life have happened to me around Asher.

I keep seeing the mix of shock and disapproval on his face as he came through the door at the club and saw me.

What must he have thought when he saw me there like that, practically naked? Then there was that guy. The neanderthal.

I knew he was going to be trouble from the moment he walked in. And he was.

He tried to grab me long before Asher arrived. At one point he got me in his lap and started asking for all manner of shit. He was drunk off his face, the violent kind of drunk.

I was supposed to do a lap dance for him, but I refused, ready to accept the consequences if I got in trouble.

I broke free the first time when his friend offered him some drugs. Then he took the chance to grab me again when he saw me staring at Asher.

God knows what he would have done to me if Asher hadn't come in when he did. Security was nearby but they weren't quick enough. It was all one big disaster.

Everything.

I sit on the edge of my bed and look across at the desk. At the opened drawer where I'd placed my contract.

At least I know how Asher knew where to find me.

I can see a slice of cake on a little plate next to my violin case. He must have dropped that off and noticed the contract in the drawer.

Figuring things out doesn't matter anymore. What's done is done.

I can't imagine what he must think of me now. Whatever it is, he's right. I spend so much time trying to change people's opinions of me when most of the time they're right.

I keep getting myself in trouble and everything I want gets further away from me.

I think Asher is going to pay the debt. It seemed like he was. If he wasn't, I don't think he would have asked for Vito's details.

If I'm lucky enough and he pays I'll do whatever I have to, to pay it back, make it up to him then get out of his hair.

Like Josh, Asher is getting married. He doesn't need me to wreck things for him.

I'm back at that place again where I'm forced to acknowledge that I have to sort out my life.

Hopefully Asher will still give me a chance to work for him. Once I have that under my belt, I'll be able to make a start on fixing things once and for all.

I curl up in the nest of pillows and watch night turn to day. It's only then that I drift off to sleep but I'm woken up by a little tap on the door.

"Come in," I call out in a groggy voice.

The door swings open slowly, and Olga pokes her head in. I sit up, my head feeling like it's going to fall off from the mind numbing worries.

She comes in carrying a tray. On it is a plate of cookies and a mug of what smells like coffee.

"I thought you could do with this," she says with a polite smile.

Does she know what happened last night?

No. I don't think so. I could imagine Olga being a nun or something like that before she worked for Asher. So if she knew, she wouldn't be looking at me with such kind eyes.

Or maybe she does know. I should stop doing that judging thing. It's funny how I thought *she* was judgy when it's me who's judged her more than anyone else here.

"Thank you." I take the tray and glance at the clock on the wall. It's nine. "Is Asher still here?"

"Yes. He wants to see you when you're up."

"Okay. I'll be down in ten minutes."

"I'll let him know." Her smile becomes warmer. "Once you guys are done talking, I was thinking that perhaps we could go into the city together and catch the afternoon matinee at the opera house."

Her request shocks me. "I would love that. I didn't know you liked opera."

"I guess I should have told you. In another life I was a prima ballerina for the Bolshoi ballet and my husband played violin in the orchestra."

My mouth drops open. "Oh my God."

She chuckles lightly. "Yes, most people have the same reaction when I tell them. My husband and I danced and played music for years. He was the music. The notes in every step I took. I became a teacher in Russia after years of performing on stage and then we had another decade of music and dance."

"Olga, that's beautiful."

"Thank you, dear. I thought you might like hearing that little story of mine as much as I enjoy listening to you play your violin."

"It is nice to hear more about your life in Russia. I didn't know you listened to me practice."

"All the time, dear. My husband died several years ago, and I came to the states. Music was never the same for me after he passed. Then I heard you and you reminded me of how much I loved listening to the violin."

My heart squeezes. I never thought Olga could fill me with so much inspiration. And at a time like this. "Thank you so much Olga. It means a lot to hear you say that. And I'm so sorry about your husband."

"Thank you. We had a great life together." She taps my shoulder. "Eat up, then go see Asher. He said you had a rough night."

"I did." My chest caves at the memory.

"Then let's hope for a better day today."

"That would be great."

"I'll do my best to cheer you up," she promises and smiles again. "This too shall pass and there will be better days ahead."

"Thank you."

It's times like these when I realize how much I miss my mother, but I'm grateful for people like Olga who impart wisdom and inspiration on people like me who need to hear it. Need to *feel* it.

She takes her leave and I'm surprised I feel a little better. It's just momentary, though. I still have to face the music.

I eat the cookies and drink the coffee before I take a quick shower and put on some more comfortable clothes. Then I stop stalling and summon the courage to face Asher.

I find him in the living room dressed in his usual business attire. He's sorting through some paperwork but stops when he sees me and sits straighter.

As we stare at each other a wave of shame crashes over me again, tightening my throat. My stomach churns with that awful regret, the sensation twisting deeper with each second of silence that stretches between us.

"Morning," he finally greets me in a voice that thankfully doesn't sound as mad as last night.

That gives me hope. "Morning. Olga said you wanted to see me, but I was going to come and find you anyway."

"Sit." He points to the space on the sofa next to him.

I make my way over and sit, folding my hands in my lap. I stare at him, deep into those blue eyes I could get lost in. There's so much I want to say but I don't know where to start. I guess somewhere near the beginning of my problems would be the right place.

"Are you going to allow me to explain myself?" I ask, searching his eyes.

He gives me a thin stare. "Is there any point in explaining?"

"I don't want you to think I'm a slut. The Dark Odyssey is the last place I would have gone to if I'd had a choice."

"But you had a choice. You could have come to me."

"I don't want to go running to you for everything."

"So, you thought the more dangerous option was better?" His brow furrows and heat floods my face, burning my cheeks with the unmistakable flush of humiliation.

"It wasn't about that. It was about figuring out my problems on my own and not turning to you or Josh. Please tell me you can understand that."

He bites down hard on his lip and eventually nods. "I understand but tell me you understand my point, too. Danger should never be an option. I also hate the fact that you know that Vito guy."

"I didn't want to know him. He was someone Nick knew. Believe me I've learned my lesson."

"I really hope so, Harper. I really do." He swallows hard then levels me a crude stare. "I paid Vito."

My spirits lift and for the first time since Nick went to prison, I feel light. Like I can be myself again and live.

"Oh, Asher. Thank you so much." My voice is heavy with emotion, and I can't stop the little tear of gratitude that rolls down my cheek. "I will pay you back."

"Well, that's the part I want to talk to you about."

"If you want me to do the PR job and work off the money, I'm totally open to that. Or anything else you want me to do." I owe him *big* time.

"I need you to do something for me, but it won't be work of that sort. We'll keep that separate."

"Okay, what do you want me to do?" I study his face, wondering what he's going to say.

"This has to do with my ...marriage."

My insides deflate and I try to hide my sullen mood. I pray he doesn't ask me to help his bride-to-be or something like that.

"I don't have a fiancée," he confesses, erasing all my prior worries. But now I'm very confused.

"What do you mean? How could you be getting married if you don't have a fiancée?"

"I'm supposed to have an arranged marriage," he explains. "I'm supposed to get married in the next six months to secure the CFO position in the company."

"*Really*? So, you don't get it if you don't get married?"

"No. It's grandfather's rule. The position would go to the next best suitable married person."

He goes on to tell me about Priscilla De Rosa and how he caught a lucky break. I'm amazed to hear he was contracted before birth to marry her and I never knew. If things had gone well with her, he'd be married by now.

I'm just wrapping my head around that when he tells me about his recent conundrum with his father and Portia Fairchild.

I know enough about her and her family to know they're high society. Way back when my parents were wealthy, they traveled in the same circle, but they were never as close to the Fairchilds as they were with the Le Blanches.

I listen to Asher and hold my breath as though I'm underwater because I still don't really know what he's going to ask me to do.

"I'm supposed to go back to my father with a name tomorrow."

"And do you have a name?"

He stares back at me, tentative and uncertain. "Yours... If you agree to fake date me."

My breath snags in my throat like fabric getting caught on a branch.

I blink rapidly, trying to process the words that just came out of his mouth but my brain struggles.

Fake date?

Fake date *him*?

Him, the guy I've obsessed over for as long as I can remember.

My heart stutters, pounding so loudly the sound clogs my ears and drowns out the world around me. It's a good thing I'm sitting because I feel like the floor has been ripped out from under me, leaving me suspended in disbelief.

For a moment I wonder if this is a joke but the longer I look at him, the more I realize it's not.

Asher's serious expression confirms that much and a cold rush floods through me.

I never saw this coming. How could I?

And this crazy idea sounds like something *I* would come up with. Not him.

"Asher..."

"Think about it," he says quickly. "You don't have to agree just because I helped you out, but I'd need to know soon."

"Would you marry Portia Fairchild if I don't agree?" I check.

"No. I won't marry her. I went on a date last night with a woman I'd most likely choose. I just feel like I need more time to get my head together."

A strange wave of panic grips me on hearing that.

If I say no he'll pick this other woman. And he'd actually get married to her.

He liked her. Liked her enough to marry her. He *just* said so.

My chest tightens painfully at the thought of him marrying someone he just met. I've loved him all my life and now I'm faced with the possibility of losing even this fragile connection.

"If you agreed I'd have some more time to think."

Think about her?

Does it even matter, Harper? Asher Le Blanche is offering you a chance to be with him. Even if it's fake.

"I'll do it," I hear myself say

At first he looks surprised then his brows furrow. "Don't you need more time to think?"

"No. I don't. I'll do it." I nod with certainty. "Does this mean my debt will be repaid?"

"Every last cent."

"That's a very expensive deal. I'm not sure it's comparable."

"To me it is. Thank you for agreeing."

It feels good to do something for him for a change. "You do realize this is a very crazy idea, right?"

"Yes. I do realize that. But it will serve its purpose."

"As long as it helps. What do we need to do?"

"We just need to act like a real couple in front of everyone."

Oh... my.

Act like a real couple... so we'd do real coupely things.

"Are you...going to be okay with that? I mean you... may have to kiss me." I feel like a shy twelve-year-old, too nervous to say words like *kiss* or *sex*.

Asher's eyes fill with that spark of desire I've seen from time to time. And like always it disappears within seconds.

"We're just acting so it should be fine." The overly certain tone of his voice makes me think he's trying to convince himself with that explanation. Maybe he is because he needs me. "Will you... be okay?"

"Sure. It's acting," I answer in near enough the same tone as him. "I've had to do things like that many times." No. Not really. And not like this.

Pretending things were fine when I was living with Nick is not like this at all.

"Then we should be good."

"Yes, of course."

"My father is the one we need to worry about most. We need to make him believe we're real. He already likes you and my mother adores you so we're halfway there."

I'm sure his parents would be thrilled if we ever got together. It makes sense now why his father was looking at me the way he was last week. He probably thought I was on Asher's list of potentials.

"The first time you'll see my family will be at a charity dinner on Wednesday evening. That's when we'll really have to perform."

"Um... what about Josh? Are you going to tell him?"

His eyes cloud with an emotion I can't quite put my finger on. "No. I want to keep this between us."

His answer surprises me. "You don't think we should say something? I'm sure he'd understand that I was just helping out."

"No, it's best we say nothing. Josh would hate the idea." The flatness in his tone suggests something more to the answer and I wonder if there is. Like maybe Josh said something about me before. "I don't want him worrying over you for nothing. This is just a temporary plan for the next three months. We still have another eight before he's back. By then I'll be married and this will be old news."

"Oh, right." The thought of us being old news tugs on my heart. "I guess you're right. Josh doesn't need to know."

"If the press gets photos of us together, they'll assume that we're dating anyway, whether we are or not. It's just something that happens. As long as we're not doing anything obvious, we should be fine."

Obvious—like kissing.

"Are you sure you don't want more time to think about it?"

And let him pick that other woman?

I don't think so.

"No. I'll be fine. I can do this."

"Then it looks like we have a deal."

"Looks like we do."

"*Oh my God.* You agreed to fake date Asher?" Beth blurts out, her eyes wide with shock.

"Yes."

She looks like she's going to fall off my bed.

She arrived twenty minutes ago, and I couldn't wait to tell her the news, and about what happened last night at the club.

Before I could tell her about my little arrangement with Asher, I had to make her sign an NDA. As per his request.

Beth is the only person he allowed me to tell. I don't know who else will know but it doesn't matter. All I have to worry about is that people need to believe we're real. To me that means *everyone,* whether they know we're real or not.

A slow grin spreads across her face. "This is huge but I'm so sorry about the club. When Diane called me to see if you were okay, I knew something happened, then she told me. Of course, that's when I called you."

I was in the city with Olga at the time, so I told Beth I'd see her later. "I'm sorry. I should have called you last night."

"No, it's fine. I totally understand. I feel bad for putting you in that position."

"Beth, please. We both know I was desperate. And if I'd done what you said in the *first* place that wouldn't have happened to me."

"Asked Asher for the money?" She gives me an I-told-you-so look.

I nod slowly. "He was so mad that I didn't come to him."

She smirks. "I could have told you he would be, but I get why you didn't want to ask him."

"I'm not even sure Asher won't get in trouble for beating up that guy at the club. I've been worrying about that."

"Do you think they want trouble with Asher Le Blanche?" She quirks a brow.

"No."

"Diane said the guy in the party broke the club rules by trying to force you. They're leaving it at that."

"Thank God."

Her expression softens and she smiles again. "Does this mean you never have to worry about Vito ever again?"

"Consider him a distant memory. I have my life back," I sigh. "This feels like a *Shawshank Redemption* moment where I've crawled out of a hole filled with shit and emerged into new hope."

"That's the best news I've heard in forever. But how are you feeling about this arrangement thing? You seem awfully calm, Harper."

I widen my eyes. "Oh, believe me I'm not calm about it. I'm going crazy. And I'm a little worried about keeping this secret from Josh."

"Don't worry about Josh. I actually agree with Asher. There's no need to tell him anything. Josh doesn't need to know *everything*."

"I suppose so." I can see what she means but I still worry because I lied a lot when I was with Nick, telling Josh things were fine when they weren't. I guess my conscience is just screwing with me.

"I also think you could use this chance to explore things with Asher." Mischief fills her face.

"Beth, I'm just going to do what I'm supposed to do. No exploring." Although I'd love to.

"Well, maybe Asher will see what he's been missing all this time." She laughs.

I look down at the fluffy rug beneath my toes as if it holds the answers then return my focus to her. "I don't think so. This is just for convenience. I shouldn't read more into it."

"I guess that's wise, but you never know." Her eyes fill with hope.

"I can't fall for him again, Beth."

"*Again*?" She chuckles. "Did you ever stop?"

"No. But you know what I mean. I have to view this thing as a business deal. I don't want to get hurt."

"I don't want to see you hurt, either."

"All I want is to get my life back on track and the chance to be happy."

She nods understanding. "I have faith in you, Harper St. John. I can imagine you doing great things with your music."

"Thank you, my friend."

"Maybe my grandma was right, and this is the universe giving you a helping hand. Vito was your last connection to Nick. Now you can be free of both of them"

I nod, agreeing. "Yes. Now all I have to do is stay focused."

"You'll be fine."

"This should be easy considering what I've been through."

"Exactly."

Focusing sounds easy but it's the part that worries me.

How am I supposed to focus when I'm going to be Asher's pretend girlfriend? Every time he touches me, and we act real for everyone else it will feel real for

me. Then I'll have to remind myself that we're not.

Sadly, the desperate girl I was in the past is excited about this new venture.

That version of myself would rather have this fake relationship with Asher Le Blanche than nothing at all.

Chapter
SIXTEEN

Asher

"I CAN'T BELIEVE YOU ACTUALLY TOOK MY ADVICE." LAYLA gazes back at me wide-eyed with her hands placed on her cheeks.

We're at the office and she's sitting across from me. I lean back against my chair and stare at her. This feels like a déjà vu of Saturday. Except I have some control over my wife problem now.

"I can't believe I took your advice either."

Layla grins, raises her hands, and claps. "Well done for taking a walk on the wild side."

"You're right to call it that—*wild*."

We both laugh.

This morning when I arrived at work I sent three messages. One to my father, and the other two to Layla and Hunter. Each of them got different variations of my news about Harper.

Like my father, Hunter called me straight after he received the message. He wanted to talk because I won't see him until tomorrow at the Astoria.

I knew I would see Layla as soon as she came in. And I expect my father will stop by too when he gets here.

Layla leans forward and bites the inside of her lip. "Alexis called me after you dropped her home. She said you both had a good date."

I dip my head. "We did."

"Yet you decided to go with my zany fake dating idea?" She gives me a narrowed stare.

"I guess so."

I haven't told her about the crazier parts that happened at the Dark Odyssey and Harper's loan. It's not necessary to tell her. The two things are completely separate matters, but I'll admit that my crazy mind—*and maybe my dick*—put them together because it gave me a reason to go with the fake dating idea.

Layla gazes at me like she can see through my shit, but her face remains stoic. "So, what's your plan?"

"As of right now I don't have a plan as such. The logical thing to do is use the time to get to know Alexis a bit more."

"You *could* do that."

"You haven't told her anything about my situation with the company, have you?" I'm aware that they're friends so she may have given her more details than the other women to keep her clued in.

Layla shakes her head. "No. The only thing I told the potentials, including Alexis, is that you'll get back to them whenever you choose to if you're interested. That's it. They don't know the time scale, details about you needing to get married to get the CFO position, or anything else."

"Good. That keeps things open." I'm glad she kept the information as basic as I requested. The only thing I wanted the potentials to know is that I was dating with a view to getting married in the next few months.

"It does keep things open. So, if you wanted to use the three months to get to know Alexis, or *anyone* else you technically could."

I don't miss the emphasis she places on the word *anyone*. As we stare at each other for a few moments, I can see her trying to assess me and figure out the workings of my mind.

"Asher?"

"Yes, Layla." I can imagine a mountain of questions brewing in her head like a pot of tea.

"I've known you for a while now and I've never seen you take an *indirect* route to get something you want. Definitely not when the stakes are raised."

Trust Layla to call me out. The only other person who will do that is Hunter. And if I lie, he'll know.

"What are you really asking me?"

"I think you know but let me spell it out. Clearly you want Harper, so what's stopping you?"

Realizing I can't lie or sidestep her question, I think for a moment on what to say. "Some women are off limits."

"There's off limits and then there is pure foolishness. This feels like the latter to me."

"It's complicated, Layla."

"Because of Josh?"

"Yeah."

"Has Josh ever warned you away from his sister?"

"He has."

She narrows her eyes with the scrutiny of a lawyer. "Yet he asked you to take care of the same sister?"

"He was desperate and he knew..."

"That you're loyal to a fault and you wouldn't touch her," she fills in giving me a knowing look.

"Something like that."

"Asher, there's a time in life when you can't allow people to tell you what to do. Or stop yourself from doing something just because it will upset your best friend."

"I know. I'm not normally like this but Josh is like another brother to me."

"I understand, but if you don't mind me saying so I'm sure you would have been a better fit for his sister than her ex."

Of course she looked up Harper's background. "When did you go digging around?"

"Five minutes after I met her and realized you were smitten." She chuckles. "But I'm right. Aren't I?"

"Yes. You're right."

She's not telling me anything I haven't thought before. Josh practically sang Nick's praises when he and Harper first got together. All I heard was how good Nick was for her and how in love they were. It felt like Josh was rubbing it in.

When he'd issued his warning, he said Harper could do better than me. Nick was supposed to be testament of that. Until he wasn't.

Josh could barely look me in the eye when he told me how Nick murdered those people and about all the things he put Harper through. I felt he only told me as much as he did because he needed someone he trusted to talk to.

"I think it's food for thought." Layla nods. "All of it. And that's all I'm saying."

There's so much food for thought going around in my head I'll be able to feed a small country by the time this is over.

"Anything else you need me to do?" she asks straightening up.

"Just the job training. I need you to teach Harper whatever you think she needs to learn. Block out a few hours a day in your schedule to accommodate whatever time you need. But that doesn't mean taking the day off to go shopping at Neiman Marcus." She's done that before. And I'm sure she'll find some loophole in what I just said so she can do it again.

Layla gives me a guilty smile and a wink. "Gotcha."

There's a knock at the door.

"Come in," I call out.

The door opens and my father walks in. He's come just like I predicted, and the proud smile plastered across his face makes me feel guilty for the lie I've led him to believe.

I feel bad, but at the same time I can't overlook the fact that he was being stubborn, demanding, and blind when it came to Portia. This plan is the only thing that's given me some clarity to focus. Now I feel like I can do everything I need to do.

Layla gives me a cautious look before she stands and acknowledges my father with one of her dazzling smiles. "Morning Preston, I'm about to do a coffee run. Do you want me to grab you a cappuccino?"

"I would absolutely love that, dear," Father replies.

Layla glances back at me with a wish for good luck in her eyes before she leaves.

As soon as she's out the door, Father steps forward with a full-blown smile.

"I just wanted to drop by and let you know how happy I am with your decision to pick Harper." The last time I saw him look so happy was when Hunter and Luna told him they were having a baby.

"I'm glad I've made you happy."

"Absolutely. You've made an excellent choice. I'm glad that you two were able to get together. It's not often that I admit that I'm wrong but if I'd known Harper was an option I would never have suggested Portia."

"I'm glad to hear that." God knows how much I am. If nothing else, I can take pleasure in knowing that I've thwarted the Fairchilds attempts to get a piece of our empire. All I have to do now is stop Nigel and Nolan from getting on the board.

"Harper and I make a better match."

"Your mother and I have always thought so. I know she went through a lot recently in LA, so I assume that's why you didn't approach her before."

This is just too perfect. I hardly have to explain anything. "Yes. I wasn't sure if she was ready for a serious relationship."

"I'm glad she is. It will also be great to have her working here. When does she start?"

"Thursday."

"And will we get to see her tomorrow at the Astoria?" He cocks his head and gives me a hopeful look. "It would be great for the press to get a better outlook on you. It would certainly tamp down any remnants of the scandal."

"Yes, she'll be there. And I agree, the press will get to see me in a *different* light."

"Wonderful. We have a few public events over the next few weeks. I'm sure there will be plenty of opportunity for them to see you as a changed man."

"Yes." I smile but inside I know that means Harper and I will be putting on the show of our lives. That's all well and good, and it's just *acting* but it means getting closer. It means touching her in ways I wouldn't normally and looking like a couple in love.

"I hope you two can make it work. I'm sure Josh will be happy to hear you're together."

"Sure." I try to sound confident but my insides twist at the mention of Josh.

"Alright, son, I better run. I have back-to-back meetings so I won't see you until tomorrow at the Astoria. I'm really looking forward to seeing you and Harper together." Father smiles again and I can see he was worried about me. Worried I wouldn't ever find my way.

"We'll be there around eight."

"Perfect. See you then."

He leaves and I stare at the wall, hoping I can pull off my plans unscathed.

I doubt that will happen since I'm already seeing potholes in this grand plan of mine.

The biggest one being me.

Number one: I'm lying to Josh by omission.

Number two: I don't want to come between Harper and her brother, and I don't want to ruin my friendship with Josh either. And that leads to number three.

When I take Josh out of the picture, I'm still my own worst enemy.

I could be setting myself up for a fall because in three months I have to let Harper go.

I'm not sure if I can handle knowing what it's like to be with her, then letting her go.

It seems foolish to feel this way when there is no marriage contract to worry about anymore. Meaning the door is open to a future if we wanted it.

I shouldn't entertain the thought, but it's there. Having this fake relationship with Harper may give me a taste of what I could have for real. *If* we wanted it.

But it's not as simple as wanting it. Because of Josh.

Deep down I'm also worried because I'd never want him to be right about me. I'd never want to hurt Harper and disappoint her the way Nick did.

I'm not him but I already blame myself enough for her accident.

I wouldn't want to break her heart too.

It's show time.

Tonight is the night to put my fake dating plan into action and reveal Harper to my family as my girlfriend.

We have everything carefully crafted to ensure things *hopefully* run smoothly without a hitch. We spent a few hours last night getting our stories straight and going over a strategy.

The essence of the plan is to go with the flow and act natural. I hope that will be as easy to do as it is to talk about.

I got home fifteen minutes ago.

Olga and I are in the living room talking about the plans for the coming week while Harper gets ready. We're leaving as soon as she's done.

Olga is the only member of my staff who knows the truth. I

also didn't need her to sign anything. She's kept far worse secrets than this for me in the past.

I felt that I had to tell her the truth about Harper and me because it didn't feel right to lie to her. She knows Josh almost as well as she knows me. And I know she's figured out my reservations regarding Harper.

"I should be back next Saturday. Are you sure you're going to be okay?" Olga asks. She's heading to Japan with her nieces tonight. It will be the first in a long time that I'll be without her.

"Everything will be fine." I smile back at her. "Please have an amazing time with your family and don't worry about me."

"Of course I'm going to worry about you. This is the first time I've left you in a...well a *situation* where I think you might need me around. As soon as the press hears what's happening they'll be camped on the lawn."

"We'll be fine. I promise." I nod with a confidence I partly don't feel.

"Okay. Well, everything here is in order. All the staff know what they're doing next week, and no one should need anything. But if anyone does need me you know where to find me."

I give her a grateful smile. She never stops working even when she's on vacation. "We know and like always we won't disturb you while you're away."

She chuckles. "I'm just giving you the option, so you *know* you have it."

"Thanks, I appreciate you."

"I know you do. And just for the record I think you and Harper will have a great time tonight." Olga looks pleased. "She's just getting the finishing touches on her make-up done. At first, she was skeptical about using an artist, but she soon changed her mind."

"She's always been that way. She's stubborn at first then she—"

The words dissolve in my mind as Harper walks into the room dressed in a sleeveless black evening gown. The sight of her steals my breath away and erases everything from my world that isn't her.

The shimmering black fabric clings to her curves, cascading down in soft, elegant waves that glisten under the light.

And that's just her dress. Her face looks like she's ready for a magazine photoshoot and her hair is swept up in a loose ponytail, exposing the graceful line of her neck.

Everything about her is beyond perfection—and I'm so transfixed all I can do is stare.

The barest hint of a smile plays on her lips as she meets my gaze, and my pulse quickens as if I've been zapped with lightning.

"I'm ready," Harper announces, bringing her hands together, a nervous habit.

I want to speak, say something that shows my appreciation, but my mind is a blank slate.

"Harper, you look absolutely beautiful," Olga says rushing up to her and taking both her hands.

"Thank you."

"Yes, you do look beautiful." I try to sound like I'm not over here holding back my drool and keeping my eyes from falling out.

"I guess it's a little different from my shorts and t-shirts." Harper giggles.

"It sure is. Ready to go?"

"As I'll ever be."

I hold out my hand to her and she moves toward me looking back at Olga who nods her approval.

I place my hand to the small of Harper's back and quickly take in the soft beat of her pulse leaping against the smooth skin on her long, elegant neck. She's definitely nervous. So am I.

And… judging from the state of my dick, I'm also fucked.

It's already difficult to control myself around her because all roads keep leading me back to what I want most.

Her.

Chapter SEVENTEEN

Harper

I'VE HEARD GREAT THINGS ABOUT THE ASTORIA BUT SEEING it in real life is something else entirely.

The building is a testament to timeless European elegance with its ornate carvings on the exterior and the tall, arched windows that punctuate the walls.

Considering where I was weeks ago—*from the broken-down motel in the middle of nowhere to the county jail*—I never imagined in my wildest dreams I'd ever be here as a guest at the invite-only association which caters for the world's elite, known by their net worth.

The press spot us as soon as Asher and I step out of our car. And when I see them the nerves in my stomach turn to rocks.

It's time. Time to act like Asher and I are a real couple.

I don't think I've ever been more nervous in my life. I feel like I'm going to implode.

A group of journalists swarms us when we walk further inside.

Asher keeps his hand at the small of my back but moves closer and I follow his lead.

"Asher Le Blanche, who is this beautiful mystery woman you're with?" a woman with thick-rimmed glasses who reminds me of Velma from Scooby Doo asks. "Is she your date for the evening?"

"Yes, she so happens to be my date?" Asher gives her a charming smile.

"Are you two in a relationship?"

Asher replies with another smile not confirming or denying the answer to her question. I smile too, realizing what he's doing.

He's allowing them to believe whatever they want. And they do. They *assume* we're dating but they won't have it on record that he confirmed it.

A flood of questions come rushing our way next.

They ask for my name. Where we met. How we met. How long we've been dating and if marriage is in the picture. But Asher remains silent and leads me away.

"They're not allowed in the hall," he mutters in my ear, making it look like he's whispering sweet nothings to me.

For a moment I wonder what that would feel like, but I shove the thought away and smile back at him.

"I'm glad because I don't know what to do if they ask me something crazy," I murmur back under my breath.

"You're doing great. Just keep doing what you're doing. Come on."

Asher leads me up the sweeping marble staircase leading to the large double entrance doors. Then we go into the grand hall which is brimming with people dressed in their finest.

There are stunning women dressed in gowns suitable for the red carpet, but it's the opulent décor in the hall that makes my head spin.

Gilded mirrors stretch high along the walls, reflecting the soft, golden light spilling from the glamorous chandeliers lining the painted ceiling.

Deep burgundy velvet drapes frame the windows and the floors shine like black crystal.

Whoever designed this place was a real master of the arts. I feel like I've been swept into some fantasy palace where every detail seems meticulously crafted to evoke the grandeur of the Rococo period.

Little old me only knows about the *Rococo period* because of a trip to Europe in my freshman year. We mainly stayed in Italy, and I fell in love with the place.

I never knew I could have a taste of it right here in New York.

"Wow," I gasp, knowing I'm drawing attention to myself for being so fascinated with my surroundings, but I can't help it.

"It's beautiful, isn't it?" Asher grins down at me.

"This room is a work of art. I've never been anywhere like this before."

"Welcome to my world." He gives me an easy grin and I get lost in his smile just as easily as I do with the place.

We spot his family sitting at a long table in the corner of the hall. There are some other people at the table I don't recognize, and I wonder whether the woman he likes is here.

I have no idea what her name is or what she looks like. Only that she exists.

Asher's hand moves from my waist and he takes my hand. His large hand swallows mine, warming my body from head to toe, and all thoughts of his mystery woman drift out of my mind.

He held my hand the other night at the Dark Odyssey but that was different. Or rather *this* is different. At the club it was the *I'm-mad-as-fuck-and-you're-coming-with-me-now* kind of hand holding. Whereas this says...you're mine.

"Ready?" Asher leans in again, filling me with the scent of his musky cologne and power.

"Ready." I look up at him this time, not realizing how close he is.

Our eyes lock, time slows, and the world narrows in the space between us.

He guides me to a stop then inches closer and I quickly realize with impending shock that he's going to kiss me. I'm going to get the answer to all those years of wondering what it would feel like to kiss him.

The sudden thought makes my nerves buzz, but I'm drawn to him like a magnetic force.

Shivers rush down my spine. Then his lips touch mine. And it's electrifying.

Asher presses his mouth to mine and fire ignites within my core, consuming

me with the raw heat of desire and longing.

The kiss is divine, filled with every dream I've ever had of Asher Le Blanche's lips on mine. But it's also bittersweet because I know that nothing will ever be the same again.

Nothing. Because... the kiss. It doesn't feel fake.

A fake kiss isn't supposed to make your head spin. Or stir need in your core that makes you think of hot wild sex.

The kiss feels as real as we are standing here.

Asher moves away and I wonder if he felt it too. The *non-fakeness* of our

first kiss.

His lips part to speak but he doesn't get a chance. His parents come up to greet us and the magical moment we just shared is sucked away with their excitement at seeing us together.

Asher's mom hugs me like I'm her long-lost daughter and practically carries me away to meet the rest of the family, leaving Asher with his dad.

I just about manage to glance over my shoulder at him before a group of people clouds him from my view. But he was looking at me too.

His mom introduces me to all the wives, friends, and acquaintances. I'm seated in between Luna, Layla, and Autumn, Luc's wife who is all talk nonstop about everything.

The excitement is infectious but all I can think about is Asher and that kiss.

When dinner is served Asher and I sit together, becoming *the couple* again.

He kisses me two more times and I don't believe there's *anyone* here who thinks we're anything other than a couple. Except of course for those who know about our plan.

The evening wears on and I have a surprisingly great time but in the back of my mind I keep wondering what next.

What will we do next?

What will happen next? What will we have to fake next that will feel real?

And is it just me who's worrying about this?

Maybe Asher is fine. Maybe this is nothing to him. After all this is his world and he's used to the attention. Since we arrived, I've noticed so many women looking at him, not even caring he's clearly with me.

I guess the irony of the situation is he doesn't really belong to me.

So, either way it doesn't matter.

Chapter
EIGHTEEN

Harper

MIDNIGHT COMES AND IT'S TIME TO HEAD HOME.
Day one is over, and we did well.
Asher and I slide into the backseat of the Maybach waiting to take us back to the Hamptons and we set off.

I look over at him sitting next to me, tall, brooding, and handsome.

He turns to face me. "We did it." His voice is as reflective and soothing as a gentle caress.

"We did."

"You okay?" He slides his hand over mine on my thigh to give it a gentle squeeze. It's a completely innocent touch but I feel it everywhere and the warmth of arousal makes moisture bead between my thighs.

"I'm good. You?"

"I am now." He smiles at me, looking like he wants to say more but is holding back because of the driver.

It's nice to see him look at me with such admiration instead of the disapproval he's been sporting since Massachusetts.

We reach home within the hour, but I don't want the night to end. I feel like if it does the magic will go with it.

We go inside the house and when we reach the corridor where we're supposed to go our separate ways our steps slow.

We stop and face each other. Conflict seems to settle in Asher's expression, but I don't know if I'm seeing what I want to see. It's hard to tell when you're dealing with a guy who can either mask his emotions or switch from one to the next as effortlessly as breathing.

"I'd say we had a great time tonight," he states with an easy grin.

"Yes. We weren't arguing and I wasn't getting myself in trouble."

"Maybe this is a new normal for us."

"It seems that way."

"Thank you for agreeing to do this… *thing* with me. It helps a lot."

"It's a small price to pay considering what you did for me." I give him a coy smile, showing my appreciation for saving me from whatever fate awaited with Vito and the debt.

"Don't worry about it. We seem to have a mutually beneficial agreement."

Mutually beneficial.

It's odd he would say that when he had a choice between me and this other woman who I don't think was there tonight.

Asher was with me the whole time and all the women he introduced me to as friends seemed to just be *friends*. I've known him long enough to know when he likes someone.

"We should probably get some sleep," he suggests.

"Yeah," I answer, although I don't want to say goodbye yet.

"See you in the morning."

"See you."

He dips his head and turns to go to his room. I watch him and I don't know what comes over me but it's like there's this urge to hold on to tonight.

It pushes me to call to him. "Asher, wait."

He stops midstride and turns back to face me.

"Do you want to hang out for a while?" The words tumble out of my mouth faster than I can think. I might be shooting myself in the foot but at least I tried. "I'm not tired."

Asher seems surprised by my question. As if I caught him off guard. Then the surprise on his face morphs into caution and it looks like he's going to turn me down.

I prepare for that sinking feeling of disappointment I hate but then his eyes darken with some unidentifiable emotion, and his gaze flicks down to my dress then roams over my body in an unmistakable sexual way.

"Sure. Let's go to my office." He nods.

I'm so stunned he agreed that I stare back at him with my eyes wide, checking to make sure I heard him right. "Really? You're saying yes?"

"Sure. I have some of that wine we had at dinner." A smooth grin slides across his lips.

"That wine was amazing." And wow… he actually agreed to hang out. It's great but now the butterflies in my stomach have goosebumps.

We go in the opposite direction and take the stairs to his office. I've only ever seen the door when Olga took me on the tour.

His office is in its own wing of the house with a separate entrance.

When he opens the door and I see inside I'm completely surprised by how big it is. It's like a separate apartment. The only thing missing is a bed.

He's got everything set up like his office at Le Blanche Global but on the left there's a sofa area with a bar. Next to that is a glass wall with a sliding door to a private terrace. The glass walls offer a great view of the beach. Against the dark the beach and the trees in the surrounding area look like a fantasy painting.

Asher goes over to the bar fridge and removes the bottle of

wine. It has a French name I can't begin to pronounce but it's fruity and absolutely delicious.

"I picked this Monbazillac up on my last trip to France," he says, grabbing two glasses.

"When was that?"

"A few months ago. I went with a friend of mine, but it was a business trip. They needed me to evaluate an investment."

"Sounds like fun."

He smirks. "Harper, *you* really think that evaluating an investment sounds like fun?"

I bite the inside of my lip, holding back a smile. "Not really. I was just being polite."

"*Clearly*. Let's sit over here."

I follow him to the large leather sofa where we sit alongside each other.

He sets the wine and glasses on the coffee table then he takes off his jacket and tie.

Embarrassingly, my eyes glue to his thick forearms as he rolls up the sleeves of his dress shirt, revealing the Japanese characters for earth, warrior, and brave tattooed on each arm.

I only look away when he picks up the corkscrew to open the wine and I'm amazed how easily he's able to uncork it.

"You make that look so easy." I giggle. "I always have a difficult time opening wine. Even with my bar experience."

"There's an art to it. My grandfather taught me. I'll teach you next time." He glances over at me.

"Thanks. I look forward to you teaching me."

He grins and pours our drinks. I watch him, getting lost in the way he looks at the glass as he focuses on the wine flowing into it. And the way his long fingers seem to caress the narrow stem.

How silly. I'm jealous. Jealous of the glass. I wish he would stroke me like that.

Asher gives me the glass and I take it, still thinking of him having his hands on me. "Thanks."

"What did you think of tonight? You got to meet everyone."

"They were great. Your parents especially are always amazing. And your mom is like my fairy godmother."

"She likes you a lot. Let me guess, she's invited you to go out, hasn't she?"

"Every weekend for the next year." I giggle. "I'm going to see her on Sunday for afternoon tea at the Ritz. Then she's taking me back to her house to try on all the dresses she got me. I can't believe she still buys me dresses after so many years of not seeing me."

"That's my mom for you," he grins. "Sorry she's so crazy."

"It's fine. I love her craziness. I think my mom would be grateful to her too."

A touch of sadness flickers in his eyes. "I think she would too, so it works out well then."

"It does."

I finish drinking the wine. He does too and pours us each another glass.

"Luna, Layla, and Autumn are all a great bunch too." I try to keep the conversation going so that awkward silence doesn't have a chance to step in and throw me off.

"They are." Asher chuckles. "I knew you'd get on well with them."

"I felt like I'd known them for years. It's different with Beth because I've known her since we were kids. I've never met anyone else that I got on so well with right off the bat." They all made an effort to talk to me. It took mere minutes for us to click.

"They were like that with each other too."

"It will be great working with them. I guess I'll see Layla more though. And Luna at the charity events." I learned that Luna owns a charity which she and Hunter run. As Le Blanche Global are huge investors their PR team gets involved with various activities.

"You'll love working with both of them. More wine?"

"Absolutely."

After pouring more wine, he starts talking about Hunter and

Luc. He talks about going to Luc's hockey games and taking me along. Then he talks about sailing with Hunter next year after he and Luna have their baby.

This is the longest we've ever spoken and either not argued or offended each other.

I hang onto every word he says, and I think he does the same with me. But when he talks, I like looking at his lips and I keep thinking about all the kisses we shared tonight.

If I'm like this now, how will I feel next time?

Next time will be Sunday. His parents are hosting a dinner party at their home. Since I'll be with his mom all day, I won't even see Asher for a regroup until he arrives with everyone else. The plan should be fine. It's just me who's nervous.

We continue drinking and talking until eventually we reach the last bit of wine in the bottle.

As Asher pours it into my glass, sadness hits me that we've reached another natural pause where we should say goodnight.

It's almost 3 a.m. Now it's super late.

He has an early start and today is my first day at work. We *should* go to bed. I just don't want to yet. The time went by too quickly.

Asher hands me my glass and looks at me as if he knows what I'm thinking. "You tired yet?"

"No." I smile back at him. "Are you?"

"I'm not but I don't think it's a good idea to get you drunk mere hours before your first day on the job."

"I can handle a few more." I cock my head, gesturing to the bar. "I haven't reached my limit yet."

"Me neither." That sexy half grin returns. "How about we make some cocktails then head to bed?"

Thank God. "Yes. I want to do that."

"Alright, come over to the bar with me." He takes my hand and tugs me to follow.

Like an obedient servant destined to follow him anywhere and do whatever he says, I go.

"What do you like?" He goes behind the bar and grabs a bottle of vodka.

"Anything with fruit and vodka."

"Perfect."

"Have you got fruit up here for cocktails?" I glance at the mini fridge.

"I do. When I'm working from home—*which happens quite often*—I love having cocktails. I like making them too. So Olga makes sure I have what I need."

He opens the fridge and shows me the little pot of fresh fruit and juices ready to go.

"Olga is amazing." I giggle, looking over the fruit.

"She certainly is."

Asher sets out the fruit, the juices and an assortment of alcohol on the counter. Then he grabs two coupe glasses from the cupboard. "Let's see who can mix the best cocktail." Asher cocks his head with a challenge in his eyes.

"Game on. You first."

"You sure?"

"Hmmm hmm."

"Alright then Miss Bartender."

Within minutes he shakes up a cocktail using a jigger of bright green liqueur that he says is made by Carthusian monks.

"Wow, this is great." I'm impressed. The start of a buzz also zings through my mind, a signal that I'm nearly at my limit. "What is it?"

"The Asher special. Do you remember that time when Hunter, Luc and I got stranded in Ibiza?"

My shoulders sag. "No. I don't remember."

He touches my cheek, and his fingers warm my skin. "It's okay. It was just a funny story that sparked a running joke for years. We all had to work at a bar. That's how I learned how to make cocktails."

"Really? What happened?"

"We got plastered as my grandfather would say—basically drunk out of our minds. Then we were robbed. Then we ended up in jail without a hope in hell of getting out. When we were eventually released, we had to find jobs to earn enough to get home. Our parents were away on one of their getaways and unreachable."

"Oh my God. That is so crazy." I laugh.

"Josh was supposed to go with us, but your dad broke his leg. Josh stayed back to look after him. You were supposed to go on a skiing trip but the two of you refused to leave your father's side."

Like always, when I hear people talking about things I should remember, I try to push against those barriers preventing me from accessing my memories. Nothing comes. Not even that hint of a familiar feeling people get when they recognize something. All I see and feel is emptiness. "It's sad that I don't remember any of that."

"It's okay. The ordinary person doesn't remember everything."

"I guess so."

"It's your turn, Miss Bartender." He smirks. "See if you can beat that."

I laugh, knock back the rest of my drink and grab a bottle of gin from the shelf. "Mine will be the best cocktail you've ever had in your life."

"Is that so?" He raises his brows.

"It will. I've never been turned down for a bartender job."

"Okay. Show me what you got then."

I mix the drinks even quicker than he did. I fix him my rendition of a Boulevardier but instead of swapping out the gin for whiskey I add both. I always find that the sweetness of the bourbon balances the flavor.

I hand him his glass and he looks interested to try it. He takes a sip and the totally impressed look on his face tells me I've won.

"Holy shit, what the hell did you put in this to make it tastes so good?" he glares at me.

I drink mine too. "You saw me. It's the way I did it."

"*Clearly.*"

"I'll teach you next time." I borrow his words from earlier.

He grins and a lock of his dark hair falls over his eye when he takes another gulp. "I'll hold you to that."

"Just say when."

"I will." He nods with an easy smile on his lips that makes my heart flutter. "And I agree. You *do* make the best cocktails. Looks like Harper St. John isn't just a beautiful face."

I was about to take another sip but he hooked me at *beautiful*. "You think I'm beautiful?" If I was ever going to find out what he truly thinks of me, it's now.

He stares back at me and my nerves twist in my stomach. I'm locked in his gaze until his eyes drop to my body, then stay there for far too long before climbing back up to meet my eyes again.

"I think any man with eyes thinks you're beautiful Harper *St. John.*"

"But… do *you*?" I'm pushing the limit and crossing a line again. *Again,* as in allowing the same madness that possessed me to throw myself at him years ago to take over my mind again.

Unlike then, my question feels like the most important one in the world.

And I want the answer my body seeks.

Asher holds my gaze, searching my eyes, knowing what I'm asking him.

Those nerves in my stomach turn to lead, growing heavier the longer I wait.

"Yes. I think you're beautiful." His voice is quiet and reverent, but the simple words of his answer hit me in my core, stirring my need for more.

More of this feeling rippling through my body like wildfire.

"What else do you think about me?"

He bites the inside of his lip and keeps his gaze trained on me. "I'm… not so sure I should answer that question, Harper."

"Because you'll hurt me?" My lungs squeeze. Given that I know he thinks I'm trouble maybe I shouldn't have asked him anything.

"No, I'd never intentionally hurt you."

I'm relieved to hear that but my interest piques. "Then tell me. What else do you think about me?"

He looks at me for a moment then reaches out to take a lock of my hair. "I'd have to show you. And I definitely shouldn't do that."

"Why shouldn't you?" God my nerves are on fire.

"Because..." He touches my cheek and leans in a little closer, wrapping me in that scent of power again. "I'm a few drinks away from not being able to control myself. I don't want to do anything that I can't explain when the sun comes up."

His words are like bait thrashing around in front of my face, screaming at me to take the hook and not let go.

So I do. I take the hook, grab the scotch and pour him another drink.

"Show me," I mutter.

That dark desire settles in his eyes once more and his hand drops from my cheek.

His gaze flicks down to the glass in my hand and he stares at it for a few seconds. Then he takes it from me and nerves scatter all over my body, making my legs turn to fiery liquid.

The moment he puts his lips to the glass, tips his head back and drinks it feels like we've both crossed another line. And we're on the same page now.

Asher closes his eyes for a heartbeat and when he opens them again, I see hunger. Raw and carnal. The kind you'd see on a wild animal starved for weeks.

"Fuck it," he rasps under his breath then leans in to capture my lips for a searing hot kiss that burns through my mind.

He tastes like sin, forbidden passion and dangerous desire rolled into one. My brain barely gets the time to process that his lips are actually on mine before Asher deepens the kiss, making it clear that this kiss is not like any of the others we shared at the Astoria. The kisses that were supposed to be fake.

There is no mistake in whether or not *this* kiss is real.

And my God does it feel exhilarating. This is the kind of kiss that rivals all kisses, leaves you breathless and wanting more.

Shivers of fire race down my spine and I relish the feel of his tongue touching mine.

His electrifying touch ignites everything inside me, and I'm consumed by the heat, lost in a whirlwind of desire and longing.

He pushes his solid body into me, pressing his hard cock into my belly.

At the feel of how thick and big he is my pussy aches with the need for him to be inside me. Every nerve under my skin comes alive and I can't stop my body responding.

The kiss turns hungry with our tongues tasting each other as if we can't get enough. I moan into his mouth, and he takes the moment to pull out of the kiss and press his lips to my ear.

"I have to stop, Harper," he groans, his hot breath burning my skin.

"Don't." I've never sounded more desperate in my life.

"*Fuck.*" The scruff of his beard brushes my cheek as he turns his head. "If I keep going, I'll want to taste you everywhere."

"What if… I want you to taste me *everywhere*?" I'm breathing so hard I can barely get the words out but there's no way in hell I'm giving up now. Not in a million years. I feel like I just strayed into a dream, and someone handed me everything I ever wanted.

Asher doesn't waste another moment. He returns to my lips and kisses me like he's starving for me.

He goes back to my neck and shoves me against the wall so he can kiss his way down my chest, pausing briefly to taste my skin.

I close my eyes, savoring the little throbbing pulse in my clit as he nibbles on my skin. Then down he goes until he's licking the skin at my cleavage.

I gasp when he shoves the top of my dress down and my breasts pop out.

He covers my nipple with his mouth and sucks so hard I feel

the pull in the tips of my toes. It makes me arch my back to press into his mouth.

He takes me deeper, sucking in more of my sensitive flesh.

I moan out loud and a flicker of a smile slides across his face before he moves to my other breast and sucks.

He sucks from one breast to the other until both nipples are so hard with arousal they feel like shards of glass.

The ache in my pussy increases, making me writhe against him.

Holding my waist with his big, strong hands, he moves down my body and crouches down to bury his face between my thighs through my dress.

I don't have to wait too long to wonder what he's going to do next. Asher rolls my dress up my legs, right up to my hips, then he pulls down my panties and spreads my legs wide.

Before I can take my next breath, his face is back between my thighs and his tongue is thrusting into my pussy. And holy hell, the impact of his tongue inside me is earth shattering.

I grab on to his shoulders and throw my head back, crying out from the intense pleasure that pulses through me like hot lava.

My blood throbs in my veins, overflowing with a lethal dose of desire and pleasure. It leaves me powerless to do anything besides surrender to the mercy of his dominance as he eats me out, tasting and taking everything from me.

The rising pressure floods my core then explodes into a mind-blowing orgasm that's like nothing I've ever felt before.

I cry out again, lost in ecstasy as Asher feasts on me, licking, sucking, drinking, lapping until there's nothing left.

Then he just stays there, breathing hard with me as if we've just finished a marathon.

I look down at him, gazing at the top of his ruffled hair. I'm too afraid to move in case I shatter this moment, so all I do is stare.

Feeling the weight of my gaze Asher slowly looks up at me. I don't know what I expect to see on his face but it's definitely not guilt.

He presses his forehead to my thigh for a few brief seconds then looks back at me.

"I have to stop now, Harper. I've already gone too far." His voice is heavy with guilt.

"No."

"Yes." The firmness in his voice snaps my awareness back into focus and I pull my dress up to cover my breasts.

"Asher—"

"Harper, we *can't*."

All the words bouncing around in my head freeze, and I realize we're back *there* again. Back to four years ago. This time might have been different but he's still rejecting me.

"Let's just stick to the plan. We need to."

The plan. Be his fake girlfriend.

Not his real one.

"But we—"

"No." His sharp tone reminds me that all I am to him is his best friend's *little sister*.

Shit. I'm so stupid. This was another foolish mistake.

Why do I keep jonesing for this guy when it's clear he doesn't want me?

A wave of embarrassment pulls me under and just like four years ago I turn on my heel and flee.

"Harper," Asher calls after me but I don't stop.

I keep going.

I keep going while hot tears sting the back of my eyes and my heart pounds in my throat.

What the hell is wrong with me?

It's not like I haven't walked down this road before. I know what's at the end waiting for me—nothing.

Stick to the plan.

I need to because I owe him, but how the hell am I supposed to forget what we just did?

The problem with crossing lines that are already so blurred

you can hardly see them is that you can't find your way back. I sure as hell can't.

I wish to God I could.

I wish this was as simple as telling myself I shouldn't fall any deeper than I already have for him.

But how do you stop falling when you're already sprawled on the ground?

Chapter
NINETEEN

Asher

FUCK.

I slam a fist into the wall and stare at the empty space where Harper stood.

What an absolute fucking clusterfuck.

God, do I have a way of making shit worse than it already is.

I've been thinking with my dick all night. Right from earlier when I saw Harper walk into the living room in that dress and all I could think of was getting her *out* of the fucking dress.

Every move she made drew my attention to her gorgeous body and when I caught myself looking at her tits I kept thinking about her at the Dark Odyssey.

Her topless for some guy who wasn't me. Then I wanted her for myself.

I knew that I wanted her. So, I shouldn't have agreed to hanging out. It's not like I didn't know something could happen between us. I felt it from the way she looked at me and I was eager to know if that part of her that used to want me still existed.

I shouldn't have wanted that, but the intense desire got the better of me and I agreed to hang out because I wanted to fall in the trap.

I wanted to be powerless to resist the temptation and the thought lured me in like an addict who can't resist a fix.

As I feasted on her perfect breasts and ate out her pussy I wanted more.

I had every intention of taking more until I heard Josh in my head.

I heard his words in my head screaming at me that I wasn't good enough for his sister. If I hadn't stopped, I'd be balls deep inside her by now.

Day one and I've already fucked up.

Now Harper is mad at me.

But what the fuck did I expect? Of course she was going to be mad.

I'm mad at myself. And look at me. I'm standing here pitching a tent and I'm not sure what I am. Am I a coward or a fool?

Cowards shy away from a fight and fools never try to get what they want.

It doesn't matter.

I messed up and now I have to try and unfuck myself. I have to focus on the plan which is working so well. Tonight was a success.

I'm satisfied that Portia Fairchild is so far off my father's radar she's pretty much an afterthought.

Harper and I stole the show and won everyone's hearts. Of course, the irony in that is that the plan worked because we aren't fake.

But those kinds of thoughts are going to get me in more trouble with her.

The best thing to do is avoid situations like tonight. Avoid Harper when I don't need to be with her.

I'm sure that's going to be easier said than done. Especially now that I'm also going to be her boss.

I didn't bother to go to sleep. Now I wish I had. Sleep would have given me the chance to rejuvenate and be ready for the meeting with Father, Hunter, and Nolan.

The morning already started off like shit because Olga wasn't there.

She would have gone to call Harper for breakfast or checked on her. I could have done it myself, but I felt that after last night I should keep my distance for a little while.

Layla has a busy schedule planned for Harper today and I have back-to-back meetings, so chances are I won't see her.

I wanted to at least make sure she was okay with me. Now I have to put all my focus on this meeting because it seems Nolan—the motherfucker—has another ace up his sleeve I never saw coming.

The meeting is supposed to be about our work with the tech company. Last week I had Layla draw up my proposals on how we should move forward and send them to Nolan, who agreed.

Except today he's saying something entirely different. Something different that has blown my father's mind.

"Merging the tech company with Ansel Software would solidify the brand and increase our profits exponentially." Nolan speaks with pride, sounding like a door-to-door salesman eager to make a sale.

This is the new thing he sprung on us this morning. He and his father have surprisingly managed to secure the leading shares in Ansel Software *overnight*.

Of course my father thinks that a merger is a great idea because Ansel Software is a development company.

If he agrees to merge our tech company with Ansel Software, Nolan and Nigel would have a formidable powerhouse.

This is their comeback at me for eliminating Portia as a marriage potential.

Although a merger wouldn't carry the same impact as marriage to me, it would be a hell of a lot more than what they have now.

I glare at Nolan as he continues talking about all the potential profits we could see from a merger of the two companies. When he's finished talking, I look at Father then at Hunter. Both of them have this transfixed expression that irritates me even more.

I've been patiently listening, trying to keep myself under control while wanting to snap Nolan's neck. It's obvious he's trying to outdo me again.

Once again I can't get violent. I'd definitely be in the wrong. Especially when Nolan has my father eating out of his palm like a dog.

"This is absolutely wonderful, Nolan," Father says, giving him the same adoration he shows us as his sons. "We'd just need to go over the dynamics and logistics thoroughly as the tech company has been a subsidiary of Le Blanche Global for many years."

"I understand completely, Preston," Nolan replies in a hearty voice. "My father and I expected you to ask for more time so we're good to wait. Just don't take too long. We have other companies in mind to merge with. I just think it'd be a great opportunity to expand our already wonderful working relationship with Le Blanche Global."

"I think you're right," Father agrees and looks at Hunter and me. "Do you boys have anything to say with regard to this possible venture?"

I have no shortage of words to bury him but the moment I open my mouth to speak Hunter taps my leg, pressing a thumb down into my knee. It's his secret signal. His way of telling me not to say anything that's out of line.

When we were boys we used to do this a lot.

I glance at him out of the corner of my eye and when he nods I decide to tamp down my rage. *For now.* "I think it's a good idea but I'd like to look into it a little more."

"Me too," Hunter agrees, switching his gaze to Nolan. "I can definitely see the business potential. Congratulations on sourcing such an acquisition."

I take note of the wary look in Hunter's eyes. It tells me he's picked up on something. That eases my rage to some degree.

Nolan smiles wide and proud. "Thank you. I actually did this on my own. So I'm very pleased with this achievement. It couldn't have come at a better time."

"No, it couldn't have." I restrain the sarcasm in my tone, masking my true feelings about this idea.

"Well then," Father says, taking back control of the conversation. If no one else has any questions let's wrap this up. I have to get to my next meeting but you boys are welcome to continue the discussion."

"Sure. Thanks, Father," Hunter replies.

"Thanks for your time, Preston." Nolan dips his head. "I'm really grateful that you heard me out."

"Of course. We're all about growth here. The more we grow the happier we all are. The guys and I will talk then get back to you."

"Perfect."

"I'll see you all later." Father smiles then he heads out.

Hunter and I have meetings to attend as well. We stand but I want to speak to Hunter.

Nolan looks at me with that stupid grin on his face. "I appreciate that I didn't make you aware of this before today, but I thought it would be best if we all discussed it together."

Bullshit. He kept it secret because he knew I would argue and want to look into it before presenting the idea to my father.

"No worries." God help me. Every time I see this guy he rubs me the wrong way.

"We'll be in touch," Hunter says, knowing I'm ready to blow.

"And I'll see you both on Sunday." Nolan grins.

"Of course."

I keep my silence. I was so glad he and his family weren't at the dinner party last night. They had a prior engagement they couldn't miss. Sunday will be different.

It will be worse because there won't be as many people.

Nolan glances at me before he leaves.

I watch him through the glass door and wait until he's out of earshot before I whirl around to face Hunter.

"Hunter, please don't tell me that didn't seem shady to you. Because it was."

"It was. And that's why I didn't want you to say anything. I think we might have just found your first lead."

Hope sparks in my heart for the first time in forever. "What did I miss?"

"I've been watching Nolan and Nigel so I asked Jericho to keep digging and he found something I felt I should look into."

Jericho Grayson. No one is better than him at finding shit out. "What did he find?"

"Nolan and Nigel have had shares in Ansel Software for a long time. I was aware that they were trying to get ruling shares, but the evidence suggests something is up with their stocks and revenue."

"Seriously?" *This is good.*

"Yeah. There were a few instances where the minimal revenue was drastically low on one day and the next day the stock price spiked. They hid it well. So, you'd only know if you were looking for something. Which we were."

"Well damn. Do you think they could have initiated a pump and dump scheme?" Low revenue on one day and high stock prices the next usually tends to suggest some sort of scam like that.

"It looks that way. If they merge with our tech company it makes them stronger, not us. It also means they get to continue their shitshow with our backing."

"We have to tell Father."

"No. Not yet." He shakes his head. "We need to watch them

and gather details. Let them dig the hole for themselves and we'll be there to cover them with the dirt."

I smile, feeling better for the first time since my encounter with Harper. "I like this."

"At least you have something to work with now. It's small but it's something. Father hates shoddy business deals. If he comes across shit like that it won't matter how long he's known Nigel or who he is."

"No, it won't. If this works it'll be perfect. It may even be the thing that will get the Fairchilds out of the picture for good."

"Agreed." Hunter nods then gives me a curious stare. "So... what about your other problem?"

"What other—" I stop myself when he quirks a sharp, questioning brow.

"Harper," he clarifies.

We haven't spoken face to face about her yet and so much has happened since I told him about my plan over the phone.

I may be able to fool everyone else, but I can't do that to my brother.

"I think I fucked myself over," I confess.

"In what way? Because you two looked great to me last night. I had a hard time believing you're supposed to be fake." His gaze intensifies.

"It's complicated."

"Why? What happened?"

"I don't want to talk about it." The worst thing is having him call me out.

"Did something happen between you two last night?" His eyes narrow to slits.

I think for a moment about how I should answer that, but I decide to go with the truth. "Yes."

"Asher—"

"Hunter don't. Like I said, it's complicated."

"Okay. I'll leave you to figure it out. Only you know what you want."

Damn it, why the hell did he say that? "Sometimes I can't have what I want."

"That's bullshit. Since when was that ever the case? We're men who take what we want. Especially when it comes to a woman."

True. But I've never been in this situation before, where my conscience is getting the better of me. "I'll figure it out."

"I hope you do." He gives me a tight-lipped smile but the gleam in his eyes tells me he wants me to be with Harper. "Let's get to our meeting."

"Sure."

We head outside and I hear Layla's voice in the other room. I know she's training Harper so I can't help but look inside as Hunter and I walk by.

There she is. Harper is standing next to Layla. She's holding a notebook and making notes.

She must feel my eyes on her because she looks around at me.

As our eyes lock, I remember us only hours ago. Me stepping way over the line and her giving herself to me.

I remember how she felt in my arms and how she tasted. The taste of her alluring mouth, her silky skin, her delicious breasts, and her sweet pussy.

It was like drinking pure honey, nectar, roses all at once in a lethal dose that hooked me with a craving I will never forget.

For those few moments that I held her and ate her out Harper St. John felt like she was mine.

She was. And she was just Harper. Not Josh's little sister. Not the woman who was off limits to me. She was Harper, the woman I wanted to bury myself in and devour until every part of her belonged to me.

Now I can feel a wall between us. Not the glass wall separating us but the invisible barrier I pulled up when I stopped us from becoming more than what we are now.

A forced, stiff smile flickers across her face. It's the kind you'd give your enemy when you need to be polite. The smile is similar to those I give Nolan and Nigel.

Harper looks away and I glance back at Hunter who's already watching me.

He says nothing. Neither do I. But I know what he's thinking.

Even if we weren't brothers and close, I'd be able to tell what he was thinking.

That this shouldn't be as complicated as I'm making it out to be.

Not when it's as clear as the hard on in my pants that I want her.

Chapter
TWENTY

Asher

MY DAY AT THE OFFICE WAS AS SHITTY AND HARD AS I knew it would be.

I couldn't stop thinking about Harper. I barely paid attention during my meetings, and I was completely off my game.

I couldn't wait to get back home to see her and clear the air between us.

But when I reach home though, I find an empty house.

I finished at eight and Harper was done before five, so I expected her to be home before me.

At ten on the mark, I get a message from her letting me know she's at Beth's. I text back, telling her to be safe.

I know Beth is her best friend and she's a nice girl, but I don't trust her with Harper.

Beth gets up to the kind of wildness that I don't think is good for Harper. I don't like the company Beth keeps and fuck, yes I'm worried Harper will see Jack or someone else like him.

I wake early the next day with Harper on my mind even more than before.

Today is the first time since she's been living with me that she's been away and as I'm not at work today I won't see her until later. Hunter and I are upstate to meet with a new client.

Once again, at the end of the day, I'm eager to get home and see Harper, but I get another message at ten letting me know she's going to stay with Beth until Sunday.

It's clear she's avoiding me. I don't even have to wonder whether she is or not, but the irritating thing is, if she were around me, I might be doing the same thing.

She's just beating me to it. This way neither of us has to feel that awkwardness of being *avoided*.

This isn't what I wanted. But what did I expect after what we did? After what *I* did.

Things were never going to go back to normal after that. I fucking ate her out, licked her half-naked body, then had her coming in my mouth. There is no going back to how we used to be. Only this. *Awkwardness.*

On Sunday evening when it's time to head to my parent's house for the dinner party I'm ready to flip my lid.

I've imagined all sorts of scenarios and things that Harper could have gotten up to with Jack.

I keep imagining her with him and feel like a fool because this is not my style.

Usually if there's a woman I'm interested in there's no way in fuck that I'd allow someone else to have her.

I'm only stuck because it's her. Harper. My best friend's sister.

I'm already running high when I walk through the doors of my parent's hall. So, when I see Nolan talking to Harper my blood spikes as if someone added a dose of napalm to it.

It ignites when he says something to make her laugh, and I see how happy she looks.

God, I hate that guy. And knowing Nolan like I do, he's only talking to Harper to fuck with me.

I march over to them like a general leading his men into battle.

When they notice me, they stop talking but Harper still has a ghost of a smile on her beautiful face.

"Asher, there you are," Nolan says with that fake-as-fuck smile plastered over his face.

"Moving in on my girl as well?" *Shit.* I can't help it. He's so obvious to me, I call it like I see it, whereas everyone else tiptoes around him. I can't do that.

Harper looks surprised by my comment. Nolan simply laughs.

"We were just talking. I just discovered that Harper is a baseball fan. It's always great to meet a woman who loves sports."

"Indeed." I return his fake smile.

"I've asked her to join me at the Rangers game on Wednesday."

I give him a death glare. Clearly, he must be on crack if he thinks I'm going to agree to that. "No. She's not going with you, Nolan."

They both stare back at me as if I've lost my mind, but I couldn't give a rat's ass what either of them think. Especially Nolan.

"Harper has already agreed to attend with me." Nolan smiles at Harper.

"Yes. I did," Harper says in that stiff tone that tells me she's annoyed with me.

"I'm sure you're not the kind of man who makes decisions for his woman."

"I'm not. But it's still a no from me."

"*Oh my God,*" Harper mumbles under her breath.

Nolan chuckles low and menacing. "Good God, Asher, loosen up a little. It's just a game."

I step into his personal space and stare him down like I'm ready to fight. We've had enough run-ins over the years that he would have wondered what it would be like to fight me.

I've held back because of my father. I'm guessing he held off because of his father too. And the threat that I'd win.

We both know I would. Unlike him, who's afraid to get his hands dirty, I'm unhinged with no off switch.

"Find another Rangers fan." I give him a clipped smile and flick some invisible lint off the shoulder of his jacket. "My girl is not going with you. *Understand*?"

I intensify my stare, silently warning him to back the hell off. From the shift in his demeanor, he seems to get the message and after a beat of silence he nods.

"Sure. See you both later."

I don't answer but Harper smiles at him.

"It was great talking to you," she says in a small, cautious voice, her embarrassment peeking through.

Nolan dips his head at her and walks away.

I turn back to Harper, finding her glaring at me. Mad as hell, like she was that day when I was rude to Jack, but all I can see is her beauty.

"What is wrong with you?" she snaps. "Do you have to be an asshole all the time?"

"Yes. Definitely with certain people."

"But Nolan was being nice to me. He invited me to a simple baseball game."

"I want you to stay away from that guy."

She narrows her eyes. "Why? We were just talking about baseball."

"I don't care."

"He's harmless."

"You don't know him like I do. He's shady as fuck and I don't want you hanging around him. Do you hear me?"

She holds my gaze for a moment with that relentless look in her eyes that makes her ballsy, but she finally sighs and nods. "Fine. Anyone else I'm supposed to avoid?"

Yeah. Me. Except doing so defeats the purpose of our plan. I need to talk to her. I need to do it now before we get to the end of the night, and I want her all over again.

We're alone so this is the best chance I'll get for privacy before everyone starts talking to us.

"There's no one else. But um…" I pause for a beat, wondering how I'm going to say what I need to say and not piss her off. "I wanted to talk to you about the other night."

"There's nothing to talk about. Obviously, we both drank too much." Her answer sounds well thought out and rehearsed. She's also trying to look nonchalant but the hurt in her eyes is evident.

I don't want to take the easy way out and agree that we drank too much because I already had a get-out-of-jail card thrown my way when she lost her memory. But maybe it's best for tonight.

"Yes, I guess we did. So, are we good?" That feels like an asshole question when I know we're not and I feel like I'm trying to fix a broken vase with paper glue.

"Yes. Of course. And we're sticking to the plan." She tries to keep a straight face, but I can see the hurt still lurking in her eyes.

"Yes. This arrangement of ours is just to give me time. Time to get to know other people."

"Sure," she says in a clipped tone. "Is she going to be here tonight?"

I give her a narrowed stare. "Who are you talking about?"

"The woman you like."

Oh. Right. I forgot I told Harper about Alexis. Except I didn't give her name.

"No, she won't be."

"Okay. Well, I guess we should get this show on the road then." Again, she gives me that not-real smile.

"Yeah."

She glances across the room as Autumn and Luna enter. They wave her over.

She waves back and faces me. "I'm gonna talk to them."

"Go, have fun. I'll catch up with you later."

"Sure," she says, then saunters away.

I stare after her like always, feeling like the coward and the fool again. Two things that are naturally against my character.

This is supposed to be the right decision. If I stay away from Harper things remain the same. She'll be free to be with someone more deserving of her and things remain cool between Josh and me.

So why the fuck do I feel like shit?

Why do I feel like everything is wrong?

Why does she still feel like mine when I keep letting her go?

This girl has always screwed with my head, so I don't know right from wrong when I need it most. But right now, I *know* this doesn't feel right.

The feeling becomes more evident as the night wears on.

And the worst thing is her kisses don't feel like they did the other night.

Every time I kiss her, I can't feel her anywhere. I find myself kissing her when I'm not supposed to, just to check. Every time I come up short and it's like I'm kissing an empty shell.

Like the Harper I want isn't there anymore. Each kiss is as empty as a void and fake.

As fake as our relationship is supposed to be.

Chapter
TWENTY-ONE

Harper

THE SCENT OF JASMINE AND FREESIA SOOTHES ME AS I stare at the sandstone walls of the relaxation room.

I'm at the Rockwood spa in the Hamptons with Layla. I'm dressed in a fluffy white robe, curled up on the sofa, waiting for Layla to finish her hot stone body massage.

The spa was Layla's idea of a Monday morning huddle. Because I've been feeling so low and drained, I didn't question it or ask whether Asher was really okay with us heading to the spa when we're supposed to be at work. Especially when I know he probably isn't.

Being here amongst the calming floral scent and peaceful ambience has been the only thing to calm me in days.

Nearly three weeks have passed since I agreed to this fake dating arrangement between Asher and me. The time has flown by, but each day has been hell for me.

Every time we launch into our act, I feel like I've stepped out of my body and slipped into someone else's shoes. Then when we're not acting things feel strange. Like the real world is the fake world.

Every time Asher kisses me, I struggle to protect my heart.

At home, when we're alone and we don't need to pretend, I keep expecting him to kiss me or hold me the way he does when we're around his family.

When he puts up that wall between us, we become two passing ships in the night. Little more than strangers. It jars me.

Sometimes I counteract it by staying with Beth. But that has its own problems.

Beth's place tends to be okay for a night or two. No more than that. There was a reason Josh asked Asher if I could stay with him and not Beth.

As much as I love being with her, I can't stand the guys she associates with. Years ago I tolerated it but now many of them remind me of Nick.

There's nothing wrong with liking a guy who has a wild streak but there's wild and then there is evil. Nick was the latter.

Being around guys like him made me feel like I was constantly sitting on the edge of my seat in a horror movie. But at times being around Asher was so much worse, thanks to my new crisis. Which I totally blame myself for.

Not only have I agreed to pose as a fake girlfriend for a man I've been in love with my whole life but having him confirm that I'm simply standing in for the real thing has made me feel more foolish than ever.

Today I feel like shit, and I shouldn't. I knew where Asher and I stood right from the get-go, but I pushed and pushed and pushed and now I can't shake this feeling.

More than anything I can't seem to get his mystery woman out of my head.

And I still don't know her name.

This isn't the first time I've known about Asher having a love interest. I grew up watching him with one girl after another, wishing I were one of them.

How sad is that? And really, can't I do better?

Is this how I want my life to be? Forever pining for my brother's best friend when he doesn't want me?

Except I keep remembering that first night weeks ago when it felt like he *did* want me. Before that night I didn't have anything to hold on to. Asher and I had never gone that far.

I blamed the alcohol because it was easier, but I was within my limit. I think he was too, but it doesn't matter because we're sticking to the *plan*.

I just don't know what's going to happen to me along the way. Things are already so much harder, and I have another two months to go.

The door swings open, cutting into my thoughts.

Layla strolls in looking more refreshed than I've ever seen her. She pulls the white fluffy robe she's wearing close and a relaxed smile floats across her face.

"Wow, you look reinvigorated," I say, observing the soft glow in her skin and the looseness of her shoulders.

"I feel it." She giggles and sits next to me, slouching against the wall. "Are you feeling any better?"

"I'm fine."

"That sounds like the same kind of lie you told me earlier when you said you were okay. The only difference is you swapped out the word okay with *fine*." She narrows her eyes and gives me a half smile. "Admittedly, that's why I thought you could use a spa break."

"So, we're here *only* because of me?" I can't hide my humor.

Layla laughs again and mischief sweeps over her face. "Not entirely. Let's just say I needed a spa break too. We're just lucky we have a *very* compassionate boss."

"Asher knows we're here?"

"Not entirely," she repeats with another giggle. "He said we couldn't go shopping. However, he didn't say anything about the spa."

"Oh my gosh." I burst out laughing. "You really are a girl after my own heart."

She raises her hands and flicks her palms over. "That's exactly what I said about you."

"Thank you for bringing me here." Layla has been great and I find it easy to talk to her.

"No worries. Any chance you'll tell me what's on your mind? It looks like serious shit."

"It's just some stuff."

"Stuff to do with Asher?" She stares back at me, curiosity filling her eyes.

"Yeah. Stuff to do with him."

Layla bites the inside of her lips. "I have a confession to make."

"What is it?"

"I know about the arrangement you have with Asher."

Oh no. God was it something I said?

"Don't look so worried." She reaches across and taps my knuckles. "All secrets are safe with me. I'm only coming clean because I'd feel bad sitting here and acting like I don't know."

"Oh." I don't know what to say. I had no idea that she knew about the arrangement but that's probably my fault for not asking. And now I feel bad for the lies I told to make Asher and I look more credible.

"Reason number three for coming here was that you looked like you might need to talk away from work. I felt that whatever was on your mind might be to do with him."

"It's... complicated. Who else knows about us?"

"To my knowledge, only Hunter. Asher wouldn't keep something like this from him."

I don't think he would keep it from Olga either. The same way I couldn't keep it from Beth.

"What about Luna?"

"No. I haven't told her and if Hunter had she would have spoken to me about it by now. Hey, like I said, please don't worry." She squeezes my hand again. "Also, me knowing about your arrangement doesn't take anything away from the truth."

"What truth?" I thought we were already talking about *the truth*.

"That you genuinely like Asher." She keeps her gaze fixed on me. "Look, I know we haven't known each other long but I'm the kind of person you can be real with, so you can talk to me if you need to."

I press my lips together, instinct wanting to deny her assumption but the desperation in my heart longing to relieve some of the angst living in my soul.

Layla also looks like the kind of person you can't lie to. Or fool. So, I don't try. "It's silly right? To like him. It's like falling for your own act."

"No. Not really. You seem to have liked him well before the *act*. Have you spoken to him?"

"No. I can't do that." Nervously I fumble with my fingers in my lap.

"Why not?"

I shake my head and relax my shoulders. "I can't."

"Haven't you two known each other for a lifetime?"

"We have but it's best if I don't go there. I understand that I'm just helping out. And besides I know there's someone else he really likes."

Layla's eyes widen slightly. "You mean Alexis?"

Alexis.

Is that her name? "He never told me her name. There's always a steady stream of Asher Le Blanche wannabe girlfriends. She's probably one of them."

Layla chuckles. "Alexis is a very good friend of mine. I actually set her up with Asher."

Oh great. I just put my foot in my mouth. "I'm so sorry. I didn't mean to sound like a bitch."

"It's okay. You weren't being bitchy. She's my friend but I get it."

"She must be nice."

"She is. And so are you. Just talk to him. You have two more months. I don't think you want to be in the worry zone that whole time. Do you?"

"Not really?" I'd go crazy.

"Then maybe you should think about it."

"Okay." I say that but I know I won't. The last thing I need is to complicate things more and make myself look like some desperate loser.

"Let's go get our manicures."

"Sure."

We end our pampering session two hours later then head back to the office.

I'm on admin duties for the rest of the day so I'll be working in Layla's office helping her to organize files.

We're about an hour in when there's a knock on her already opened door. We stop counting the files and turn around to find a stunning woman with long black hair standing in the doorway.

The woman has model features, bright jade-green eyes and a smile that would have photographers lining up to take her picture.

I can usually hold my own in the beauty department but she's the kind of woman who will make you feel like second best.

"Hey, girl," she beams at Layla.

"Oh my gosh, *Alexis*." Layla glances at me with an awkward smile and silent confirmation in her eyes that *that's* the friend we were talking about earlier.

Holy shit. This is the Alexis I was worried about.

I can see exactly why Asher likes her. She's beautiful. There's absolutely nothing not to like. I might as well sign myself off the Asher Le Blanche girlfriend wannabe list because I have no chance.

Layla rushes over to greet Alexis. "I can't believe you're here."

"I was just dropping by. I had an unexpected job offer in the Maldives. I'll be gone for a few days so I wanted to say goodbye."

"You're such a good friend to me."

"Right back at ya." She looks over Layla's shoulder and smiles at me. "Hey there."

"Hi," I reply, forcing a smile and hoping I don't look as jealous as I feel.

"Where are my manners?" Layla laughs. "Alexis, this is Harper. Harper, Alexis.

"Nice to meet you, Harper," Alexis says, and she looks like she really means that.

"You too."

"You're absolutely gorgeous. I have a photographer friend who would love your high cheekbones." Alexis nods.

My God. I can't even be a bitch. This woman is beautiful *and* a nice person. "Thank you. That's such a nice compliment. You are gorgeous too."

"Thank you. I appreciate that." Alexis turns back to Layla. "Is Asher around? I have something to give him. We had this running joke the other week."

Okay, back to hating her now.

"Yeah, he's around. Come, I'll take you to his office?"

"Thanks." Alexis looks at me again. "Nice meeting you, Harper."

"You too." I'm lying now, meeting her has made me feel even worse.

"See you in a minute Harper," Layla says with a soft smile.

I nod and watch them go.

A minute later that wild streak of mine kicks in and beckons me to follow them. So, I do.

I act like I'm going to the water cooler near Asher's office. There I wait. I can't hear them but it's a good spot to observe.

I'm there for about two minutes before Layla comes out of the office. She spots me and heads over.

"Are you okay?" she asks, looking uneasy.

"I'm fine."

Moments later, Asher and Alexis emerge from the office laughing.

He doesn't see me watching.

They look good together. Their names even go together: *Asher and Alexis.*

Asher must really like her. He's a man who's booked out for weeks on end, but he's dropped everything just like that to hang out with her.

I watch them head toward the elevator and I wonder if this will be what it will feel like in a few months' time when he picks her to be his wife.

They'll get married. And I'll be at their wedding watching them take their vows.

Then that will be it.

I'll lose him forever.

Chapter
TWENTY-TWO

Harper

I DRIVE UP THE LONG WINDING DRIVEWAY TOWARD ASHER'S house, cursing the pain brewing in my head. It feels like the start of a mega migraine. I haven't had one of those in months. They always seem to come about when I'm too stressed and anxious. And when I haven't had much sleep.

I can't say I'm surprised to have a headache. I actually expected it. I just didn't want it sneaking up on me tonight.

Asher and I are attending Luna's annual wine auction. We'll be at the Astoria again, which I always love. What I don't love is the idea of socializing when I just want to roll into bed.

I had an excessively long day which saw me at NYU from nine o'clock this morning. It's after seven now.

Today was orientation day for the transfer students. Classes start in exactly one month. There were three hundred students starting their senior year. Twenty of whom were in my music program.

Although it was nice to be on campus and immersed back in

college life, the day was intense. Especially for me who's been out
of the game since last year, if I'm being honest.

There was the shit with Nick, the court case, then the after-
math with Vito. I feel like I've been on a roller coaster to hell, suf-
fering through loop after loop and big drops. The worst thing is I
don't know when it's going to stop.

Admittedly, being away from Asher and Le Blanche Global
today was good for me. Asher is going to be in Hong Kong on a
business trip with his father from tomorrow. So that will be another
welcome break where I don't have to be jealous of him and Alexis.
I just have to get through tonight.

At least I know Alexis won't be at the event. She's supposed to
be off on her exotic trip to the Maldives. *Good for her.*

What still irritates the hell out of me is that she and Asher were
away for over two hours yesterday. That put me in a bad mood all
day and I know poor Layla must have felt like she was caught in
the middle.

I don't want anyone to feel like that. After all, this is my battle and my agreement to be Asher's fake girlfriend was the way I
chose to pay the debt I owe him. I agreed knowing full well that I
was signing my sanity away to something that was likely to screw
with my head.

The garage door rises and the automatic lights snap on, chasing away the darkness. I drive in and get out, wincing at the sharp
pang that pulses behind my eyes.

Damn it. I should have stopped at the drugstore. I thought I
had some painkillers in my purse, but I must have used them some
time ago.

When I get inside the house I can tell that all the staff have already left and Asher isn't here.

The house gives off that blanket of silence that suggests it's
been empty for a few hours. Asher should be home soon, though.
We're leaving at eight.

By the time I reach the kitchen the pain has doubled. I grab a glass of ice-cold water and down it before I head to the main bath-room to search for some aspirin.

It's just my luck that there's none in there.

I think for a moment on where I saw some and it comes to me. It was inside Asher's office. A place I haven't been since that night we made our *mistake*.

It's off limits to me but I don't care about that right now. Better to apologize for the intrusion than be in pain and grumpy all night.

I head down there, turn on the light and walk in. The room smells like furniture polish and Olga's rose scented perfume. It's a nice combination.

I head over to the desk where I saw the aspirin next to some foolscap folders.

The desk is clear now but I assume they must be in the top drawer.

I open it and thank my lucky stars that something is going right for me when I find it.

"Hello, lifesaver." I grab the box, take two pills out and pop them in my mouth. They should work in about fifteen minutes but just swallowing them makes me feel better.

When I put the box back I notice a newspaper with Asher's picture on the front page.

It gets my curiosity going and I wonder if this is an article about us. The press went wild for the first two weeks of us *dating* but they seem to have calmed down now.

Mostly because they couldn't confirm if we were dating or not. I think it was because they haven't managed to get any pictures of us kissing. That's been good for us because of Josh.

Lisa, his fiancée, mentioned seeing us in the tabloids the other week but we laughed it off as nonsense. I gave her the explanation Asher and I agreed on. That the press was always going to assume we were dating from the moment they saw us together. I knew she would buy it, so our plan is still safe.

It's strange how Josh will have been away for almost a year by the time this is all over and so much will have happened without him knowing.

I read the article and realize that it's not about Asher and I, but about him and some actress. Of course she's beautiful but the woman was also under investigation by the feds for drugs.

The date of the article was the weekend before Asher picked me up in Massachusetts.

The article was written to make it seem like Asher might have been involved. He certainly was *involved* with the model. There's a picture of them together, kissing.

Seeing them flares my jealousy. It seems that he can be with everyone, even someone clearly bad for him, except me.

"How did I not know about this, Mr. *I Can Do No Wrong*?"

"Because I kept it secret." Asher's voice nearly makes me jump out of my skin and I end up dropping the newspaper.

I look up to find him approaching me with that hardened look on his face.

"Sorry. I needed some aspirin. I remembered seeing some in here," I explain.

When he reaches me, he crouches down and picks up the newspaper and my mind takes me back weeks ago to when he bent down just like that to eat me out.

He rises slowly with the paper in his hand and his gaze drifts between my thighs. The unmistakable look pulls at my core and that ache in my pussy returns.

As he rises I try to school my thoughts, remembering that I'm not supposed to think about him like that ever again.

His eyes darken, looking stormy with unrestrained emotion as he keeps his gaze on me. "Did you find it? The aspirin?"

I point to the box in the drawer. "Yeah. I have a migraine coming on. It was a long day."

"Are you going to be okay later? We can cancel if you need to rest." Although he's asking me a specific question, his eyes tell a different story. Like he's thinking about something else.

"I'll be fine." I've said those three words so often I'm tired of hearing myself.

Asher holds up the newspaper. "This was the reason I needed a new publicist."

"What happened?"

"She was paid off to follow me and get dirt that would make me look unfit to run the company."

I raise my brows. "Really? That's terrible."

"Yeah. It's worse when people you trust double-cross you."

"Of course."

"Hunter and I managed to do damage control. I guess I kept this as a reminder to be careful and watch my back at all times. So you see I'm definitely not Mr. *I Can Do No Wrong.*"

"No. I suppose not." No matter what happened with the publicist Asher still dug the hole for himself.

We stare at each other for a moment until he straightens. "You sure you can go out tonight? Everyone will understand if we can't make it."

It's strange; it's almost as if he wants me to say I can't go. It makes me wonder if he's finding this act of ours as hard as I am. But as usual I can never be sure of anything when it comes to him.

"Let's go. Honestly, I'll be fine. Luna is looking forward to seeing us there."

"Alright."

"I'm going to get dressed."

He gives me a clipped nod. "See you in a little while."

"Sure."

I make my way out and his eyes follow me every step I take. It's only when I reach the corridor that I don't feel his gaze burning into me.

What is he thinking?

Maybe he's become close to Alexis and wants to cut me loose. If that's the case, I'll let him.

It would be easier than this.

The Astoria is as beautiful as ever.

I've enjoyed studying the style of décor at each of the events. The party planners must have a field day choosing how they want the place decorated.

Tonight, there's a black and silver color theme that highlights that underlying elegance of the place. It's also the dress code so Asher and I are both dressed in black with hints of silver.

He has silver cufflinks, and I have a Tiffany bracelet around my wrist that cost more than I've ever earned in a year. Asher handed it to me before we left the house as if it was nothing more than a last-minute prop. Apparently, he bought it for me to wear to this event.

His parents are the first to greet us when we reach the main hall. Both his mother and father have the same endearing smile on their faces as they look at us.

"You two look so good together," his mother says.

"Loving the color coordination," his father agrees.

"We were going for subtle," Asher explains. "The less-is-more effect."

"Well, you both nailed it."

I smile at them, trying to keep my game face on. "You both look wonderful, too."

They're almost matching like we are. The only difference is that Asher's mom has more silver streaks on her dress.

"Thank you, dear."

"We've got to sit with the Caldwells tonight," Preston explains. "But join us later at the bar for a drink."

"Of course, Father."

"See you both later." His mother smiles back at us and blows us a kiss.

Asher and I exchange glances when they leave. A silent confirmation that we managed to fool them again.

"There you are." Layla rushes up to us. I didn't even see which way she came from. "You two look amazing."

"Thank you," Asher and I say at the same time.

"Boss man, if you don't mind, I'd love to borrow Harper. She needs to see my ice sculptures. They are to die for."

"Sure." Asher nods. "Meet me at the gala when you're done."

"Okay," I reply.

Layla grabs my hand and off we go but I look over my shoulder at Asher as she ushers me away. He gives me a little smile, but I can tell he's troubled.

Again, I think about the Alexis situation.

Would I really be okay with being terminated?

I can't deny that it would be for the best but that silly part of me is still hanging on to... What?

Nothing.

I have nothing but the air and the fake kisses we share.

But it's something. No matter how small.

Layla takes me out into the garden where Luna and Autumn are standing by a gorgeous ice sculpture of a girl holding a bird.

It's so beautiful it takes my breath away.

"Oh, wow," I gasp.

Luna and Autumn smile at me.

"We knew you'd like it." Luna chuckles. "I can't believe that a year has flown by since I last did this event. I wanted to go all out this year to make it more special."

"It certainly is special." Autumn nods her approval.

"Agreed."

"Come, let me show you the rest," Layla prompts us, reminding me of an excited child at Christmas. "We have half an hour before the auction begins."

She takes us to view the other masterpieces, then launches

into a deep conversation about babies and shopping with Luna and Autumn.

I don't mind the talk about babies although something like that is way, way, way down my list.

When we go back inside, I leave the girls and look for Asher.

My heart sinks into my stomach when I gaze across the room and find him talking to Alexis.

What the hell is she doing here? Isn't she supposed to be on the other side of the world?

Sure, she might be nice but she's clearly here for him.

Surely, she must know by now that he's with me. Or maybe she doesn't.

Regardless, it's irritating the hell out of me that she's here with him, looking so good in her sleeveless silver dress.

And Asher is smiling at whatever she's saying to him.

"Thought you two were together," comes a menacing voice from over my shoulder.

I turn to find Nolan smiling at me. He glances at Asher and places a hand at his heart. "If you were mine there's no way I'd leave you standing around all by yourself."

"I was with Layla," I reply.

"He looks busy." Nolan glances back at Asher who is now laughing with Alexis. "Doesn't he?"

"Yeah. I guess."

"How about we go sit in the balcony and watch the auction, then maybe we can play some pool if your dearly beloved is still... busy."

Asher doesn't want me talking to Nolan but to hell with that. I'm supposed to sit tight looking like a fool while he flirts his ass around with Miss Supermodel?

I don't think so.

"Okay, that sounds great." I nod and Nolan smiles wide and toothy, reminding me of a shark in an Armani suit.

"Right this way then, Miss St. John."

Chapter
TWENTY-THREE

Asher

A LEXIS IS LOOKING AT ME AGAIN OUT OF THE CORNER OF her eye.

I never expected to get stuck with her tonight. I didn't even know she was going to be here.

I lost Harper just before the auction began. I thought she would meet me in the auction hall after Layla showed her the ice sculptures.

Since I know how excitable the girls can get when they're all together, I thought I'd allow them the time to hang out. Admittedly I also wanted Harper to spend time with the girls because I'm in a weird mood tonight. Alexis' presence has only amplified it.

She's here because she managed to rearrange her flight to the Maldives.

I told her about the event yesterday, not knowing she'd use it as a way to get closer to me.

Yesterday after we hung out, I got a rude awakening. I realized that as much as I like her, she's not who I want.

The weeks have flown by since I entered this fake arrangement with Harper and there is still only one woman I can't get out of my head. The woman who continues to be off limits to me.

Something I was reminded of by the email I got from Josh earlier today, which I still haven't responded to.

Lisa told him the press ran a wild story about Harper and I dating. Although Josh was his usual lighthearted self and joked about the idea being ridiculous, I know him. So, I knew he was testing the waters and trying to find out without asking if it was true.

The message felt like a reminder of the warning he gave me years ago.

I didn't reply because I didn't feel like it. I didn't feel like lying. Or like justifying myself.

The auction ends ten minutes later, and Alexis and I stand with everyone else.

"Do you want to grab a few drinks?" she asks.

I give her credit for trying even though I set her straight yesterday. I told her that Harper and I were dating. Alexis seemed to understand but I knew she was disappointed. Obviously not enough to deter her from coming here tonight.

"No. I should go find Harper."

"Of course. She's a lucky girl."

"I think it's me who's lucky."

"I'm jealous I missed the mark." A light chuckle falls from her glossy red lips. "Here's hoping you'll still keep me in mind if... things don't work out."

Everything about her body language and the way she's looking at me tells me she wants me.

Logic is still whispering to me that Alexis would be the easy option, but as I stare at her I know deep down that if I pick her, I'll feel trapped for the rest of my life.

I'm about to answer Alexis and tell her that I'd like for us to remain friends when I spot Nolan and Harper walking across the third-floor balcony. The asshole has his arm around her and is guiding her toward the pool lounge.

What the actual fuck?

What the hell is Harper doing with him? I thought she was with the girls.

A glance to my left reveals that the girls are still together. Harper must have left them. I just don't know when. And I can guarantee Nolan whisked her away.

I look back at Alexis who's staring at me, waiting eagerly for an answer.

"Sorry, Alexis, I gotta go. There's something I have to take care of." I try to keep the irritation out of my voice.

"Oh." Her smile fades and disappointment takes its place. "Of course."

"See you later." I move away before she can say anything more, my eyes glued to Nolan and Harper as they continue their pursuit to the lounge.

I keep going, watching them until I'm at the wide sweeping stairs that will take me up to them.

I take the stairs two at a time then rush past the guests in the archway.

Once I'm in the pool lounge, I spot Nolan and Harper at the furthest table. Harper is leaning over the table with her cue, getting ready to take her shot while Nolan is blatantly staring at her ass.

My blood heats and I want to rip his eyes from their sockets then squish them under my shoes like bugs.

I know I can't blame him for looking at Harper. She's beautiful and literally perfect, but he's clearly *still* sniffing around her because she's mine.

And she is. *Mine.*

Regardless of whatever arrangement we have, a part of me claimed her years ago and has never let go. That's why I always get so worked up whenever I see her with another man. It's because that part of me thinks she should be with me.

I march up to them. Nolan spots me first.

"Hey, Asher, just keeping your girl company while you were busy." He gives me that stupid smile I can't stand.

Harper straightens and the instant I look at her I can tell she's pissed as fuck at me.

I want to ask her what I did but I want to deal with this douche-bag first.

"Nolan, the next time you think it's a good idea to steal my girl when we're at an event be prepared to pick your teeth up off the ground." My jaw clenches and I hope to God he doesn't say anything I don't like because I *will* answer him with my fist.

"Jesus, Asher. You need to take a chill pill. We were just playing pool."

I step into his personal space. "I don't care. I see what you're trying to do here and it's not going to work."

He smirks. "You're being paranoid."

"No. I'm not. I'll tolerate you at work but that's as far as it goes. So, stay the fuck away from my girl."

"You know what? I'm going home," Harper speaks up in a firm voice then sets her cue stick down and storms away.

I give Nolan a hard glare before I follow Harper. I know from the quickness in her pace and the tension in her shoulders that she's definitely mad at me.

"Harper."

She doesn't stop. I catch up to her and take her arm but she wrenches it free of my grasp.

"Just leave me alone."

"What the hell did I do now?"

She casts me a scathing look and walks even faster.

"Harper."

"I said leave me alone."

"No. Not until you tell me what the hell I did."

She stops short and whirls around to face me, her eyes dark with anger. "Are you serious?"

"Please don't tell me you're mad about Nolan. There are things going on between us that you don't understand."

"This isn't about Nolan."

"Then what is it about?"

"Okay. Tell me if you think it's acceptable that you act like I'm yours one moment then throw me away the next to pick up some woman who's clearly after you."

Shit, this is about Alexis. "Harper. I didn't throw you away."

"Yes, you did. I came here for *you*. And if you think that ditching me to hang out with whatever the hell her name is isn't throwing me away, then I don't know what planet you're on."

"I didn't know she was going to be here."

She shakes her head and drags in a slow breath. The slow, steady kind of breath a person would take to stop them hyperventilating. "I can't do this anymore. Find another way for me to pay you back. At this rate I'd rather owe Vito than you."

Before I can answer she turns on her heel and carries on walking.

I follow her into the elevator that just opened its doors.

"Asher, go back to your family and leave me alone."

The doors close and the elevator starts moving. As I look at her and the tears brimming in her eyes I just know that if I let her go again she won't just stay with Beth this time. This time she won't come back.

Thinking quickly, I do the first thing that comes to mind and press the emergency button, stopping the elevator mid-descent.

"What are you doing?" Harper gasps, looking from me to the big red button with wide eyes.

"Is everything okay in there?" comes a deep, businesslike voice through the intercom. It's Archie, the head of security.

"Archie, it's Asher Le Blanche. I need a private moment. Don't move this elevator or open the doors until I say."

"Sure thing, Mr. Le Blanche."

It's a good thing I am who I am and that my name carries so

much power in the circles I travel. The Le Blanche name can some-times act as an all-access pass to requests like these.

"This is crazy. You can't trap me in here, Asher." Harper balls her hands at her sides.

"I just did. We need to talk."

"There's nothing to talk about."

"Yes, there obviously is."

"What are you going to tell me?" Her gaze intensifies. "That I'm the fake girlfriend so I should feel nothing? Or that I should be *totally fine* with *Alexis* turning up here, there, and everywhere to throw herself at you?"

"I told you I didn't know she was going to be here."

"It doesn't matter. You like her. You told me. So why the hell am I here? Why the hell am I here, Asher? She's not exactly hard to get. Why didn't you just pick her from the start if you like her so much?"

There it is. The question of the hour. It seems more pertinent now that we're three weeks into our arrangement.

"I needed more time."

"Well, I think you've had quite enough time. You obviously want to be with her, so let me make things easier for you and back out now."

God, she has everything all wrong. "No."

She presses a hand to her heart as if she's in physical pain. "I can't do this again with you."

Her words grab my attention, and I instantly think of the past. She said *again* and it didn't sound like she was talking about weeks ago.

I gaze into her eyes. "What do you mean by *again*, Harper?"

"Years ago."

My stomach knots then clamps and my heart stops beating in my chest.

Years ago. The night of the accident. "You remember?"

"I never forgot." Her voice lowers to a cautious whisper.

I stare back at her in disbelief, my heart beating again but faster than normal while my lungs lock.

Harper never forgot what happened. God. I want to rip into her and trash her out for keeping such a secret, but reasoning stops me.

Because didn't we both take the easy way out? She pretended to forget, and I never mentioned it. It was like the incident never happened so neither of us had to face it.

Pretending to forget is such a Harper thing to do but unlike her other antics, I understand *why* she did it. At the same time, I want to hear it from her lips.

"Do you remember everything else?"

"No. How crazy is that? When I woke up from that coma, I remembered that night with you but nothing from the six years before that. I didn't even remember that my mother died. But I remembered that night."

"*God . . .* Why didn't you tell me?"

"It hurt less to pretend."

"Harper—"

"Don't. I already feel bad enough and I can't take any more. Please go be with Alexis so I can be over you." A tear slides down her cheek. The sight pulls on my insides like a thick rope.

I stare at her, taking in her distress and the wealth of hurt in her eyes. That hurt does something to me, pushing me to be the ruthless man I normally am who takes what he wants. It's time to become that guy again. The real me. Fuck the consequences.

"I can't be with Alexis," I rasp. As soon as I speak those words, I feel free. They feel like the first right thing I've said in years.

Harper stares back at me, confused. "Why not?"

"Because . . . I want you."

Her lips part and she stares back at me in shock. She seems frozen in my confession. The slow rise and fall of her chest is the only thing moving.

"What?" Her voice is small and soft, her tone careful, as if she's scared the question will change the moment.

"I want you." I reach out and touch her cheek, tracing my thumb over her smooth, silky skin.

The contact sends my mind into overdrive, and I find that I can't take any more either. My pretense ends here.

The urge to taste her and take her overwhelms me so I move closer. She moves toward me, too, and I crush my lips to hers.

I taste her desire and the need in her hot little mouth, as I explore her like I want to conquer every piece of her. Then, fuck, I kiss her back the way I've always wanted to. Without restraint, without limit, without all the reasons that made her off limits to me.

I'm taking what's mine tonight.

Her.

Chapter
TWENTY-FOUR

Harper

THE SEARING-HOT KISS ASHER GIVES ME BREATHES LIFE into my tired soul, filling me with his taste, his desire, his lust.

Nothing has ever felt like this moment. Not even when he kissed me weeks ago. This feels like swimming in uncharted waters fueled with passion and delirious pleasure.

My entire body throbs from head to toe but there's an ache deep in my core that craves him. Craves *more* of him. Everything he could ever give me and more.

My hands roam his chest, clutching the sinew of corded muscles beneath his shirt. Touching him like this—the way I've always wanted to—feels like pure magic.

Asher pushes me against the wall of the elevator car and deepens the kiss.

Then he presses his hard body into me, allowing me to feel his massive erection digging into my belly.

Knowing I made him so hard sends thrills over my body and the need in my pussy grows for him, yearning for his touch.

As if he knows, he reaches through the split in my dress and cups my sex.

Arching my back, I mold myself against his hand, grinding shamelessly.

"*Fuck*, Harper. You're soaking wet," he growls in a deep, raw voice I've never heard before, then pushes his fingers into my pussy.

"*Oh God,*" I moan as he strokes my pussy lips and pumps in and out of my passage.

He curls a finger around my clit and squeezes, then pumps harder, pushing deeper into me.

I can't believe this is us.

I can't *believe* what he said—that he wants me.

This might be another fluke of passion, but I'm taking it. I'm seizing it by the horns and claiming it because, damn it, I want him, too. I never stopped.

"Asher..."

"Just feel me."

I do. And just like that, I lose myself. I savor every thrust of his fingers, my body bowing in order to devour every pulse of pleasure that races through me.

He parts my legs and crouches so he can nuzzle his face between my thighs, then he thrusts his tongue into my pussy. He's barely in when a gush of wetness bursts from me and I come in his mouth, moaning out loud.

Grabbing my hips, Asher gazes up at me with wild fascination and continues licking and lapping my pussy as I come undone in his arms.

When he's licked me clean I expect him to stop but he doesn't. Instead, he pushes to his feet and returns to my lips, pulling me back to him and devouring my mouth like he has no intention of stopping anytime soon.

I taste my arousal on his lips and his tongue. It sends more heat pulsing through me. Then he rolls up my dress to my hips and his warm fingers run across my bare skin, charging every nerve in my body with electricity.

I press into his erection, noting that he feels bigger than before. My simple contact makes him groan deep in his chest. The sound sends a flutter through my heart and I marvel that I made *him* groan.

Asher pushes me harder into the wall as his kiss becomes consuming, sending shivers of fire racing throughout my body.

God, I've been waiting for this moment forever. I've dreamt of this moment so often I can't believe it's really happening. My brain hasn't even fully processed it yet.

His touch becomes rough and then we're tearing at each other's clothes while we kiss like we're starving.

Asher shoves the top of my dress down my body, exposing my breasts to the air, and I push his jacket off and undo the buttons on his shirt.

When his shirt lies open, I barely get the chance to run my hands down his chest and trace the definition in his hard muscles before he latches on to one of my rigid nipples and sucks it greedily into his mouth.

He sinks his teeth into the swell of my breast, taking as much of the flesh into his mouth as he can. I groan, relishing the waves of pleasure surging through my body.

He moves to my other breast, doing the same thing. Then he yanks my dress down my hips and legs and rolls down my panties. Seconds later I'm naked.

Asher stares at my naked body with wild, mesmerized eyes.

The thought suddenly hits me that we're in the elevator—and I'm naked—but at this point I'm beyond caring. My body is aching with desire and the emptiness of wanting him all these years.

The tension inside me rises, making me mindless to everything but him. All I want to do is be with him in this moment and seal it away in my heart forever.

Seeing him looking at me like that fills me with an emotion

I've never felt before. It feels like desire and contentment and euphoria rolled into one.

I realize this is the first time in my life that I've truly felt wanted. Wanted for being me and everything that makes me, me. My scars, my flaws, my imperfections.

Asher is looking at me as if he wants to take it all.

His lids become heavy when his gaze drifts back to the puckered nipples of my breasts.

He returns to take another mouthful, then kisses his way down my body, tasting me as he goes along. When he reaches my toes he stands again and rips open his fly then pushes his pants down his hips. My eyes snap wide as his cock juts free, long, massive and hard.

He reaches for me again, cupping my face. "I need to be inside you now. And I won't be able to stop."

"I don't want you to stop."

"Good." His voice comes out low and ragged.

Pulling me close again, he lifts my leg and hooks it around his waist. Then he takes his cock and rubs his straining erection back and forth along the slit of my pussy, making me even wetter.

A needy moan slips past my lips, husky with undiluted desire.

Holding my gaze, Asher pushes into me and I gasp from the feeling of his length filling me.

He shoves deeper inside, stretching me until pain invades the haze of pleasure. He pulls out, then he's back inside me again, but this time he buries himself deeper and I feel nothing but intense pleasure.

The penetration is so powerful we both shudder and groan at the same time.

"Holy fuck," he gasps, tightening his grip on my hips.

"Asher…"

"Stay with me."

I know I'm tight. It's been a while since I had sex—and I don't want to think about last time, or Nick, right now.

I just want Asher in my head. He seems to know exactly what to do with my body. He moves inside me slowly, then as my walls stretch to take his huge, hard cock, he speeds up, moving faster and faster.

Then it's like whatever restraint held him back all these years unleashes with a vengeance, and he owns my body with his savage pounding.

He starts fucking me, deep and hard, and I dig my fingernails into his back to hold on as he drives into me over and over.

I climax again, my entire body straining.

Pressure explodes in my ears and my heart as he hammers into me, pushing me closer to another ravaging orgasm. The intensity turns me inside out, sending tremors of shock rippling across my flesh. It robs me of air.

I arch back and clutch at his shoulders, opening my mouth to scream but the intensity of his relentless pounding kills the sound in my throat.

His strong arms crush me to his powerful chest as wave after luscious wave of pleasure courses through me.

Then he pulls out and flips me around so that I'm facing the wall. I just about manage to catch my breath before he plunges back into me and pounds into me from behind.

This position amplifies the pleasure rippling through my body. I come again, shuddering and moaning.

Asher speeds up again and I feel his cock harden inside me. I see stars speckling before me and my head feels light.

We stay like this for another spellbinding pocket of time where I soak up his desire for me before he growls out his own release.

I come again and we share the insatiable climax.

God… I'm on fire. My skin feels like it's going to combust and burn right off my body.

I've never experienced anyone or anything like Asher Le Blanche.

He slips an arm around my waist and presses his chest to my back. His touch brings my awareness back and it hits me that *we* just had sex.

Us—him, the man who was always forbidden, and me.

I chance looking over my shoulder at him, hoping beyond hope that he'll still look like he wants me.

The lust-filled fire surrounding his blue gaze tells me he does. He catches my face and pulls me back for a kiss—further confirmation.

"I've always wanted you, Harper," he breathes into my hair. His words tell me that he knows what I'm thinking.

"Have you?" I whisper.

"Always. Fucking always, so please… promise me you'll never get over me."

His words sink into my soul and my heart swells with every dream I've ever had of this man. "I promise."

A smile tips the corners of his sensual mouth. "Let's go home. I need you in my bed."

Asher

Hey Asher

I've got so much to tell you, bro! Life on the submarine has been more exciting than I ever imagined. Every day brings a new challenge, whether it's navigating deep, uncharted waters or working with the crew to solve problems.

I freaking love it.

I think you'd love the thrill of adventure, too. But I know living under the sea for almost a year isn't your jam.

What's driving me insane is not seeing my girl. Now that Lisa and I are officially engaged it feels wrong to be away from her for so long.

Anyway, how's life? Did you find the woman of your dreams?

I hope you did, and you managed to sort everything out with your father.

I also hope Harper isn't getting into too much trouble. I still can't thank you enough for looking after her.

Lisa told me the craziest story about you two. Apparently, the press believes you're dating. Those fuckers.

I laughed my ass off. The press will make up all kinds of convincing shit.

I guess it's a good thing I know Harper isn't your type and is like a sister to you. You wouldn't go there with her, so I have nothing to worry about.

I can't wait to catch up properly when I'm back on dry land. Keep me posted, buddy.

Talk soon,

Josh

I take a drag on my cigar and stare at the email from Josh. On the laptop screen it looks like a spotlight competing with the shroud of darkness filling my bedroom.

It's three in the morning and I'm sitting at the desk by the window, smoking and torturing myself.

I should be asleep because I have to leave for Hong Kong before six. But I couldn't sleep because my fucking dick is still hard for Harper, despite having had her four times over the last few hours. And because of this…

Josh's email.

It screwed with me yesterday when it first arrived, too.

I only looked at it again because it slipped back into my mind the instant Harper fell asleep.

I glance at her in my bed, wrapped in my silky sheets. Her breasts are exposed, and her hair is sprawled out on the pillow around her.

She looks like the goddess of trouble again.

Trouble for me.

Josh would kill my ass if he saw us now. When I first read his email, I felt guilty for the sinful thoughts I'd been harboring for his sister. Then I felt irritated by his message.

Knowing him the way I do, I imagined him rewriting the last two paragraphs to get his message across without sounding like an ass. The rest of the message sounded upbeat to cover up his true worries—that I'm back home fooling around with his sister.

'I guess it's a good thing I know Harper isn't your type and is like a sister to you. You wouldn't go there with her, so I have nothing to worry about.'

Sorry, Josh. Harper has always been my type. She's never been like a sister to me, and as for going there, well...

We've had unprotected sex four times. Right now, she could be pregnant.

I don't know. But I'm that fucked up to impregnate her and use it as an excuse to keep her.

My baby. My girl. End of story.

But knowing Josh it wouldn't end there. So, baby or not, that's something I have to think about—him.

Not now, though. Because I can't answer the email yet. Every time I've tried to formulate a response, I come up short and don't know what to say. It feels wrong to lie and it feels wrong to act like nothing is going on.

At the same time, I know that I can't tell Josh the truth just yet.

Knowing Harper never forgot that night years ago feels like I've been given a second chance to make it right. Not just for her but for myself, too.

It's like someone took us back in time and put me back on that path.

Right now, I know I'm running on sex and adrenaline. I'm not thinking beyond this room. I also know I have to make a decision on *everything* once and for all.

But it can wait. All of it can fucking wait.

Harper rolls onto her side, drawing my attention to her breasts as she moves. Her nipples are hard, a sign she's aroused and wants me.

I smile when she stretches her dainty hand across the bed, feeling for me.

On seeing that, my greed and need take over so I glance at the email again before I close it.

I switch off the laptop and decide I'm going to spend the last few hours I have left in New York buried deep inside Harper. I'll be gone for five days so I want to make every minute with her count to keep me going while I'm away.

So... Sorry, Josh, but I'm not sorry at all. And I'm about to make your sister mine all over again.

I get up and make my way over to the bed where I run a finger over Harper's lips.

When a sexy smile slides across her mouth, I lower my head and suck her breasts.

The sound of her moans hardens my dick even more.

"I'll never get tired of you doing that." Her voice is a sultry hum filled with pleasure.

"Good, because I'm always going to enjoy sucking your tits."

I take her deeper into my mouth and she runs her fingers through my hair, holding my head to her breasts.

Her body bows at my wild suckle and I move the sheets away from her bottom half so I can see her pussy.

She's already wet, with her arousal leaking down her thighs.

The sight of her writhing against me with her slick, wet pussy is something I'll never forget. I don't know how the fuck I'm going to leave her and be away in a whole other country for so long.

When she moans louder the very best idea fills my head.

I stop sucking her breasts and she pouts.

"Don't stop," she giggles.

"Don't worry, I won't. I just have other things in mind."

"Like what?"

"Sit on my face and you'll find out."

Her eyes light up and the silver moon casts an ethereal glow on her body as she pushes herself up.

I take off my boxers and climb on the bed, then I pick her up and guide her to sit on my face.

I grab her hips and thrust my tongue into her pussy, eliciting mindless moans from her lips.

What I love about Harper is that she always knows what to

do and she's not shy, so I'm not surprised when she leans forward, reaches for my dick and takes me into her mouth.

We both feast on each other. Her sucking me off while I eat out her pussy.

I could stay here forever, getting drunk on her sweetness. She's my new addiction and I've developed a craving for her that keeps me wanting more and more.

I flick her clit with my tongue and suck hard on it, making her body tense. She stops sucking me and throws her head back to let out a scream. Then her sweet juices pour into my mouth.

Fuck.

She tastes even better. I don't know how it's possible for everything to be different every time I take her. She's like a new adventure waiting for me to explore and unlock all the secret parts of her.

I lap up her juices and when my balls draw up, I know I'll have to take her now if I want to finish inside her.

I lift her off me and settle her on her back like she was at first, then I part her legs and guide my dick into her body.

She's not as tight as she was the first time. Now she fits me perfectly, like she was made for me.

I like having her on her back like this so I can see her beautiful face and watch her breasts bouncing while I pound into her.

I drive into her body, sliding deeper, then pumping faster and harder.

Then I'm hooked.

My mind cuts out like someone short-circuited my wires and nothing else matters besides her.

Her in this moment where she's mine to devour and fuck however I want.

I gaze down at her beneath me. Harper looks so beautiful and right now, she's all fucking mine. *My girl.*

Her walls clench around my dick and a burst of madness shoots through my veins. It makes me lose control. Then I'm gone.

Something primal takes over and I can't stop. Even after we come, I find myself hard all over again and I *can't* stop.

My fucking dick is in a perpetual need to be inside her and own her in every way possible.

I take her on her back, I take her from behind, I take her to the shower and fuck her against the wall.

We're like that for hours and still, even as I pull orgasm after orgasm from her body, I want more.

Harper St. John has me under her spell and I feel like if I stop touching her, I'll never have her again.

When the sun comes up, I have her cocooned in my arms with her hands pressed against my chest.

We only stopped a few minutes ago. It's five thirty. The jet leaves with Hunter and my father in an hour and a half.

I consider missing the flight and heading to Hong Kong on my own later, but I'd miss the whole purpose of the trip.

We have a meeting with one of our biggest clients. A property development company my father wants me to handle because of my asset management background. He's even allowed me to bring Knight and Jericho Grayson on board as my team because they have unrivaled experience in real estate. They'll be in Hong Kong, too.

This is a billion-dollar project, so as thrilled as my father is that Harper and I are together, he won't understand that I missed the biggest opportunity of my life because we couldn't get enough of each other.

The second alarm goes off, meaning it's now five forty. I have twenty minutes to be out of the house.

Harper lifts her head, and we stare at each other.

"I don't want you to be late, but I also don't want you to go," she whispers.

How crazy is it that I'd stay if she asked me to? "I'll be back in a few days."

"I know. I just don't want to break…"

"*This?*"

She nods slowly. "Yeah."

"It won't. How about we get back to *this* the moment I get back?"

"Really?" Her eyes brighten with hope.

"Yes."

God help me. I'm digging a deeper hole for myself. But I'm the poor fool who will happily fall into the abyss for that smile on Harper's face and the kiss she plants on my lips.

Yes, I've lost my mind.

But I can't turn back now.

Chapter
TWENTY-SIX

Harper

"OH MY GOD, *MY HEART*." BETH STARES BACK AT ME FROM across the park bench, looking utterly mesmerized.

I've just told her about what happened between Asher and me last night.

I've only ever seen my best friend look that way when watching one of her classic chick flicks, like *Only You* or *When Harry Met Sally*.

Honestly, I feel like I've been walking around in a romantic movie. Things seem to have flipped around for me to get the guy—even for one night.

I've had a busy day, but I couldn't wait to see Beth to talk to her.

"So, what happens now?" Beth squeaks.

My shoulders slump and I gaze out to the swans swimming in the river. In the waning afternoon sun they look like sailboats sailing on the open sea.

I shake my head and look back at her, feeling the doubt I experienced earlier stirring in my heart. "Asher promised to pick up where we left off, but I don't know if he means it. Of course, that's exactly what I want but there's a lot to think about."

The excitement in Beth's eyes dims and she nods. "Like the fact that he has to get married to secure his position in the company."

"Exactly." My heart feels just as heavy as it did earlier when I first thought about the *marriage thing*. The bubble of last night popped the instant the thought slithered into my mind.

"Maybe you could talk to him about it." Beth bites the inside of her lip.

I laugh without humor. "Really, Beth? We spent one night together, and you want me to ask him about marriage?"

"You don't have to talk to him about it right away. But as this is an unusual circumstance it's a conversation you're going to have to have at some point."

I hate to admit it but she's right. "Yeah, I guess I should see how everything plays out first."

"Yes, absolutely. I wish you could have gotten together before."

"Me too. That's the other thing that's troubling me. Asher made it sound like he'd always wanted to be with me. So why didn't he try? He knew how I felt." I keep hearing his voice telling me that he always wanted me.

"Maybe he had his reasons."

"Like Josh?"

She narrows her eyes. "I doubt that."

"There was something Asher said when we first agreed to our arrangement that made me think he believed Josh wouldn't approve of us being together. I didn't think too much into it at the time but now I am."

"But Josh left you in his best friend's care because he trusts him. I'd say he'd be happy if you and Asher got together."

"I don't know. Throughout this whole time Asher has been careful to make sure there were no pictures of us that the press could use to confirm we're dating."

Outside of when we're around his family we don't hold hands, kiss, or anything like that. We do just enough to make sure people don't ask questions.

"If Josh is the reason, then perhaps Asher never tried to be with me because he doesn't want to ruin their friendship."

"If that's true, would you really step aside for their friendship? I think it would be quite selfish and controlling on Josh's part to stand in the way of you being with the guy you want."

"It would. While I don't want to upset my brother or disrespect him, I wouldn't allow Josh to stop me from being with Asher. Of course, that's if we do get together." Asher could still change his mind.

"Are you going to talk to Josh about this?"

Again, I laugh without humor. "I don't know. I guess it depends on what happens when Asher gets back. All I want is for things to work out." I bring my hands together and set them on my lap.

"You never stopped loving him," Beth notes with a small smile.

"No. I *know* that now."

"Then hang in there and don't worry about what you can't control." There's her mantra again.

"It's just hard. I've never felt this way about anyone. And I don't think I ever will for anyone else."

"I hope it works out for you. But, um... can you just take a moment to be happy about last night?"

I bite back a smile, and I know I'm blushing from head to toe just thinking about how Asher and I were with each other. He claimed me over and over, and I can't wait for him to get back. "Yes. I can *definitely* be happy about last night."

"Good." Beth giggles. "Keep that thought. This is the guy you've loved your whole life. You were with him."

"I was. And he wanted me. Not Miss Perfect Alexis. That part alone will keep me smiling for years."

"Exactly. When does he get back?"

"Next Thursday." That's almost a week away but it feels like forever.

"The time will go quickly. Especially if you agree to go to my party on Saturday."

It's her birthday. Normally, I wouldn't miss her parties for the world, but I told her I'd think about it because this one is at a club and Jack is going to be there. Jack, who is still trying to get with me despite my numerous attempts at turning him down. The last thing I need is for the press to picture us together and create some cheating scandal. Asher specifically warned me about that.

"Come on, Harper. It'll be fun." Beth clasps her hands. "I can't have a party without my best friend at my side. That's literally *never* happened."

She's right. We've always been at each other's parties. I would feel bad if I didn't at least make an appearance. "Okay, I'll stay for an hour."

She pouts and rolls her eyes at me. "Two hours. Harper, no one goes to a club and stays for just an hour."

"Alright, two hours then."

"Yay, thank you! We're gonna have a blast. I think you need something like this to take the edge off and keep your mind occupied."

"I can't argue with that."

"Let's go shopping tomorrow."

"Okay."

We spend the rest of the time talking, then head home when night falls.

I keep myself occupied with my violin and play for hours.

When I stop, I snuggle on the sofa in the living room and watch reruns of *Friends*.

I'm two episodes in when I get a text from Asher.

My heart leaps when I read his name on the home screen and I'm so excited I can hardly read the message.

It says: *Hope your evening is more exciting than mine.*

I smile and type back: I'm *watching Friends. What are you doing?*

Him: *Listening to my father talk about breeding guinea fowl.*

I burst out laughing and my heart flutters. We never talk like this. All his previous messages were so businesslike and lacked humanity.

Me: *Your father is a very interesting man.*

Him: *He is. But you interest me more.*

My breath catches and my toes curl.

Me: *Do I?*

Him: *Yes. So much more. What are you wearing?*

My entire body heats at the question and I think of taking a walk on the wild side again.

Me: *Nothing.*

The blue dots start jumping like they're going to leap off the screen.

Him: *Fuck.*

I laugh, probably sounding crazy because I'm all by myself.

Him: *Send me a picture.*

I bite the side of my lip. I've never done that before but for him I would.

Me: *Okay, but only if I get a picture, too.*

Him: *What kind of picture do you want?*

Me: *A dick pic.*

Him: *Give me an hour. Now send me yours.*

It's a good thing I do have the house to myself because the next few hours see me sending naked pictures of myself to him.

And he, Mr. Serious Billionaire, does the same.

It's Saturday night. Time for Beth's birthday party.

She and I just walked into the Blue Ridge, an underground techno club in Lower Manhattan that seems to have attracted the most eccentric of partygoers.

The club itself is eccentric with its grungy décor, crazy strobe lights and the punk rocker bouncers and staff at the door and bar.

I love dancing the night away, but this isn't the sort of club I'd go to on my own.

It seems like the kind of place where anything goes, and *anything* can happen. Perfect for Beth.

Joining us tonight are Mara and Denise, our friends from high school who are just as zany as Beth. There's also Jason, Beth's current boyfriend, a few of his friends, and Jack and his friends. There are twelve of us.

It's been a while since I hung out with a group this large or since I saw my friends from high school—who I only vaguely remember.

I feel terrible about that because we've been friends since junior high. All I remember about them is the last few months of high school after the accident when I was able to return to classes.

As luck would have it Mara and Denise both go to NYU so I'm hoping to reconnect with them there.

As for tonight, I'm struggling to not think about Asher. The last few days have ended with either phone sex or us sending each other naked pictures.

I can't believe it's us. I have four more days until he's back and I'm dying to see him.

Beth leads us to the VIP area and we start the night with a few rounds of drinks while we get to know the new guys and catch up on old times.

When we're done drinking we head to the dance floor where Jack tries to dance with me. Thankfully I'm saved when Mara slips between us and starts dancing with him. The moment she hooks her arms around his neck and whispers something in his ear all thoughts of trying to hook up with me are forgotten.

Thank God.

Beth and I dance like we used to when we were kids. Like we don't have a care in the world and like no one is watching. We have a lot of fun until Jason whisks her away.

I finish dancing to the song because it's a 90's mix I like, then suddenly I find myself dancing among strangers. Everyone has left me.

I know the drill. When Beth disappears like that it means I won't see her again for the night. The same for our other friends.

I've been here a little over two hours anyway, like I promised, so it's time to go home.

When I turn to head toward the exit I feel eyes on me. There must be hundreds of people here, but these eyes feel different from the crowd.

I look over my shoulder, following the pull of the stare, and find myself gazing straight at the man of my dreams.

Asher Le Blanche is leaning on the balcony of the second floor watching me.

Our eyes lock and I'm instantly trapped within his bright blue gaze.

Oh. My. God. He's back.

He came back early. And he's *here.*

I told him I was going to be here for Beth's party. Knowing that he flew back and came to find me is the best surprise ever.

I turn around fully to face him and the brightest smile spreads across my face.

His eyes roam down my body, taking in the black bodycon dress molded to me and my red heels. I study him, too.

He's dressed in a black button-down shirt and black slacks. His hair is ruffled in that just-got-out-of-bed way and the sexy smirk on his face sets me on fire.

Asher straightens, raises a finger and twirls it around slowly, emulating the way I was dancing previously. He wants me to dance.

Dance for *him.*

My body heats up at the realization, but I start moving again with the change in the music.

It's a slow sexy piece that guides me to move in a more sensual way. I raise my arms into the air and move with the beat.

My hips sway slowly, rhythm and arousal pulsing through my body like a heartbeat.

His eyes are riveted to me, and I lap up his attention as though I've been starved for centuries.

I trail my fingers lightly down my sides, teasing my movements with deliberate control. Then I tilt my head back, exposing my neck as I wrap my arms around my body.

We're about twenty feet apart but even from here I can read the lusty look in his eyes.

I keep dancing—for him. He watches me for a little while, then he moves away from the balcony and makes his way through the crowd, heading toward me.

He keeps his eyes on me the whole time and when he's right in front of me, shivers of desire course through me.

He doesn't speak. I wouldn't be able to hear him anyway because the music is so loud. But we don't need to speak to understand each other.

Asher slips his arm around me and pulls me flush against him. I slip my arms around his neck when he leans down, we sway to the music together.

Our bodies move like they were made for each other. The way his hips move with mine, the way we follow each other's lead, the way we touch each other.

Asher pulls me closer, and his hands wander over my breasts, my stomach, and my ass as if he wants to undress me right here in front of everyone.

I never want him to stop touching me.

On seeing I'm enjoying his hands on me he lifts my chin and captures my lips for a kiss. The kiss I've been starving for since we left his bed mere days ago.

The kiss becomes the kind other people shouldn't see. But we don't care.

When he pulls away dangerous heat roils through me as I take in the hunger in his eyes.

Without words he guides me off the dance floor. At first, I think we're leaving, but then he's ushering me up the stairs and taking me down one of the hallways.

It takes me a moment before I realize he must have been here before.

The music up here is still just as loud as on the dance floor, until we reach a dark empty hallway where the volume is lower.

He continues to a little alcove with an archway and then pulls me back in for another searing kiss.

"I need you. I need to be inside you, now," he whispers over my lips through kisses.

"Here?"

"I don't care where I fuck you, just as long as I do."

We crash into the wall and his kiss becomes consuming.

My God, this is sheer possession. All of it. And I want him to take everything from me.

He pushes my legs wider and rolls my dress up to my hips.

He cups my pussy and slides my panties to the side so he can push his fingers into my already wet passage.

"Good girl, always wet for me." He smiles.

"Maybe it's because I'm always happy to see you. Especially... tonight." I try to talk but I'm restrained by the moan laced beneath my words.

"After seeing those pictures of you I couldn't stay away for another minute."

He gives me a savage kiss then turns me to face the wall.

I hear the clink of his belt buckle and look around to watch him undo his pants. The sight is so hot it makes me even wetter.

He takes out his cock and grins back at me as he fists his length, making pre-cum bead at the tip. "This is what you do to me, Harper St. John."

Asher grabs my hips, and I turn back to face the wall.

He bends me over then the head of his cock presses against my entrance.

He eases into me, pushing deeper, an inch at a time, until he fills me up.

My pussy tightens around him, and he groans. "Jesus, Harper, you feel so good."

He thrusts even deeper, and I moan out loud, feeling my orgasm rising.

He starts to fuck me, and I come instantly, reeling with pleasure.

Every thrust of his cock has me utterly lost in the sensation.

As he fucks me into the wall all I can do is press my hands against the cool surface to take his relentless pounding.

"Oh God," I cry out, coming again.

Asher hammers into me and I hold my breath, feeling like I'm falling and flying at the same time.

Moments later he comes, too, growling his own finish.

Hot cum floods me and I relish the sensation of heat—his heat—inside me.

We both slump against the wall and when my knees buckle, he slips an arm around me.

My mind is spinning from the impact of him.

Asher pulls out of me and turns me to face him. He tucks himself back into his pants then rests his forehead against mine, our breaths mingling as we share the same air space.

"That was worth the long flight," he mutters, licking my lips.

"You mystify me."

"Good, you won't ever be bored."

I laugh a little. "Asher... we just had sex in a club."

"Yeah. The only man who gets to fuck you in a club is going to be me." He kisses me briefly and I smile at the memory of what I said to him weeks ago. "Let's go home."

"Home." It's the first time I've said that word in years and felt like I actually had a home.

I realize it's because home is wherever he is.

He is my home.

Chapter
TWENTY-SEVEN

Asher

I WATCH THE COOL SPRAY OF WATER FROM THE SHOWER RUN down her body.

I like this.

Watching Harper and being close to her.

We haven't stopped since we got back from the club last night. I brought her in here because I like taking her in the shower up against the wall.

It's the early hours of the morning. Although we've calmed, that ravenous desire to have her is still swimming in my veins.

It was that same thing that made me fly back early from Hong Kong.

Hunter is covering the next few days for me, so I get to spend the time with Harper.

I keep losing myself around her. At the same time I keep pushing aside the elephant in the room that's growing bigger and bigger.

But now that I've had time to think I've decided to talk to her and lay the cards on the table.

The moonlight coming through the skylight shines down on her, turning her hair silver. She leans against the wall, and I press my hand to the flat of her stomach, allowing the water to trail over my hand and down to her pussy.

I crouch and lick her from her stomach to her clean-shaven mound. Then I gaze up at her and savor her smile, wanting to take that, too.

I stand, rest my hand above her head and gaze down at her. "Are you tired?"

"No." Her smile widens.

"You should be. I've kept you up every night." I cup her chin with my free hand.

I've had barely any sleep myself. Our crazy rendezvous of phone sex and naked pictures kept me up all night. God knows how I managed to sound sensible during my meetings.

"I like spending time with you." He sweet voice is a tender whisper that floats over my skin.

"Me too. With you." I sigh and trace the line down her elegant neck. I stop when I reach her cleavage, feeling myself getting hard again.

If I keep going, we'll be back in that bed, and I'll have her there all day. "I need to talk to you, Harper."

"Don't worry, I have an implant."

"Implant?" I give her a narrowed look, not quite catching her meaning.

"Birth control."

"Oh." The crazy part of me is still keeping the pregnancy plan open as an option. "I'm sorry. I should have checked. I'm clean." I felt that I should tell her that because she knows about the scandal with the actress.

"Me too."

Quickly, I realize she's stalling. This is definitely a conversation we need to have but she knows I wasn't going to talk about that.

"Harper, there's some other stuff I need to talk about. We—"

"No." She shakes her head vigorously and her eyes fill with sadness that grips me. "Every time you say anything that sounds like that, we lose each other."

She's right. This is going years back. But that changes tonight. "Not today. I'm not leaving and if you run from me, I will always chase you. So, let's talk. Okay?"

She presses her lips together and nods with hesitation in her eyes. "Okay…"

"Let's go downstairs and I'll make us some coffee."

"Alright."

We get out and she pulls on a fluffy white robe while I dry off and put on my boxers.

We head downstairs to the kitchen. She sits at the breakfast table, and I switch on the coffee machine.

Within minutes I have two steaming mugs of coffee ready for us. I set them on the table and sit opposite her, leaning onto the wood surface.

She takes a sip of her coffee and watches me over the rim. "What do you want to talk about first?"

"Everything." She is the only person I've ever struggled to talk to when I have a mountain of things on my mind. This is different, though. Different from everything we've ever spoken about.

I drag in a deep breath and decide to start with the most important thing. The beginning. The night things changed. "I shouldn't have rejected you."

"Which time?"

"The first time. The time that counts the most."

"Why did you? I was eighteen."

"I know."

"Was it Josh?" Harper searches my eyes. I'm not surprised she guessed he had something to do with my decision. "Did he say something to you?"

"Yes. He did. The year before he warned me to stay away from you. He caught me watching you."

Her eyes widen and a soft rose color spreads across her cheeks. "Okay I was seventeen then but telling you to stay away from me sounds *way* harsh. Nick was ten years older than me. Josh seemed fine with that. He never even mentioned it, so it can't be our age difference—which is hardly anything anyway."

"He has his reservations about me." I sit straighter and level her a hard stare.

"But he knows you more than anyone."

"I guess that's why."

She thinks for a moment and the curiosity in her eyes intensifies. "What gave him those reservations?"

"High school." I swallow hard. I haven't spoken about Natalia in years. It always gets me when I do, but I will myself to keep going. "He doesn't want me to hurt you, the way I hurt an ex of mine who ended up killing herself."

Harper's skin pales and her hands go so limp I fear she may drop the cup. She sets it back on the table, but her hands are shaking.

"What happened, Asher?"

"Her name was Natalia. We dated for nearly a year. I broke up with her in senior year when we grew apart. I was already bound by my marriage contract so I knew I couldn't have a future with her anyway. Knowing that, my biggest mistake was getting involved with her in the first place." I pause for a beat as my mind goes back to that difficult time. "I guess I wasn't really thinking about that at seventeen. She took our break-up harder than I expected and turned to hardcore drugs. It ruined her life. She killed herself months later when she saw me with someone else."

Harper's hands fly up to her cheeks. "Oh, Asher. Oh my God. I'm so sorry."

"I blamed myself." Guilt stirs deep in my soul like a tumultuous maelstrom waiting to swallow everything that goes near it.

"But that wasn't your fault."

"Maybe not technically, but I still blamed myself." I press my palms to the table, allowing my fingertips to touch the hot coffee cup. "People like Josh blamed me too."

Harper shakes her head and stares at me with sad, worried eyes. "That's incredibly unfair. I'm shocked that Josh would do that."

"Josh thinks of me as a playboy who has no regard for anyone's feelings. That's why he blamed me and the reason he wouldn't want me to get involved with you. That night I rejected you I didn't want to hurt you. But I ended up hurting you anyway."

She presses her lips together and frowns. "The accident wasn't your fault, Asher. It's something uncontrollable that happened to me."

"You could have died."

"I didn't. I'm here."

"One more minute could have saved you from heading into danger."

"We don't know that."

"I wanted you. If I'd kept you with me, you wouldn't have gotten hurt. I let you go because I knew Josh didn't approve of me and I didn't want to cross a line like that with you and end up proving him right."

"I understand how you feel, but you thought you were doing the right thing." She rests her hand on top of mine. "You can't blame yourself for that any more than you can with your ex."

I hang my head for a moment then look back at her. "I won't let that happen again. Not ever. I allowed Josh to stop me from being with you. I tried to stay away from you, but it messed with me."

"Then don't stay away from me." A weak smile glides across her lips. "Josh is my brother, but that doesn't mean I have to do everything he says."

The warmth returns to my heart. "I know. It doesn't mean I have to either. So, I decided not to. Not anymore, because he's wrong. I would never hurt you." And I *am* good enough for her because I'll never stop trying to be better than what I am.

The soft twinkle in her eyes enriches the vibrant green. Deep within them I see the intense desire and longing that reflects my own.

"I want us to be real, Harper. Not fake anymore. I think I only went with that crazy idea because I wanted to be with you. I just didn't know how much."

She grins back at me. "So, you don't want me to be your fake girlfriend anymore?"

"No." I reach out and caress her cheek. "I want you to be my *real* girlfriend. What do you think about that?"

"Yes. I want to. More than anything."

"More than anything?"

"Yes, more than anything."

"Well, I'd like you to be my girl more than *anything*."

"Then you have me." She smiles wider and I lean in to kiss her.

When I move away, she gazes up at me with excitement, but then her smile falters.

"Are we going to tell Josh?" she asks cautiously.

"I want to wait awhile before I tell him. And I think he should hear it from me."

"Are you sure? I am his sister. If I'm dating his best friend he should hear it from me, too."

"I know but I feel that this is something I need to smooth over between him and me first. I want him to trust me."

"Okay. I guess that means we'll still have to be careful around the press?"

"Yes."

She places her hands in her lap and looks more worried. "What about the company? You... still need to get married."

Of course, I knew she'd ask that question. But I don't want to download too much on her. I told her a lot tonight.

"I don't want you to think about that."

"But it's important. Isn't it?" She smirks.

"It is, but I just want to be with you without the worry of the company hanging over our heads. I want normal with you first. Not a contract or an arrangement to get my legacy. I want to do *normal* and make up for the time you could have had with *me* instead of Nick."

My words stun her, and she stares back at me with tear filled eyes. The sight pulls on my soul. "Oh Asher. I would love that."

I reach for her and pull her into my lap. "Then let's do this. We can think about the fine print after."

She touches my cheek, and I touch hers, too. "Are you sure."

"Absolutely. All I want is you."

"I want you too."

"Then don't worry about anything else."

She smiles, looking more like her usual self. "Okay."

I'm glad she looks in awe at the idea, but what she doesn't know is that I've already thought about the things she might not have considered.

Specifically, to do with Josh.

I might have decided to risk my friendship with him, but he *is* her brother.

Harper is a strong-minded woman. Even though she wants to be with me, it will break her heart if she's put in the position where she might have to choose between Josh or me.

Here's me being selfish again and hoping that if that happens, she'll choose me.

If she doesn't—because I won't make her—then I've made my choice.

Which is to take whatever time I can get with her.

Staying with Harper means cutting off all other avenues to finding a wife.

I have six weeks before my father's deadline then I'm locked in for three months.

If Harper and I don't work out, I'll have one big decision to make. *Marry Portia or forget the CFO position in the company.*

I'm not marrying Portia—*or anyone else*—so... I'd choose the latter.

It's not what I want, but while I was away, I realized that I can't see myself with anyone else but Harper.

That is my truth.

"How about we start with you going with me to St. Barts?" I say, knowing she'll be excited to getaway for a while.

She gasps. "What? Where did that come from?"

"I need to be there for a little over two weeks on business. I landed the deal in Hong Kong. I fly out Friday. Come with me?"

"Really?"

"Yeah. You start classes the week after. It's perfect timing."

She laughs. "You've thought about this already."

"In detail."

"I haven't been on a vacation in years."

"Then come with me. Let's get away from here and spend time together. It will be fun." And I'll have her all to myself.

"Yes. A million yesses."

I smile and pull her in for a kiss. "Thank you."

"No. Thank *you.*"

We fall into a deeper kiss, and I think of all the things I want to do to her and with her.

In my heart I know I'll never be able to let her go.

Even if she wants me to.

Chapter
TWENTY-EIGHT

Harper

THE SUN DIPS BELOW THE HORIZON, CASTING A WARM glow over St. Barts' pristine white sand beach and turquoise sea.

Asher and I walk along the beach barefoot, holding hands while we admire the picturesque scenery and listen to the gentle crash of the waves.

Behind us is our beach house. An exotic three-story villa that looks like it was pulled from a travel magazine.

I breathe in the salty sea air, excited to be here with him. I can't believe we get to stay here for two weeks.

Two weeks of us being together. *Alone.* Every time I think about it my body warms and thrills of excitement race through me.

We arrived half an hour ago, dropped our bags off and headed out here to bask in the scenery.

"It's absolutely gorgeous here." I look from Asher to the sparkling sea. "St. Barts is one of the places I've always wanted to visit."

He gives me a worried glance but attempts to mask it with a smile. "You've been here before." His voice is a low rumble.

I look up at him and my breath catches. That's clearly another thing I don't remember.

"Oh God." I shake my head at myself. "When?"

"For your fourteenth birthday. It was a few months before you lost your mom. We went on one of our joint family vacations."

My steps slow and we stop. "That would have been the last vacation I had with my mother."

He nods with a dull look in his eyes. "It was strange. She never looked sick while we were here. Your mom was the life of our group. Every day was an adventure."

"That sounds like her."

"Sounds like you too."

"Yeah."

When people tell me I'm like my mother, I believe them. I just wish I could remember all the years we spent together. It always feels unfair that I can't access those memories given I had so little time with her.

"I think she'd be happy to know we came back." He smiles. "And she'd want us to have fun and do something spontaneous."

I laugh. "Spontaneous? Like what?"

That sexy mischief I love lights up his eyes. "Like this."

Asher suddenly scoops me up and tosses me over his shoulder. I shriek, then I start laughing as he runs toward the sea and keeps going until he's waist deep in the water.

"Asher, you are so crazy." I laugh out loud.

"Looks that way."

"We still have our clothes on."

"Yes, we do. Haven't you ever wanted to do that? Just run into the sea?"

"Yes."

"Well now we've done it together."

With a deep chuckle he ventures further until we're both

immersed in the warm soothing water, then he lets me go so I can swim.

"My clothes are stuck to me."

"Yes, baby. They certainly are."

He looks down at my breasts, which are entirely visible through my white tank top. You can see *everything*. From the shape of my breasts to my soft pink nipples poking through.

We look at each other and start laughing.

I slip my arms around his neck, and we frolic in the sea with our clothes on, as if we don't have a care in the world. A little while later we head back to shore for lunch.

Asher hired a chef to cook us gourmet meals. He explained that he'll come by twice a day to have our food ready. We also have two maids who will clean.

Outside of that we have the house to ourselves, and the beach is private. Meaning we can get up to all sorts of sexy fun.

And we do.

We return to the beach at night and swim naked, then we have sex on the beach right there under the stars.

I feel like I'm in heaven and I don't want to leave.

The next few days are amazing. The only break we have from each other is when Asher has to go off on his business assignments, which will end the following week.

We've been here long enough for me to feel like I live here. It's hard to believe that we'll be heading back to New York in a few days. Back to life.

I love Asher's idea about us being a normal couple without the stipulations of an agreement keeping us together. At the same time, it's hard not to think about the requirement for him to get married to get his position in the company.

I want him to choose me, but I know we have to take baby steps.

We've only been real for the last three weeks. It's not a long time at all, but I'm aware he doesn't have much time. He has a little over four and a half months before he has to make the big choice. I worry that he'll be forced to be with someone else. That would crush me.

Then there's the whole matter of Josh.

Honestly, I'm still processing everything Asher told me about Josh and the past.

Josh has been on my mind a lot. More so than ever because in my last email I felt like I lied to him. Lying by omission is still lying. I talked about everything except the most important thing— Asher and me.

I know Asher did the same thing.

I feel bad that I don't feel bad when I probably should. Josh and I have always been honest with each other. Well… for the most part. There are many things that happened to me that I should have told him yet kept to myself.

This doesn't feel like one of them. Especially given what I know about Josh's warning to Asher. It was wrong of him to blame Asher for his ex's death. I can't begin to imagine Josh being so insensitive. Then again, I know his rules seem to change when it comes to me.

I love he's protective and I know I can always count on him but sometimes he acts more like my father than my brother. I understand why but we've reached the point in my life where I just need him to be my brother.

On Saturday night Asher and I eat dinner on the terrace. We sit at a beautiful candlelit table. Before us is a glorious exotic feast the chef prepared for us of grilled chicken, lobster, and vegetables.

I enjoy the meal and looking at him. He's allowed his hair and his beard to grow out while we've been here. With his sun-kissed skin he looks like a bronzed god.

"I'm going to miss this place like crazy when we head back to New York," I say, piercing my last piece of chicken with my fork.

"Me too. It's always hard when I leave paradise places like this and get back to the hustle and bustle of Wall Street life." Asher smiles.

"I can just imagine. You're always so busy."

"I need to be. We should come back when I don't have business here."

Dare I hope for such a chance? "Really? You'd bring me back here?"

"Of course, I want to come back here with you." His smile melts my heart.

"Then I can't wait." I sound like an excited child, because that's exactly how I feel.

"What were you thinking about earlier when we went to the market?" Asher reaches across the table and takes my hand. "You looked worried."

"I'm okay. I was just thinking about stuff." I saw some newly-weds and it made me think about Asher and me.

"What kind of stuff?"

"Life." That answer sums up *everything*. "Is it bad that I don't want to go back even though I get to finish my last year of college?"

He smirks and takes a sip of his wine. "Definitely not. In fact, you're allowed to feel like that."

I smile back at him. "Thank you."

"You've come a long way. I think it's impressive that you've reached this point. Next year at this time you'll be a graduate."

My heart lifts at the thought and I savor the feeling. That feeling inside me is what has kept me going all this time.

"I'm really hoping to get a placement with the New York Ballet or the New York Strings Orchestra. Daniella thinks I have a good shot." One thing I can trust about Daniella is that she'll always be honest with me. She's not the kind of teacher who sells her students false hope.

"I believe her. You have a good shot."

"I worry about the things I don't remember. I feel like I wasted time when I was with Nick in more ways than one. Life was hard when I was with him."

Asher's expression hardens, but his eyes remain warm. "I wish

I could have done something more about him. It felt like he got off too easy."

"I know but I'm glad he doesn't have a hope in hell of early release. He'll be behind bars for the rest of his life. That's some compensation for me."

Asher nods. "Life will get better, I promise."

"It's already better. You've given me so much." Including himself.

"Doesn't feel like much to me."

"It's everything."

"I'm glad you think so."

"I do. And I'm excited we get to work together." I keep forgetting that part. My training has finished now so Layla will allow me to take charge of all the projects that come in.

"Forgive me in advance if I become the office grump when we get back. Nolan is going to be around more than usual." He frowns and clenches his jaw.

"You really don't like him, do you?"

"I guess that's no secret."

"Not even a little bit. What the hell did he do to you?"

Asher sits back and relaxes his shoulders. "It's not just him. It's the whole Fairchild family."

The only thing he's told me about the Fairchilds is his father's idea for him to marry Portia.

"They were as close to your family as mine was." I always thought it was odd that we never mixed but figured it was because my mother was his mother's best friend and Nigel Fairchild was his father's best friend.

After being around Nigel and Nolan over the last few weeks I've had the impression that they kept up that line between us because they came from old money. My family's money wasn't new, but it wasn't old enough. Now we have no money.

"Nigel and Nolan want to be part of the board at Le Blanche

Global. I don't trust either of them. I never have. Right now, they're pissed that I don't want to marry Portia."

I like hearing him say that, but I wonder whether he would marry her if he had no choice. The one constant I know about Asher is that he's a Le Blanche through and through. He won't allow anyone to stand in the way of his legacy.

"According to my grandfather's terms of inheritance, if I marry her, she'd be entitled to half of everything he left me, including my shares in the company. That would benefit her and her family greatly."

"That's one hell of a deal."

"It's not going to happen. I also found evidence that suggested it was Nolan who paid off my publicist to get dirt on me."

My mouth drops. "Why didn't you tell me it was him? There's no way I would have ever spoken to Nolan if I'd known."

"I was trying to keep the peace. Especially because we both have to work with him. However, it's become obvious that he's trying to push me out of the company, or at least away from the leadership, so he can take my place."

That's even worse. "Can he actually do that?"

"He *is* doing that. My father likes his ideas. Nolan has already infiltrated a deal that I've been working on for years. He would have gotten his dirty hands on the Hong Kong project, too, but the clients specifically asked for me."

"My God. I didn't know all of that was happening."

"Unfortunately, it is. It shouldn't be but Nigel and my father have this bond of friendship that makes my father blind to everything he should see. Because of that both Nigel and Nolan get away with all sorts of shit."

"Now I understand why you wanted me to stay away from Nolan."

"That's one reason." He leans forward and gives me a seductive smile. "The other is I don't like to share my things. I don't like anyone touching what's mine or even looking."

"You sound like a very possessive man," I tease.

"I am when it comes to you."

I stare at him and wonder how in the hell I went through all the years of my life without him.

"I hope that won't be a problem." He searches my eyes then his gaze drops to my breasts.

"No. Not at all."

"Good." He meets my gaze again. "I think I'm ready for dessert now."

"Me too. Do you want the cake or the ice cream first?"

"I was actually hoping to eat you."

My skin flushes and arousal claws through me, making my nerves scatter.

"Me?" I try to bite back a smile but fail.

Asher stands, looking like the god again and guides me to stand. Then he clears a space on the table and sets me on top of it.

"I want you, Harper St. John." He husks. "I want to eat out your pussy until you come and you're aching for more."

My pulse leaps at the rawness in his words and the greedy look in his eyes. "Then take me, Asher Le Blanche."

With a wicked smile Asher slides my skirt and panties down my legs then he takes off my top, leaving me naked on the table.

He picks up a strawberry from the basket of fruit, parts my legs, and places it inside my pussy.

I gasp at the cool sensation which is swiftly replaced with the heat from his mouth when he starts nibbling at the strawberry. He eats it and licks me at the same time. Then he's eating me out and it's glorious.

He grips my hips and feasts on me as if I'm the only meal he'll ever eat for the rest of his life.

It's not long before I'm moaning and coming in his arms, rubbing my pussy against his face as I climax.

Once he's drunk my arousal he stands, leaving me lying on the table, breathless.

"Ready for more?" he asks, undoing his pants.

"Always," I pant.

He takes off his pants and his shirt, showing off his masterpiece body, and my mouth waters. I'll never get enough of looking at his perfectly sculpted body with all those artistic tattoos that enhance his perfection.

Lord, he is beautiful. A fantasy come to life.

My fantasy.

He grabs his fully erect cock and guides it to my entrance then slides into my body, consuming me.

"You're mine, Harper," he husks, his voice thick and coarse with desire. "You are *all* mine."

"You're mine, too." I search his eyes, getting lost in the wealth of desire I see filling them.

"Always."

He speeds up his pumps and pounds into my body as if he wants to brand me from the inside out. Making sure I know I belong to him.

We spend the rest of the night indulging in each other, as well as the remainder of our days in St. Barts.

On Tuesday, as the jet takes off and we head home, I pray that we really do come back. And that when we do, I don't have the worries I have now on my mind.

I wish for happiness with the man I love and the freedom to be with him.

The first few weeks back are hectic. But in a truly exciting way.

I get off to a great start at NYU and Layla assigns me the task of arranging Asher's appearances for an interview and fundraising event with *Finance Magazine*.

I finally feel like I have a balance between everything. And like I have my head screwed on.

When I think back to only months ago when I sat in that jail cell in Massachusetts, I feel like a new person.

Back then everything was full of doom, and I couldn't see my way out. Honestly, I didn't even know if I was going to live to finish college let alone afford college.

Vito and all the money I owed him plagued my mind day and night. But thanks to Asher I got my life back.

And I have him, too. Of everything that I have he's the best part of my new life.

The universe waved her wand in all the right ways and gave me everything I wanted.

On Friday, Layla and I decide to close the week by doing all the high priority admin work that has to be completed before next week.

We plan for a long day so, in typical Layla style, we head to the spa first thing in the morning. She maintains that we'll be less stressed if we enjoy a good back massage and some pampering. I can't argue because she's right.

We get back before lunch and work straight through until five.

"We just have these files left." Layla points to a stack on her desk. "But they could take up another two hours. I have to take some stuff down to the mailroom. Are you good to start without me? It's the same error checking task."

"Sure, I can do that."

"Thanks. The first one is Nolan's company's financial assessment."

I cringe inside on hearing Nolan's name. I've seen him around a few times since we got back from St. Barts. Even though Asher warned him away, Nolan still flirts shamelessly with me as though he doesn't care about the consequences.

"He's supposed to stop by with some more files." Layla rolls her eyes. "If he comes by while I'm away, just take them and don't engage in any conversation. Hopefully he'll leave if he sees you're not in the mood to talk."

We both laugh. Nolan flirts with her, too.

"Don't worry, I've learned how to deal with him."

"Perfect. See you in a bit." She grabs the bag with the mail and heads out.

I sit at her desk and grab Nolan's file. I'm supposed to go over them to see if the checks came back with any errors.

I make a start and become quickly impressed by how squeaky clean and profitable everything looks in the report.

It amazes me that these men make so much money. It's unreal. The type of wealth they have is something I could never conceive of.

Nolan may be a creepy asshole, but he knows how to do his job. The company I'm looking at is a subsidiary of his father's company. Because he's requesting a merger with Le Blanche Global's tech company all his financials have to be checked.

I'm about to sign it off when I notice something.

A name.

Benjamin Deffort.

Why do I know it?

Oh God.... as soon as I think of the question, the answer comes to my mind.

I knew a Benjamin Deffort who worked with Nick back in LA. He was a broker. A shady broker. He used to arrange Nick's back-door drug drop deals before the two of them fell out.

It can't be the same guy on this report. His checks have come back clean.

Maybe it's someone with the same name.

I check out his details and my stomach squeezes when I confirm the address is indeed in L.A.

I decide to look it up on Google Earth and when I see the white brick building near the port, my insides tighten. It's the same guy.

He's passed all the checks but there's *no way* he could.

"See something interesting in my file?" comes Nolan's slithery smooth-talking voice.

I snap my gaze up to him and nearly jump out of my skin when I realize he's practically right next to me.

How the hell did he get so close without me hearing him?

I can't even pretend that I wasn't looking in his file because he knows. He can see it open before me. And he said *my file*.

Quickly, I paste on a smile and think of something to say. "My God, Nolan, you scared me half to death."

"Thought you heard me come in. I did say hello."

I must have been so engrossed in what I was looking at that I totally didn't hear him. "Sorry. I'm a little tired. I've been working on these all day."

I can't let him see the computer screen. If he sees it and knows the true nature of Benjamin Deffort's work—which I'm sure he does—he'll know that I know something's not right with his report.

While holding his gaze I manage to slide my finger across the keyboard and click out of the Google search window.

Thankfully I manage to do it before Nolan comes closer, and the screen shifts back to the Chinese menu Layla was looking at earlier.

He glances down at the screen and smiles. "Hungry?"

"Famished."

"We could grab a bite to eat when you're done." He looks me over, pausing to stare at my breasts before his gaze climbs back up to meet mine.

This guy really doesn't give up. "No. Asher and I have dinner plans."

"You know what?"

"What?"

"I feel that you can do a whole lot better than dear old Asher. I worry about him and that temper of his. You need someone more sophisticated. Someone like me."

What a snake.

Since Asher told me about Nolan it's occurred to me that Nolan might have been trying to break us up. If he did so at this stage, Portia would be Asher's only option.

"I'm very satisfied with my man, thank you very much." I smile back at him.

"Okay. But if ever you become *unsatisfied* you know where to find me."

I don't answer.

His gaze flicks down to the report but because it's just a list of names there's no way he'd know I singled out the one that mattered most.

Unless I outright told him I doubt he'd figure out that I noticed anything wrong anyway, because I'm me. The violin-playing college student who's dating Asher and working for him part time.

"I needed to drop these off. Layla is expecting them." Nolan hands me the manilla envelope he's carrying.

"Thank you." I accept the envelope and place it beside the file.

"See you later." Nolan steps back.

"See you."

He backs away then walks out the door. I release the breath I'm holding and glance back at Benjamin Deffort's name on the file.

I need to tell Asher.

Even if everything is okay, this man worked with Nick. It's guaranteed that something is wrong *somewhere*.

Because Nick was the devil.

Asher

"**B**ENJAMIN DEFFORT IS A FUCKING FRAUD BROKER AND a con man," I say to Hunter with a triumphant smile on my face.

We're in my office. I arrived at the office early just so we could talk.

I point to the listing Harper showed me on Nolan's report and hold up a file I got from Jericho last night after I asked him to check things out.

"No fucking way." Hunter leans forward with his mouth open in shock as he scans the document. "Looks like this guy has worked with Nigel and Nolan for over a decade."

"Twenty years," I clarify. "More importantly, I now have the shit to take that motherfucker down. Jericho confirmed the checks we got from Benjamin Deffort are for another company. He has an elaborate system set up that he accesses when he needs to be verified.

That's why our systems and analysts didn't pick up anything untoward. Jericho was able to bypass all that."

"I don't believe this." Hunter frowns.

"I do, and there's more. Jericho found Benjamin Deffort's name linked to all sorts of cartel and mafia shit. He seems to be their go-to guy when they need to cover up their shady deals."

"How in the hell did Harper recognize this guy's name?"

"Nick." I was as shocked as Hunter when Harper told me, but the instant she mentioned Nick's name I understood.

"Jesus."

This intel feels like another miracle that's fallen right into my lap.

We haven't been able to find anything out since Hunter suggested the possibility of Nolan running a scam. This fits right into the theory and adds a solid layer of proof.

"We have to show Father this." Hunter's brows furrow.

"Yes. I'm just waiting for one more thing from Jericho. With this new discovery he's certain he can show Nolan's involvement in a scam. Once I have that, I can show Father that Nolan was trying to use us." I want extra hardcore evidence when we take this to Father. That way he won't be able to find some excuse to absolve Nigel and Nolan. "We should have that info by tonight."

"Alright, I'll organize an emergency meeting tomorrow morning. We can all meet with Nigel and Nolan and lay the cards on the table."

Finally, things are going the way I want. "Thanks, bro."

"No. Thank you. Your instincts were right."

"They've never failed me."

"That's why I never doubted you. Looks like you're the new Wall Street Shark." He smirks.

I laugh, feeling lighter for the first time in months. "I learned from the best."

Hunter shakes his head. "No, you did this on your own this time, Asher. And it was a close call."

"You can say that again. Father has no choice but to listen now."

"He does. I'm glad we could wrap this up before I went on paternity leave. It makes me feel better."

He's taking six weeks off to be with Luna and the baby.

I would have sworn that the baby would have been here already, but Luna is now overdue. She's going to the hospital next week to be induced.

"Don't worry, now I can truly hold the fort."

"I'm just glad this shit is over."

"Me too."

"I guess you have room to think of *other* things now. Like Harper."

"Yes, like Harper." She was already living in my mind, but now I can truly focus on her.

"You two look happy together."

"We are very happy." I smile, thinking about the last few weeks. It's great to know that you made the right decision when you take a risky leap of faith.

"I guess Alexis is out of the picture then." Hunter already knows the answer to that.

"Yes." Because she's Layla's friend and a nice person I called her and let her down gently.

"Happiness is all I want for you, little brother. You *and* Harper. You'll be surprised to find that when you're happy together nothing else matters."

He's right. I just have to get past my issues with Josh. I ended up writing that email after days of careful planning on what to say. In my response I made sure I touched on everything he spoke about in his email. Especially the stuff he said about the press and me and Harper.

I never confirmed nor denied it. I just said the press will be the press. That left it open for me. Josh doesn't know me the way I know him.

He doesn't know the side of me that can easily manipulate

words or a situation to work in my favor. That's the artful part of me that landed me my spot on the billionaire list before the age of twenty-five. That had nothing to do with my family name.

"I'm going to tell Josh in a few weeks," I say with conviction in my tone. "A month, tops. That should give Harper and I enough time. I know I also need to start thinking about the endgame."

Hunter smiles wider on hearing that. "Yes, you do. The clock is still ticking. Portia will be out of the picture once this scandal hits about her father and brother."

"I know. But Father will still try to find someone for me if things don't work out with Harper."

"How do you feel about that?" Hunter's brows furrow.

"I won't do it."

He sits straighter, realizing what I'm saying. "But that means..."

"Yeah. I know. I don't get my legacy. So, here's hoping things work out between Harper and me."

"Why wouldn't they work, Asher? She adores you."

"That's not what I'm worried about. If shit hits the fan with Josh, she won't go against him. He's her brother. She won't do anything that will ruin her relationship with him."

Hunter bites the inside of his lip as understanding forms in his eyes. "I see. Asher, we fought for our legacy."

"We did but I know if you had to make a choice between getting the company and being with Luna, you would choose her a million times over. And you wouldn't want to marry anyone else."

He nods and I see the extent of his love for his wife gleaming in his eyes. It's all over him. I sense it inside and outside of him.

"I hope you don't have to make that choice. This company was for us. You and me."

"I agree."

He stands. "I've got to get to my meeting. Let's do lunch later."

"Sure thing."

"Well done again. Can't wait for tomorrow."

I give him a proud smile before he leaves.

I stare at the blank gray wall and think about how the tides have shifted in my favor.

Harper.

Good things started happening to me the moment she came back into my life.

While we were in St. Barts all I could think of was what life would be like if she were truly mine.

My wife.

I never thought about having an actual marriage until her.

People say you shouldn't find pleasure in other's misfortune.

I'm fairly certain those sorts of sayings and rules of society never applied to the Fairchilds.

I walk into Le Blanche Global the next morning a happy man with all the aces I'll ever need up my sleeves.

The meeting starts in five minutes. Everyone should be there by now. I decided to arrive right on the mark for effect.

For today's meeting we also invited Luc because we're supposed to involve him in emergencies like these.

With the exception of Hunter and Luc, everyone there will be wondering what this meeting is about.

Father called last night to probe me for answers. It was difficult keeping what I know from him, but I hadn't heard from Jericho at that time.

I'm glad I waited because Jericho was able to find so much more than I was expecting from him.

It fascinates me how one little name can put all the pieces of a puzzle together and enable you to unveil the clear picture of lies and deceit.

I will enjoy being the Grim Reaper today.

I reach the meeting room. Everyone is there just like I imagined and even Layla is on time, ready to take her minutes.

She'll get a real kick out of today's meeting.

I glance at Father talking it up with Nigel in his usual joyous way and I almost feel bad for what I'm about to do. Nigel has been like a brother to my father.

When Luc's father died Father was devastated—he still is. I think he turned to Nigel more to have someone to lean on.

"Oh good, you're here, son," Father says with a dip of his head to acknowledge me. "Are we okay to make a start? As you know, I'll be flying back to Hong Kong later. I have a million things to do before I head out."

"Don't worry, this meeting won't take long, and we're good to go." I smile back at him then glance at Hunter.

I avoid looking Nolan and Nigel in the eye. I may be happy I got them where I want them, and they have no idea, but I'm enraged by what I've found.

I stand next to Hunter and Luc but don't sit.

I set the envelope I'm carrying on the empty space on the table before me and give Hunter a nod. As CEO he is actually going to open the floor.

He clears his throat in his habitual manner and sits forward, resting his elbows on the table. "I've called this meeting because there are some extremely important matters that have been brought to my attention. These are matters that will jeopardize the company and our good name if left unattended."

"What sort of matters?" Father asks, his brows knitting.

"Matters to do with Nigel and Nolan Fairchild."

Both father and son look at each other.

"I can assure you nothing of the sort exists," Nigel scoffs with that stupid fake innocence on his *stupid* face.

"That's where I beg to differ." I imbue my voice with power and resilience.

"What do you mean?"

"I have evidence that you and Nolan have not only been

embezzling money from *us* for months to fund your pump and dump scheme, but you're also on the verge of bankruptcy."

His face drains of all the blood and his eyes widen.

"There must be some mistake," Nolan cuts in, his skin as pale as his father's.

"Oh no, Nolan. There's no mistake. But don't take my word for it. Why don't you all look at the evidence for yourself." I pull the copies of the documents from my envelope and hand them one each.

I give Father the last copy. As he accepts it, he looks at me with a hardness in his eyes I've never seen before. I know it's not directed at me, though.

He takes the paperwork and reads through.

"May I draw your attention to the name Benjamin Deffort. You may want to check the full listing of his criminal activities in the back," I add.

I glance at Layla, who is loving this display of mine just as much as I thought she would.

Father's face is red with the fire of rage when he looks up from the document. I'm sure that's from the part where he saw his best friend stole fifty million dollars from one of our smaller subsidiary companies.

Jericho checked out why we didn't notice the money was missing and found that Nigel had hired someone on the inside to mess with the audit. The police picked up that guy from his desk an hour ago and took him into custody.

We wouldn't have known anything until we did a manual audit, and we only do those at the end of the year.

"Nigel, tell me this isn't true." Father's voice quivers as he stares at his lifelong friend.

"I can explain." The moment Nigel says that I know I've snared him and Nolan. Those three words—*I can explain*—are as good as a confession.

"What is there to explain? You and your son stole from me,

then you both wanted to be on the *board* and worse, you wanted your daughter to marry into my family. For money."

"Preston, I was in trouble with some dangerous people. You wouldn't have helped me with so much money."

"So, you decided to steal it from me."

"You're loving this, aren't you?" Nolan snaps at me as if I'm the one who did something wrong. "You've hated us from day one."

"Yes, I have," I reply, cold and callous. "I never trusted you. I may not have had evidence until now, but I've always known that you were all up to no good."

Jericho found more evidence of them doing shit like this before, to other associates and destroying their companies. So, this isn't a recent thing or some act of desperation.

"You didn't just come up with this. It was your little bitch girlfriend, wasn't it?"

I ball my hand into a fist. "Say that again."

"You heard me." He stands and makes his way over to me. *Big mistake.* "I saw the way she looked when she was checking my files. Then she acted suspicious when I spoke to her. She spotted something and alerted you. Didn't she? That bitch—"

Mistake number two—calling Harper a bitch *twice* to my face.

I land a fist smack in the middle of his face, hitting him so hard he drops backwards to the ground.

I've always wanted to do that.

He gets up, snarling like a feral beast, ready to fight me but Hunter and Luc step in, body checking him into the wall.

They hold him down. There's no way he's going to escape them.

"Layla, please escort the cops in. They're next door," I say.

"Certainly." Layla gets up and rushes away to get the three police officers who arrived earlier and spoke to Hunter.

They enter and relieve Hunter and Luc of Nolan. Nigel doesn't even put up a fight. He goes with them willingly when they read him his rights.

"I'm sorry, Preston," he says to Father as he's ushered away.

I'm glad Father doesn't answer. Finally, he can see Nigel for who he is.

Father turns to face me with a lost look in his eyes. His lips part to speak but no words come out. We all stare at him, seeing he's hurt and disappointed.

"Father, are you okay?" I ask even though the question feels foolish, and the answer is obvious.

"No."

"I'm sorry. I never wanted to be right, but I exposed them because it was the right thing to do."

He walks over to me and rests a hand on my shoulder. "You wouldn't be my son if you didn't know when to do the right thing. I'm sorry I doubted you. I should have known better, but I didn't want to believe it."

"It's okay."

"It's not. My stubbornness could have destroyed everything we worked so hard to build. That will not happen again. I will *never* doubt you again."

He gives me a quick hug and I look at Hunter and Luc watching us.

It's over now. This battle of my life.

I don't have to worry about the Fairchilds anymore.

Now to the next part of my agenda.

Harper.

The moment I step into the house, the sound of violin music wraps around me like a welcoming blanket.

As the harmonious sound captures my mind, I can't help but stop by the door and close my eyes, allowing the melody to wash over me.

I recognize it as one of Franz Schubert's compositions, one of her favorite composers.

Each note is like a whisper filled with emotion vibrating through the air.

This always happens to me when I listen to Harper play. She soothes the inner turmoil in me with her music and her enchanting power.

I stay there for a moment and allow the angst of the day to drain from me before I open my eyes and continue down the hallway, deciding to follow the sound.

I'm home early. After this morning's victory I decided I'd earned a half day.

I left after lunch, knowing Harper would be at home practicing. She spends Fridays working on her project—which is what she's doing now.

I follow the sound of her music to the back hall. There I find her playing her heart out and the walls alive with every note.

I don't interrupt her. I never do. I always hang back and listen.

I like watching her in her element, where she seems to be her strongest. As if she's stepped into another world. One she owns, where everything, including me, is under her control, her spell.

She's facing the glass wall, staring at the woods with intent as she plays. I wonder if she gets inspiration from looking at the scenery. Some people do. I've never been like that.

My mind has always worked in a mathematical way with equations, probabilities and possibilities. I don't know what it's like to be touched by creativity and have the ability to create art. The kind of art that reaches past the mind and speaks to the soul.

I want this always.

When I look at Harper, I see more than just right now. I see forever. It's the only thing that's ever scared me because I have no control over what happens to us. This has to work both ways. For her and for me.

Harper finishes playing and pauses for a moment to gaze outside, then she turns slowly to face me.

A smile spreads across her face, and she sets her violin down on the table then rushes toward me, practically skipping into my waiting arms.

"You're home early," she says through a soft kiss she plants on my lips. "Please tell me nothing bad happened." She pulls out of the kiss, looking worried.

"No. Nothing bad happened. Thanks to you, I no longer have to worry about Nolan and his father."

She smiles brighter. "I'm so happy to hear that."

She has no idea how happy she's made me. "No more talking, especially about them. I need you now, Harper St. John."

"Then take me, Asher Le Blanche." She giggles.

I return to her lips for a needy kiss, desperate and hungry for her. The world fades away into insignificance and I'm sucked into her potent passion.

Fuck, listen to me. But it hasn't just been today that I've been thinking like this.

My world changed several weeks ago on the night of fake kisses that shouldn't have felt real.

I pick her up and carry her to my bedroom, where we strip off our clothes and I make love to her. It's not just sex anymore or fucking. It's love.

I spend the rest of the day and night buried inside her every chance I get.

I'm glad the next day is Saturday because I wouldn't have been able to leave her to go to work. And even if I had, my mind would have been fucked from the lack of sleep.

We sleep in and at lunch we head out to the terrace and eat. After a feast of gourmet sandwiches Olga prepared for us, I place Harper on the table and feed her strawberries. It's my attempt at rec-reating the wild fun we had during our last days in St. Barts.

"Do you just like watching me eat?" Harper laughs.

"I do. And I can imagine you doing *other* things."

"Like what?" The little minx knows full well what I mean but she's playing with me.

"I'd have to show you. But not here."

"Where?"

"I need to take you back to St. Barts as soon as possible."

"I would truly love that." Her eyes fill with awe and excitement.

I hold out a strawberry for her to take but she leans forward and kisses me instead.

"What was that for?" I cup her cheek.

"To thank you for making my life better and taking such great care of me."

I hold her gaze, feeling my heart beating like it never has before, and I know it's time to cross another line and tell her something I've felt for so long. "I love you."

Her eyes fill with tears and her smile radiates with happiness. "I love you, too."

I lean forward to kiss her again but stop when I feel like we're being watched.

I look around to find Josh standing by the doorway.

Harper looks around, too, and sees him, then instantly goes rigid in my arms.

Josh's eyes blaze as though fire burns beneath them and his face is stone. With his hands at his sides, balled into fists, I don't have to ask if he's mad.

"I guess it was true, then," he states, speaking up so his voice carries through the air. "You two *are* seeing each other."

Chapter
THIRTY

Harper

O H MY GOD.
 Of all the things that could happen now. Why *this*?
 Josh looks from Asher to me, then it's like his gaze splits between the two of us and he's looking at us both as if we've committed some heinous crime.

What is he even doing home? Or *here*?

Josh is supposed to be thousands of miles away under the sea in a submarine. And it hasn't been freaking *nine* months yet. He has a good six months left to go.

Asher straightens and I slide off the table, fixing my top.

"Josh," Asher speaks first. "I—"

"Don't. What are you going to say? You can explain? Fuck, there is no explanation. You lied to me." He glares at Asher, seething, then switches his gaze to me. "Both of you."

"We were going to tell you," I speak up, hating the disappointment in his eyes.

"*When?*" He smirks, then he looks back at Asher with disgust. "Let me guess, *friend.* You used my sister as some pretend girlfriend to buy yourself some more time with your old man. She was an easy option because you knew she'd say yes. You know how she's always felt about you."

I'm not surprised he was able to guess the backstory of Asher's plan but he's not entirely right.

"It wasn't like that," Asher replies.

"I was helping him out," I cut in because Josh needs to know the important details before he jumps to conclusions. "Asher paid a debt I owed some dangerous loan sharks Nick got me mixed up with."

Josh glares back at me, now knowing I hid that loan from him before he left.

"I didn't tell you because I didn't want you to worry," I add in a shaky voice.

"So, you chose to do this? What the hell is wrong with you?" He's never spoken to me like that before.

"Josh—" Asher attempts again but Josh holds up his hand.

"Don't talk to me. I can't believe I was so stupid as to believe you wouldn't touch her. My sister is not one of your fucking women."

"You need to listen to me and stop it. I love her."

"The only thing people like *you* love is money and power," Josh snarls. "Harper, get your things. We're leaving."

My God. He's talking to me like I'm a child he's come to collect from a playdate gone wrong.

"I'm not going anywhere, Josh." I shake my head at him, shocked by his request.

"Yes, you are. Get your things now."

"This is ridiculous. You can't come here and demand that I leave. I'm not a child."

"You say that after your disastrous track record with men? Nick almost killed you. You lied about him, too. Every time you told me you were fine, you lied! Now he's behind bars for murder and all

kinds of other shit. Someone needs to take charge of your life before you get yourself killed."

My cheeks burn with hot embarrassment, and I can't argue
because he's right. I did lie about Nick when I shouldn't have but
Asher is not Nick. "I'm safe with Asher. It's not the same thing. You
know that or you wouldn't have left me with him."

"Asher will use you and he won't care how badly he hurts you.
He'll check out when you need him most."

"That's not true," Asher cuts in. "You know me better than that.
I would *never* hurt Harper. I have always been there for her when
she needed me."

"You believe that but you forget that I *do* know you." He shoots
Asher a death glare. From the sharpness in his tone, I know he's re-
ferring to the past. To the girlfriend who died. Had Asher not told
me, I would never have picked up on that. "I know you're a selfish
motherfucker when you need to be. You throw women away when
you get bored and all you think about is yourself. You're not going
to do that to my sister. She's been through enough."

"I told you I'm not going to hurt her." Asher walks up to him.

The moment he gets close enough Josh throws a punch in his
face. And another.

"Stop it, Josh. No!" I scream and rush toward them but Asher
places me behind him so I'm not in the way.

"You fucking asshole. How dare you lie to me?" Josh gets up
into Asher's face. "You have everything and you can have anyone.
Why do you want her?"

"I told you. I *love* her."

"Fuck you." Josh throws another punch and Asher just takes
it, not fighting back. I know he can, but he won't because it's Josh.

"Josh, stop," I cry out again, but he ignores me.

Josh grabs Asher's t-shirt and rips it. I see another punch coming and just about manage to move away from Asher's protecting
arm and slip in between them.

"Stop it, Josh," I cry out louder. "I'll go with you. I'll go. Just let him go."

Going with him is the only thing I can think of that will stop this madness.

"Harper, you don't have to go anywhere." Asher stares at me with pleading eyes, blood pouring from his nose and his face already swollen.

"I'll figure this out," I promise but I know he thinks I've chosen Josh instead of him. I haven't.

Josh releases Asher and backs away. "Come with me now, Harper."

My heart aches as I look at Asher, then I turn and head toward Josh.

I don't look back. I can't. If I do, I'll fall apart.

Josh marches away and I follow, feeling Asher's eyes burning into me, begging me not to go.

What a disaster.

Josh takes me to a hotel on the Upper West Side. When we walk into what's supposed to be a suite, I can tell it's been cheaply done up because of the budget secondhand store décor and the hint of Febreze in the air covering up the moldy smell. Maybe I've been in the Hamptons too long.

We drove here in silence. Not the kind of awkward silence you'd normally experience after a blowup like what happened back at Asher's place, but the kind of silence that's heavy with dark tension, doom and unexpected endings.

It's the sort you experience when you have no idea what's going to happen next.

It's funny: I understand now why Asher suggested we take baby steps. It was because of this. He saw this coming, this situation where I'd be the one stuck in the middle.

I used to think that no one knew Josh as I did. I was wrong. Asher knew this would happen before it did because he knows my brother better than anyone. Even me.

"Your room is the last on the corridor." Josh's stern voice cuts through the thick layer of silence.

"Aren't you even going to tell me how come you're back early?"

"The sub had technical difficulties. We had to return to base to get it repaired. I head out again in four months."

"So, you'll be back in New York?"

"For the moment. I'll sort us out a place to stay by next week."

"*I* already have a place to stay." I steel my spine and level him a hard stare.

"You're not going back to Asher."

"*Yes.* I am."

Josh's face reddens with rage, and he grits his teeth. "Harper, you don't know what's good for you."

"This is ridiculous. You know that. You're just freaking out and not listening to me. Asher is your best friend. How can you behave this way and beat him up?"

A pained look enters his eyes but it's only there for a fleeting moment before it fades. At least my words seemed to have some effect on him.

"Asher gave me a hundred thousand dollars and saved me from whatever the hell might have happened to me."

"Why the fuck didn't you tell me about that loan?"

"Josh, you're getting married. You have sacrificed a lot to take care of me. There comes a time in life when a person needs to figure out stuff for themselves."

"Not if you have people who care about you."

"Yes. Especially then. Especially when the same person is always saving you. And please, I know you didn't have a hundred thousand to give me."

"No, but we would have figured it out. You wouldn't have had to go to him."

I laugh without humor. "You are such a hypocrite. You *know* you would have turned to Asher for help. He would have been the first person you would have thought of because we don't know anyone else with that kind of money."

That shuts him down even though he looks like he wants to argue.

"It doesn't matter. We'll find a way to pay him back, then we're done."

"What do you mean by *done*?"

"You won't see him again. I promised both our parents on their deathbed that I would look after you. So, I will."

"This is not looking after me."

"Yes, it is."

I can't talk to him when he gets like this. He's only hearing what he wants to hear, and his mind is already made up.

"Make yourself comfortable. We're going to be here for a few days. I'm going to get you some clothes."

I don't bother to tell him that I have enough clothes to open my own store back at Asher's.

"I'll grab some food, too," he adds. "What do you feel like eating?"

"I love Asher. I love him. I never told you that I loved Nick. Not once. Everyone, including me, assumed that I loved him. Maybe I did. Maybe I tried to because I could never have who I truly wanted. But I am telling you now that I love Asher and I know he loves me, too. You know you've taken this too far."

"Harper—"

"I'm going back to Asher tomorrow evening." I keep my voice firm, although he stares back at me openly surprised.

I need him to know that I only came with him to reason with him. I'm not going to allow him to take charge of my life the way he said he would. I know I've made mistakes and have landed myself in more trouble than most, but every time I fall, I pick myself up off the ground and keep going, stronger than I was before.

I'm different now. Different from the sister he left behind months ago. I need him to know that. "Things are different for me now. I have a different life and I'm happy with Asher. I'm happy with *him*, Josh. Surely that must count for something. I know you'd want happiness for me."

"Of course I want you to be happy."

"Then you must know you're wrong."

"I was desperate when I left you with Asher. This job opportunity came up and I knew it was going to change everything for me. It already has. That's why I left you with him."

"But if he's the person you're trying to make him out to be now, you wouldn't have done that."

"That was before I knew he was going to make a move on you while I was away. And how convenient for you two to be together while I was in a submarine."

"Maybe that's just how things worked out so we could be together. I've made my choice. I'm going back to him tomorrow evening. I hope we can talk about this properly before then and you can see things from my side and remember that Asher is like a brother to you. Please don't make me choose between the two of you. You have been my rock and such a good brother to me. I love you with all my heart. But I won't let you stop me from being with the man I love."

The ache in my heart worsens when Josh doesn't answer. The knife twists deeper when he turns and walks away, leaving me feeling torn.

It's ten o'clock at night when I hear Josh come in.

I've been lying in the uncomfortable bed in my room which feels no better than the little slab I had in the jail cell in Massachusetts.

I came in here earlier when watching TV could no longer distract me.

I've no phone to call anyone. I left my phone and purse behind at Asher's. And the phone in the suite won't call out unless Josh authorizes it—*I tried.*

All I could get was room service, which I did because I was hungry.

I get up, hoping that Josh and I can talk in a more reasonable manner.

When I open the door I smell food. It's Chinese.

I make my way out to the little kitchenette where I see a small carton of food has been placed on the counter.

There is, however, no Josh.

He's in his room. I can hear him. From past experience I know that means he's retired for the night and doesn't want to be disturbed. If I knock he won't answer, and if I try to force my way in he just won't speak to me.

Josh can be such an asshole at times. I know he stayed away all day to cool off and most likely so we wouldn't have the conversation I want to have, but I wish he would talk to me.

I open the food and see it's one portion of sweet and sour chicken and chow mein, just for me.

If he bought some for himself, he's eating it in his room.

Fine. I'll just eat out here. Maybe I'll catch him if he emerges to go to the bathroom or into the kitchen for water.

But two hours pass without him coming out. I wait and eat, and I wait some more until my eyes are closing.

It's after midnight now and all I hear is silence.

Reluctantly, I head back to bed.

The next morning I wake at eleven. Super late for me.

A quick scan of the suite tells me Josh isn't here. He's gone again and I can't even call him.

My deadline is eight p.m. That's when I'm leaving.

If he's away all day like yesterday, well…

Well, it will break my heart, because I'm leaving anyway.

I shower and change. While I'm drying my hair, I hear the front door open and I feel relieved that Josh is back.

Good, now maybe we can talk.

I quickly put my hair up into a bun and walk out to the lounge, but I stop mid stride when my gaze lands on Vito Morales.

The loan shark from L.A. who Asher paid off and made him promise to never contact me again.

My heart slows, my lungs collapse, my skin shivers.

What the hell is he doing here?

"Miss St. John, we meet again," he booms in a hearty voice, slicking his greasy black hair back.

"Why? Why are we meeting again?" *What the hell is happening?*

"A little bird brought it to my attention that I should have demanded more money from you." He taps his chest. "I was inclined to believe they were absolutely right when they told me whose arm you'd latched on to. *A billionaire.* Asher Le Blanche." He holds up a copy of the *New York Chronicle* which has a picture of Asher and me at the Astoria, taken weeks ago.

Oh my God, this isn't happening.

"You were paid what you were owed. Even the interest."

"But I want more. I was good to you. I gave you time and I'm sure you know that time is money. I need compensation for that."

"No. Get out now before I call the police." I'm trembling and I can't hide it. He can see how terrified I am.

"I don't think so, angel face." He laughs in that deep gravelly tone that sounds like rocks moving around in his throat.

"Neither do I." Nolan steps out from the bathroom, shocking me further. I'm so shocked any air left in my lungs evaporates. "I know you had something to do with Asher's findings on me, so I did a little digging on my own and found your friend here."

Oh. Fuck. Nolan is the fucking bird Vito was talking about. "You asshole."

"Yeah, I am. I figured out that you must have recognized Benjamin Deffort's name. My research reveals that he worked with your ex. Because *you* told Asher to dig deeper, he was able to piece together everything I wanted to hide."

"You're blaming me because you didn't get away with stealing more money from the Le Blanches?" I give him an incredulous glare. "You were bound to get caught one day."

"No, I wouldn't have. I made sure of it. Until you happened and blew in like a fucking wild card. First, you knocked my sister out of the running to marry Asher, then you fucked over my plans and ruined everything. There's no way you're getting away with this."

"You need to get the fuck out of here and leave me alone."

"Ballsy. Oh, so ballsy. The short answer to that is no. I've thought of the perfect way for *you* to fix this situation, so I get the money I need. Vito here is the muscle. What's that saying? *The enemy of my enemy is my friend.*" Nolan laughs. "I'm so glad your brother brought you here. There's no Asher or his entourage of guards or whatever the fuck he has to protect you. You have *nothing* and no one will hear you scream when we take you."

I have to get out of here. I can't allow them to take me.

Blind panic closes my throat, and I spin around to run. But another man steps out from behind me, grabs my arm and holds a gun to my head.

Chapter
THIRTY-ONE

Asher

"Any contact from Josh or Harper?" Olga asks, setting the glass of lemonade down on my desk.

"Nothing." My voice has a faraway sound that I don't recognize. It's as unbecoming of me as my actions.

All I've been able to do since Harper left with Josh is confine myself within the walls of my office at home and wait it out.

I don't know where Josh took Harper because he's not answering his phone, and she left hers here.

I couldn't even try to find them because I wouldn't know where to start. I could enlist some expert like Jericho and have him track her down, but then I'd end up looking like some crazy psycho boyfriend and make things worse for myself.

"Let's hope you'll hear something soon." Olga offers a kind, hopeful smile. "If I know Harper, she'll be just as worried about you as you are for her."

She knows what happened. Even if she didn't, she could have

guessed from the mess my face was left in after I allowed Josh to beat the crap out of me.

"This is a difficult situation."

"I understand but I know she loves you. You have to believe in that."

It's nice of her to say that but I worry my fears have finally come to light. Harper might have chosen to keep the peace because she doesn't want to upset Josh. The lack of contact might be her way of trying to come up with something to tell me.

"I can only hope."

"Is there anything I can do for you before I head out? I'll be away for a few hours."

"No. I'm good."

"Let me know if you hear from Harper."

"Of course."

She dips her head and saunters away, allowing the still silence to reenter the room and taunt me like it did before. It screwed with me right from the moment Harper left. Last night was worse when I went to bed alone.

I couldn't sleep. I watched night turn to day and when I didn't hear from her I got the sinking feeling that things were a lot worse than I imagined.

I decided to distract myself by doing some work that's due next week, but I've hardly been able to focus on that.

I resume going over the contract for the resort in St. Barts.

An hour later I'm still reading page one.

Fuck. What the actual fuck am I going to do? What am I supposed to do?

I shouldn't have allowed Harper to leave. But what if she made her choice then and decided to leave me?

My thoughts are interrupted by a tap on the door. It's already open and when I look up, I expect to see one of the maids.

Instead, I find Josh standing there. I'd almost think we were back to yesterday when I first saw him, except his clothes have changed. It's also later in the day and the bruises from his fists are on my face.

I stare at him, wondering why he's here.

Yesterday changed everything between us and I'm not sure I know him anymore. But if he's here it means he wants to talk. There's only one thing I want to know.

"Where is Harper?"

"She's at a hotel I booked for us." He keeps his gaze fixed on me as if he's waiting for me to strike back and retaliate in vengeance for yesterday.

"Why are you here?" I decide to get to the point. "Come to fight me again?"

"No."

"Really? Because if you do it won't be like yesterday, and you won't win. I wasn't going to hit you in front of Harper. And I allowed you to hit me because I lied to you."

"I know." He breathes out a sigh and walks in, stopping by the desk. I hope like hell he's not going to tell me some bullshit because I won't sit here and listen to it. This whole thing is outrageous.

"She's in love with you," he finally speaks after what feels like an eternity of waiting.

He pulls out the seat in front of my desk and plants himself on it.

"I always knew but she's never had the guts to tell me the way she has now."

I'm ready for another fight but decide to tamp down my rage so I can speak to him in a calm manner. He seems to want to talk it out with me.

"Josh, for years I tried to respect boundaries and keep my distance, but I wish I hadn't. If I had done what I wanted to there's no way in fuck she would have ended up with Nick."

He bows his head for a moment and when he looks back at me, I can see in his eyes that he's acknowledged what I said and the rage from yesterday is gone.

"I always worried that you'd hurt her. You've never been serious with anyone. The only time I saw you try was with Natalia. She
was the longest relationship you ever had."

"You blame me for her death." The words feel worse outside
my head. "I know people did. I know you did, too."

"I didn't blame you."

"You could have fooled me. Years ago, when you warned me
away from Harper, you mentioned Natalia and cursed me out."

"I shouldn't have done that."

"If you didn't blame me, you wouldn't have mentioned her at
all."

He breathes out a ragged sigh. "I mentioned her because I was
being an asshole. I knew how Harper felt about you and I never
wanted you to hurt her. What happened to Natalia was the worst
thing ever. I knew it was a sensitive topic for you, but it was the
only thing that would make you listen to me. So, I thought that reminding you about Natalia would keep you from screwing around
with Harper."

I can't even believe what I'm hearing. "You knew how hard I
took Natalia's death, Josh. I didn't need anyone to blame me because
I blamed myself enough. I was fucking eighteen years old when she
died, and it's haunted me every day since. How the fuck could you
use that against me?"

"I was used to you hooking up with a different girl every week.
Sometimes less than that. I didn't want you to treat my sister like
that. Not when I knew she had real feelings for you. I'm her brother,
Asher. I'm supposed to protect her from guys like you."

"I would never have treated her like that."

"I didn't know that. I *still* don't."

"Yes, you do. You just don't want to accept it." I glare at him.

"Then maybe I just need you to humor me, on account of
the fact I've had to take care of her pretty much from when our
mother died because our father was sick. Then she nearly died in

that accident that took her memories. She survived that only to be with Nick, who nearly killed her. Now I have to trust you with her."

I understand where he's coming from and why he did what he did but it still irritates the hell out of me he fucked with my mind in such a crude, selfish way.

"You already trust me with her. What you need to do is trust that she'll be *okay* with me."

He nods. "You're right. That's the part I need to work on. She chose you and I realized there was nothing I could do. If I continue, she'll shut me out, and I'll deserve it."

I almost smile. Harper chose me. "She *will* be okay with me, Josh. I swear to you."

"I guess I'll just have to take your word for it." He nods again but this time he seems more positive. "I'm sorry about yesterday. For hitting you. I shouldn't have lost my shit like that."

"Like I said, I let you do it because I lied."

"That doesn't make it right. How do we move past this? I said and did a lot of things I shouldn't have, then I took Harper away."

"We just move past it and try to be the guys we used to be." I'm not a man who forgives easily. In fact, I don't at all. People never get second chances with me because I don't believe in them. I'm only extending the olive branch because I don't want to throw away years of friendship and I know it would make things easier on Harper if Josh and I can remain friends.

"Thank you. And thanks for taking care of Harper's loan. I want to pay you back."

"No. That's not something you need to repay."

"It's a lot of money."

"It doesn't matter."

My phone rings on the desk, buzzing like it's going to take on a life of its own. I notice on the home screen that it's an unrecognized number calling me. I hate calls like that. Especially on a Sunday.

Since my number is delisted, I know the call must be legit. "I have to take this."

"Sure."

I answer the call. "Hello."

"Asher Le Blanche," says a deep rusty voice I recognize but can't place.

"Who is this?"

"Vito Morales."

What the fuck? I glance at Josh, who straightens when he catches me looking at him.

"What do you want?" I don't try to hide my annoyance that he called me.

"I have your girl. Picked her up in the hotel room where her brother left her."

All the blood drains from my body and I stand, suddenly feeling lightheaded, like my head will fall off and crack on the floor.

"What the hell are you doing with her? I paid you your money."

"What's going on, Asher?" Josh stands too and glares at me.

I can't answer him. I have to focus on why this motherfucker has Harper.

"Here's what I want. Ten million in cash, not a penny less. You give me that and you get her back in one piece. I'll send over the instructions in a text."

"I'll kill you if you hurt her."

"Listen friend, you're not in a position to be making demands. Do as I say, and she'll be okay." He laughs as if he were telling a hilarious joke. "By the way, Nolan sends his love."

Holy. Fuck.

"Nolan?"

The line goes dead.

Chapter
THIRTY-TWO

Asher

Come to the old shoe factory on the wharf at two and bring the cash.
Ten million dollars in a black case.
Alert the police and your girl is dead.
Any attempt to fuck with us and your girl is dead.
Make sure you come alone. Or else…
Vito.

I stare at the phone in my hand and re-read the message, the ball of nerves in my stomach expanding to the size of a planet.

It's ten minutes to two.

We've just arrived at the wharf and parked on a residential block close to the factory. Josh drove because his car is more inconspicuous than mine.

He kills the engine and we both stare out the windows, scanning the perimeter of the derelict run-down surroundings. I can just imagine what the meeting point must look like if this area looks so bad.

We—Josh and I—ignored the warning in the message to come alone.

At first, I tried to get him to stay but he insisted, then he awakened my senses by pointing out the obvious. That this was a trap that would most likely see both Harper and me dead.

The threat that Harper could still die is the only reason I allowed Josh to come.

The clues of a trap with the end result of all our deaths are *all* there. The most prominent clue being that I know who the kidnappers are—*Vito and Nolan.*

They wouldn't have allowed me to know it's them if they didn't want me to know. And I'm sure they're not just going to allow me to walk away with that knowledge. Especially that fucker Nolan.

I feel like such a fool now for thinking I'd seen the last of him after I exposed him and Nigel.

That was just the beginning. Nolan and Nigel got bailed out the same night they were put in jail. Of course, that was pending trial, but Nolan got working quickly with a grand idea on how he could still get money from me.

Take the person who matters most to me and hold her for ransom. I assume he got Vito involved because he had the resources and know-how to pull off a kidnapping like this.

I glance at my phone again, checking the time. It's five minutes to the hour.

Josh looks at the time, too and his frown deepens.

"I'm gonna go," I tell him, reaching into the back of the car to grab the briefcase with the money.

In all my years I've never carried around this much money. As expected, the bank questioned it but thought nothing when I told them I was heading to a poker tournament in Monaco.

"I feel completely unprepared. I don't like this one bit," Josh scoffs, glancing around worried.

"Neither do I. And we have no plan."

"I'm right behind you. Just wait for my signal, then get yourself and Harper out of danger."

I nod, trying to reassure myself with the knowledge that I have someone with me who has military experience.

While I went to get the cash from the bank, Josh got his guns. There are two colleagues of his around somewhere to back us up but that's it.

I didn't risk calling anyone on my phone or making contact through any other means just in case Nolan or Vito had found a way to listen in. With everything happening so fast and in a short space of time, I never got the chance to check anything out.

All I knew was that they were clearly watching Josh and Harper at the hotel.

The only thing I may have on my side is I don't think they know Josh is with me. At least that's what I'm hoping. If they're watching us now and detect I didn't come alone, I'm fucked.

Dragging in a deep breath, I open the door. Josh grabs my arm and stares at me with pleading eyes.

"Be careful, Asher. Please don't let anything happen to Harper." It must be killing him that this is a situation he can't control.

"I will protect her with my life." I tap his shoulder then summon courage and leave.

I want this over and done with. And I want Harper back in my arms. I don't care what it costs me.

I just want her back.

I walk toward the meeting point, which is in a worse state of abandonment than where Josh and I parked. It's clear the place is used as a dumping ground for waste. I'm sure all sorts of criminal activity takes place here, too.

The fact no one is around at this hour of the day is a dead giveaway. I assume the area is mafia territory or something of that nature.

I glance at my watch. It's two on the dot but there is no one here but me and the stench of piss and shit wafting through the air.

A few agonizing minutes pass before the crunch of heavy boots grabs my attention. I follow the sound and find Nolan and one I assume is Vito walking out from the side of the building. Both carry handguns.

Vito looks exactly how he sounds.

Big and burly with a warthoggish face and a wide mouth that looks like a wide-mouth bass when he smiles at me.

Behind him two guards appear holding Harper, bound and gagged.

Her eyes are red, a sign she's been crying. She's also shaking and looks beyond terrified.

Jesus. I wish I were the one with the gun.

If I had one, I would kill Vito first, then I'd take my time shooting pieces off Nolan's body until he begged me for death. Then I'd torture him a little more before I ended his ass.

Looking at him standing next to Vito seems unreal. I can't believe they found each other. One guy from my world, the other from Harper's.

"Asher Le Blanche, we finally meet in person," Vito booms in a welcoming voice as if we're all gathered here for a family reunion. "I must say you're so much taller in real life than your online pictures make you out to be."

"Cut the fucking shit." I stare him down, trying to keep my temper under control. I hate talking about nonsense at the best of times, let alone in serious situations.

"Not so brave and pumped with power now, are you?" Nolan taunts, glaring at me with malice in his eyes.

"Just give me Harper."

"You think you're some kind of god, don't you, Asher Le Blanche?"

"Don't fucking talk to me. Just give me my girl."

There are two things I can't do right now. The first is listen to the sound of Nolan's mocking voice and the second is to look at Harper. I can't look at her and see her so terrified. It jars me.

Right now, I need to focus and get her out of here.

"Hand over the money." Nolan smiles.

Vito smiles, too, and snaps his fingers to beckon me to come forward.

I move, focusing on putting one foot in front of the other. I keep my head up and back straight, never faltering even for a second.

As I get closer, I think of all the times I've wanted to kick Nolan's ass. I wish I had gotten the chance to do it before the other day. The mere punch I gave him was nothing.

There's a chance that if we'd fought in our younger years it might have stopped our fathers from being as close as they were. It might have stopped this shit happening now.

If only I could go back in time.

When I reach them, Nolan points his gun at me while Vito's smile widens.

"Open the case," Vito orders.

I hold it out and flick it open, revealing the rows of bills stacked neatly together.

"It better all be there."

"Do I look like the kind of man who would play with his girl's life?" I risk glancing at Harper. She looks at me, too and tears stream down her cheeks.

"That's what makes you so good." Nolan pipes up. "Always the boy scout."

Fuck. I can't fucking stand this. *Josh, what are you doing? When are you going to give me the signal? What even is the damn signal?*

He said I'd know it when it happens.

"Close the case," Vito orders.

I close it and he takes it from me.

"Give her to me."

"There's actually been a slight change of plan."

Here we fucking go. This is the trap.

"Surely you didn't think we were going to just allow you to walk away, did you?"

"I hoped you would. I guess you're not." *Come on, Josh.*

"Nope." Vito raises his gun and cocks the hammer. It makes a *click-clack* sound.

Harper mumbles against her gags, pleading for me and crying harder.

"Say goodbye—"

He doesn't get to finish the sentence. A bullet lodges in his head, and he drops to the ground with blood pouring from the wound.

I take that as *the* signal and rush to get Harper but Nolan and the guards are already jumping into action.

"Take her away!" Nolan orders.

One guard tries to drag her away, but a bullet takes him down. And when the other guard tries to grab her, she runs.

Nolan swings a punch at me, connecting with my jaw, but I feel nothing. I unleash and send a round of punches his way which knocks him to the ground. I lunge myself on top of him and continue pummeling his face.

He's still holding the fucking gun. I try to get it away from him but he's gripping it like a vice.

Bullets sound around me, and I realize that the other guard is shooting at Harper.

Fuck. I need to get to her.

I amplify my punches, giving Nolan all I have until his face is a bloody mess and he finally passes out.

I grab the gun from him and look for Harper and the guard. I spot her hiding behind the column across from me and the guard rushing toward her.

I shoot him in the chest and another bullet comes from the left to take him down.

Seeing the way is clear, I run as fast as I can toward Harper. I'm almost with her when the sound of harsh laughter stops me.

I whip around to find Nolan standing between us. And he has Vito's gun.

Shit.

"Say goodbye to your little girlfriend," Nolan shouts, pointing the gun at Harper.

I throw myself at her, pushing her to the ground as he fires the bullet. Another shot rings through the air but the sharp pain that pierces my body steals my senses.

I know I've been hit.

Nolan shot me in the back. Still, I cover Harper.

Everything around me becomes a foggy haze. Harper shuffles from beneath me, covered in blood. My blood.

She's screaming and crying through the gag on her mouth.

Moments later I see Josh's face. He grabs me and starts calling my name, but I look at the girl. The girl I love.

If this is it—my last moment on this earth—then her face is the last thing I want to see.

I look at her, hold the image of those jade-green eyes in my heart and try to tell her that I love her.

But then I see nothing more.

Everything slips away from me.

Including her.

Chapter
THIRTY-THREE

Harper

THE STERILE SCENT OF DISINFECTANT FILLS THE AIR, SHARP and overwhelming.

It's the standard clinical smell most hospitals have.

I've been sitting in the waiting room for so long the scent feels like it's become a part of me.

Five hours.

The clock on the wall confirms I've been waiting here for five agonizing hours, and still there's no news.

Asher has been in surgery all that time. I've been out here going crazy with worry and terror, waiting for the doctors to tell us something. Anything.

Anything besides *bad news*.

I want to scream and tear the walls down. But all I can do is sit here, helpless, waiting for someone to tell me whether I'll ever hold him again.

Josh is sitting next to me. Across from us is Asher's family.

His mother hasn't stopped crying. She has her head on his father's shoulder while he has his arm around her. Hunter and Luc are next to them; both wear the same solemn expressions of grief.

I was the one who called them to tell them what happened. Josh wanted to do it, but I felt they should hear it from me.

After all, I'm the reason Asher is here. He got shot saving me.

He threw himself on top of me and now he's fighting for his life while I can't do anything but wait.

Telling his family that Nolan kidnapped me and shot Asher while he was trying to save me felt like I was trying to take the blame off myself.

I know the truth is the truth and Nolan is fully to blame but deep down I feel like none of this would have happened if I wasn't around.

There would have been no Vito, and Nolan wouldn't have thought to use me in such a way. Heck, Nolan and his father would have gotten away with their scheme if I hadn't meddled. If I hadn't, Asher wouldn't be here.

He'd be fine. He'd be his usual amazing self, living his life. God, maybe he would have chosen Alexis. Regardless, he just wouldn't be hurt. No one can tell me that wouldn't be better.

Now he's undergoing lifesaving surgery.

Asher was shot in the back. Not near his spine, but close to his heart. That's the problem.

When the paramedics got to him, he wasn't breathing and his pulse was extremely weak. I thought I'd lost him.

When they brought him back, I promised I would do anything to keep him alive.

We thought Nolan was dead because Josh shot him in the chest, but the paramedics brought him back, too. I hear he's awake and under police supervision.

What a cruel act of fate that *he*—the fucking villain—woke up, whereas Asher is still fighting for his life.

I try to breathe through the constriction in my chest, but each breath is shallow and hollow. My chest is so tight it feels like it's caving in on itself.

The buzzing of the fluorescent lights and the distant hum of hospital machines taunt me as badly as that smell.

I glance at the door for the millionth time, waiting, hoping, praying for it to open and the surgeon to come back and tell us Asher is fine. That the bullet didn't take him from me.

I should be the one in there. Not him.

I wrap my arms around myself, trying to hold in the pieces of me that are breaking.

If I cry again, I'll fall apart completely, and I can't. Not here when he's in there.

Josh holds me closer, and I look up at him. I know he feels bad, too, especially after he and Asher argued and fought so badly yesterday.

I don't know what happened between them earlier, but they must have figured out a way to work together to save me.

The door opens and I snap my gaze up.

It's the surgeon.

No one is quicker than me to get up. I was already told that Asher's family would be getting details first, but I don't care. He is my family.

"Please tell me he's going to be okay," I blurt, the tears I've been holding back streamline down my cheeks.

The doctor gives me a sympathetic stare, then he looks at everyone else as they gather around him.

"The good news is we were able to extract the bullet," the doctor explains, keeping his tone measured. "But there is some damage to Asher's internal organs. We've done everything we can for the moment. Now we just have to wait and see."

His words grip me to my core and the ground feels like it's being ripped away from beneath my feet.

Wait and see?

No.

That's not good at all.

The last time I heard those words was with Dad. He never came back.

"What can we do?" Hunter steps forward. "There must be something I can do. He's my brother."

"I'm sorry. There's nothing right now. Asher is still in a coma. The next forty-eight hours will be crucial."

Asher's mom breaks down and Preston holds her up. Luc moves to her other side and tries to comfort her.

"He's going to pull through, Auntie. I know he is." Luc's voice is barely audible.

"Can we see him?" Preston asks.

"Yes, but two at a time and just for a few minutes. I understand you're all worried but it's important that Asher has the time he needs to rest and recover without worrying about anyone else. I would advise you all to go home and get some rest after you see him. You can come back first thing in the morning."

I'm not leaving. I can't.

The doctor shows us to Asher's room, and I wait my turn to see him.

His parents go in first, then Hunter and Luc. It feels like eons pass when realistically it's only ten or so minutes.

The moment I see Asher my heart shatters. I gaze at him in the bed attached to so many tubes and machines. He already looks like he's far away from us. His skin is so pale and there's no life in him.

God, this shouldn't have happened to him. It shouldn't. I can't believe that just hours ago he was walking around, healthy and able. Now he has forty-eight hours to pull through.

The thought breaks me, and I fall apart.

Josh takes me back outside where everyone else is waiting. I'm surprised

they waited for us.

"Sweet girl, you need to go home," Preston says.

I shake my head. "I can't leave."

"You must. You've been through a lot, too."

"It's my fault. The least I can do is stay."

"Don't you dare say that. If anyone is to blame, it's me. I failed to see Nolan Fairchild for the monster he is." Sadness swells in his eyes and a tear runs down his cheek. "Please go home and get some rest. If Asher was able to talk, he would say the same thing."

I want to answer him, but my voice is stuck in my throat. More tears come. I can't hold them back.

"Take her home Josh." Hunter steps up. "We can all come back first thing in the morning."

Josh nods and ushers me away.

I'm glad we don't go back to that horrible hotel but head to Asher's place instead—home.

While Josh fills Olga and the other members of staff in on what's happening, I go to Asher's room.

Since we've been together, I've hardly slept in my room. Now I lie in his bed seeking comfort in the scent of his sheets. They smell like him. The whole room does, so it feels like he's here.

I close my eyes and imagine that he is. It's the only thing that soothes me.

When I open my eyes, the sun is spilling through the window, and I realize I fell asleep.

Josh has his hand on my shoulder. He woke me up.

"Hey." There's a rasp in his voice.

"Is there any news?"

"No. It's seven. I was thinking if we leave in half in hour we could beat traffic."

"I'll be ready." I sit up and run my hand through my hair.

"How are you feeling?"

"Just awful."

"I'm sorry. I guess we never got to have that talk you wanted."

"Josh, so help me God, if you say anything—"

"I was wrong," he says quickly. "I was so, so wrong. I met with Asher before we knew Nolan and Vito took you and we talked about you and him. I accepted your decision to be together, but of course I was still worried. Then I saw him push you out of the way to save you, and I knew he would do anything for you." He pauses for a moment and brings his hand to his head. "It shouldn't have taken a bullet for me to believe that. I should have done it just on his word. So, I'm sorry. I shouldn't have taken you away. I only made it easier for Nolan to get to you."

I feel reassured at hearing his words, and I'm glad he accepts us. But all of that only matters if Asher pulls through.

"I understand why you did what you did."

"But I overreacted and was such a jerk to my best friend. I'd be damn proud to see you with him, Harper. He has to pull through because there is no one better for you."

He pulls me into his arms and holds me. There I try to find hope.

It's night again. Everyone has come and gone throughout the day. The doctor has allowed us to spend more time with Asher now.

I'm not sure if that's a good or bad thing, but I'll take what I can get.

I've been sitting by his bedside for close to an hour. There are two more hours to go until visiting time is over.

His family are still around. They've been here all day too. Josh is sorting some stuff out, then he'll be back.

I stare at Asher's still form and attempt a smile just for show. I've been talking to him about everything and anything, hoping he'll answer.

"I remember how mad you got when Jack first brought me home that day. I thought you were an asshole but deep down I loved how protective you were over me." My breath hitches and I swallow hard. "I loved that you took such great care of me even though it seemed like I was annoyed. During those times you felt like mine. I wished you were."

As I remember it all the memories become too much, and my eyes fill with tears. I lay my head on the bed next to Asher's hand and cover his hand with mine.

"Come back to me," I whisper. "Come back to me, please. Please come back to me."

I keep repeating those words as if they're a magical spell, but nothing happens.

I lie there for almost another hour until I feel a soft grasp of my hand on the bed. It's more like a tap than a squeeze. Like a heartbeat.

It takes me a moment to realize it's Asher.

The sudden thought makes me lift my head. I look at him just as his eyes flutter open. He stares back at me, and I wonder if my mind is messing with me.

Maybe I want him to wake up so badly that I'm seeing things.

"*Har...per.*" Asher's voice is so weak there's a quiver in it. But he's talking. He's back. He came back to me.

"Oh God, you're awake," I shriek, unable to contain my excitement and relief. Both overwhelm me to the point where I feel faint.

"Harper. You're here." His voice is a little clearer and his focus sharper.

"I'm here."

"I heard... you."

"Asher, I'm going to get the doctor." Dr. Shape said that it was crucial to notify the medical staff the moment Asher woke up.

"Wait, don't go." He holds my hand tighter and my heart leaps. "You're my wife."

Wife.

That's the dream. Hearing him call me that sends a surge of joyous energy swelling within me. I smile down at him, feeling happiness rise inside my soul like a rolling tidal wave. "We didn't get married."

He gives my hand another squeeze and a weary smile floats across his handsome face. "We... should do something about that."

His words send a thrill of excitement rippling through me, awakening my desire to be with him. "Yes, we should."

I laugh and love him even more.

Asher was released from the hospital three weeks later, but it was another three weeks before he seemed more like himself.

It was a mission to make sure he got the rest he needed because he was eager to get back to his usual daily activities from the first day he came home.

The last few days were the first that things seemed more normal. He went back to work on Monday, doing a few hours before lunch, but today was his first full day.

Tomorrow is Saturday and I'm looking forward to spending the weekend with him.

The time has flown by so quickly. Next week is the first week of November.

So many things have happened in our lives and to those around us. Hunter and Luna had a beautiful baby boy they named Noah, Layla got engaged to her boyfriend, Josh got a temporary apartment where he and Lisa will stay while they're in New York, and Beth actually found a boyfriend. An ice hockey player on Luc's team. Beth has been with him for an entire month—a *long*, long time for her.

The only unpleasant thing we had to deal with was attending court for Nolan's sentencing. Now that asshole is behind bars where he belongs.

As for me, I took a few weeks off college while Asher was recovering but now I'm back on track. Thanks to my music professors I also got a place with the New York Theatre's orchestra for their Christmas and New Year shows. Me and two other students were selected to join them this year.

Things are definitely changing in all the wonderful ways I wanted.

I walk into the house with a smile on my face because I know Asher is home. I've just come back from a long day of classes and all I want is my man.

I find him out on the terrace sorting through some paperwork in the waning sunlight.

Asher smiles when he sees me and my spirits lift. Every day since he woke from his coma has felt like a miracle to me because I know I almost didn't have this.

"There she is." He stands and meets me halfway, pulling me into a warm embrace so he can give me a tender kiss. "I missed you."

"I missed you, too."

He steps back and stares at me. "I have something for you."

I chuckle. "What?"

"Something I've been carrying around for a while."

His smile brightens as he reaches into his back pocket and pulls out a little pink ring box.

My eyes snap wide and I look from him to the box. He pops open the lid, revealing the most beautiful engagement ring I've ever seen in my life and my heart stops.

"Asher..."

He lowers to one knee and takes my hand, staring at me as if I'm the most important thing in his world.

When he first woke from the coma and called me his *wife*, I was so excited. But I was happier he was going to be okay.

Of course, I've thought nonstop about us getting married as the weeks have gone by. I just trusted that he would take the next step when he felt ready.

That time is now and I'm just as swept off my feet as if I were none the wiser.

"I wanted to take you away and propose, then I thought there was no better place than here." A proud smile brightens his face, filling his eyes with the radiance of hope and anticipation. "This is where we shared our first real kiss. And it was here that I first decided to fight for you."

A joyous tear rolls down my cheek. "I drove you crazy here."

He laughs. "You've always driven me crazy. And I don't want you to ever stop. Will you marry me, Harper? Marry me and drive me crazy in love with you forever."

"Yes. Absolutely yes," I squeal.

He slips the ring on my finger and stands to kiss me.

"Thank you," he whispers over my lips. "I love you."

"I love you, too."

He holds me and I relish the moment, allowing everything to sink in.

I always thought I would never get what I wanted, but that's not true. I just had to wait.

Asher Le Blanche is my something good and I can't wait to spend the rest of my life with him.

Finally, the future looks alive, filled with all the dreams I now know I can have.

Because I have him.

Chapter
THIRTY-FOUR

Asher

I T'S OUR WEDDING DAY…

Finally, the day has arrived. And we're in St. Barts again. We're getting married on the beach.

It's the first week of January and I feel like I'm making the greatest start to my year.

I'm in the hotel dressing room getting ready. The ceremony will begin in half an hour.

I stand in front of the full-length mirror. After adjusting the collar of my shirt I stare at my reflection, feeling happier than I've ever felt in my life.

It feels surreal that things worked out for me. And *how* they worked out.

For a start, I'm alive and I'm marrying the girl of my dreams.

I remember feeling doomed several times over the last few years, but nothing was as dark as the day I got shot and thought my life was over.

That day, as I watched Harper's face fade away from my mind, I thought that was it.

When I got my second chance, I decided that nothing was going to stop me from having the life I wanted and doing everything I always dreamed of with her.

It starts today. The instant Harper and I take our vows.

A knock on the door interrupts my thoughts. My father steps in, his suit perfectly pressed, his tie neat. I give him a nod in the mirror, and he steps closer, resting a hand on my shoulder.

"You ready, son?" His voice is steady but there's a softness in his eyes.

I meet his gaze through the mirror. "More than anything." My heart beats a little faster just saying it out loud.

He chuckles, low and deep, as if he's remembering his own wedding day. "I'm proud of you." He pauses and I can already feel the warmth of what he's about to say next surrounding my heart. "You found true love. I can't tell you how much I wanted that for you. It worked out in the end."

"It did."

"You've come a long way. I've already started the process of transferring the CFO title to you. It should be done by the time you get home."

I smile back at him, my heart beating faster with the thrill of finally achieving my goal. "Thanks, Father. I really appreciate that."

"It is the least I can do. You more than deserve it." His grip tightens on my shoulder briefly before he lets go. "I still can't believe all that we've been through. I almost lost you."

"I made it back."

"I know, and I'm grateful. During the time Nigel and Nolan were around I put you through unnecessary stress, which led to everything else. All the bad that could have taken you away from us."

He's not wrong but at least he's seen the error in his ways. "It's okay. They're out of our lives now."

"For good."

Nothing gave me more pleasure than putting Nolan behind bars. Nigel is locked up for his crimes, too and will probably die in prison. The last I checked, Portia had moved to Switzerland and hooked up with an eighty-year-old man with a sizable fortune.

The best part is that I don't have to think about any of them ever again.

Father's smile grows. "Let's get you married, son."

"Let's go."

We both laugh and he ruffles my hair like he used to when I was a kid.

The bright afternoon sunlight casts a golden hue over the guests before me.

I stand between the priest and my best men: Father, Hunter, and Luc. I have one left to join us: he'll take his place after he walks my bride down the aisle.

I look at my guests and smile at them. Everyone is here to witness this magical day.

The violin music begins playing the Wedding March. And then I see her.

Harper appears at the top of the aisle, her hand resting lightly on Josh's arm.

My heart stops and the world slows down.

She looks radiant with her hair flowing down her shoulders in long graceful waves.

Her white sleeveless dress makes her look like she just stepped out of a fairytale and into my life.

Her eyes are fixed on me and for a moment, everything else fades away.

I can't breathe. I don't want to. I just want to watch her, to memorize every detail of this moment. And her.

I think of every adventure we've had and the ones that haven't been written yet.

I'm eager to see what those will look like.

When Harper and Josh reach me, Josh hands her over to me. He gives me an added blessing with a quick hug I appreciate. Then he takes his place next to my groomsmen.

Harper stands before me now, her eyes locked on mine, and I know we're meant to be.

We take our vows, pledging to love each other forever, and she finally becomes mine.

My wife, my girl, my everything.

The goddess of my heart.

EPILOGUE

Harper

Eighteen months later

T HE FINAL NOTE LINGERS IN THE AIR, HANGING BETWEEN the rafters of the theater like a soft, fading echo.

I hold my violin close to my heart, reveling in the accomplishment of finishing another performance. For a heartbeat, everything is still, and then the applause erupts.

People stand, clapping and cheering, the sound touching every corner of the theater.

Tonight's performance of *Sleeping Beauty* was epic. All the dancers on stage made the ballet come to life but down here in the orchestra pit, there was a different sort of energy that transported me out of this world.

My heart swells around me at the continued cheers and when I look at the front row and see Asher's smiling face, I feel his joy deep within me.

There's nothing quite like watching that pride shining in my husband's eyes and the way he looks at me like I'm the star of this entire night.

Asher knows how hard I worked to get this place with the New York City Ballet. I got my acceptance letter just a few months after graduating NYU. It was another dream my heart longed for.

Tonight's show was my first time playing in the group of first violinists.

I switch my gaze from Asher and look at Josh and Lisa, who is now pregnant, and Beth, who married her hockey player a month ago.

They all smile back at me.

I meet Asher backstage fifteen minutes later.

He scoops me up into his arms and spins me around.

"You were amazing, Mrs. Le Blanche." He kisses my forehead, then gives me another kiss on my lips.

"Thank you, Mr. Le Blanche."

"Ready for your secret surprise?" He pulls back and takes both my hands into his.

"I'm ready. You have to tell me what it is though."

"If I did it wouldn't be a secret surprise. You'll just have to wait and see."

"Okay. I'll wait."

"I promise it will be worth it. Consider it an extension of our anniversary."

I laugh. "Oh my gosh. Now I'm even more intrigued."

We went wild for our anniversary. Asher took me to all the amazing places I couldn't remember visiting before and we formed new memories. We spent six weeks traveling around Australia, Mexico, England, Italy and Spain.

In the time that we've been married every day with him has been amazing. I'm sure whatever he has up his sleeve tonight will be just as good.

"I love you."

I grin back at him, never tiring of hearing those words. "I love you, too."

He pulls me in for a kiss that's filled with all sorts of wild promises.

An hour later he has me boarding our private jet for Tahiti.

Our next adventure.

EPILOGUE

Asher

I've just gotten home from a game of pool with Hunter and Luc.

For once, Hunter didn't win.

The babies teamed up against us and wrecked the game. I spent the night chasing after them in their little car.

Noah, Hunter's son, and Paul, Luc's son, are both almost two. I can imagine them in the years to come being as crazy as Hunter and Luc.

Noah likes to take charge and be the mastermind—just like Hunter.

Paul follows along like the dutiful sidekick.

I was the guy who was allergic to the words *marriage* and *babies*. Now I'm lapping it all up.

I find Harper in our bedroom writing in her notebook. She has her violin out so I assume she must have been practicing. She's back at work next week.

We had a crazy amazing time in Tahiti, and like always, it was difficult to leave.

She smiles at me when I walk into the room and rushes toward me.

"You're back."

"Yes, I am. And I want you."

She giggles when I pick her up and carry her over to the bed where I lay her down and feed her hungry kisses.

"I have a surprise for you," she says, kissing the bridge of my nose.

"*You* have a surprise for me?"

"I do." Her eyes brighten.

"What is it?"

"It's time for the next adventure."

I sit up and stare at her, knowing what she means but not quite believing it.

Kids are supposed to be our next adventure.

"What are you saying to me?"

She sits up, too, and slips her arms around my neck. "I'm pregnant."

"Oh my God." My heart pounds and for a second the world tilts. I can't stop the grin spreading across my face. "I'm going to be a father?"

"Yes."

My chest tightens but in the best way, like I'm holding on to something I never want to let go of.

"And I'm having twins," Harper adds with a sheepish grin.

My mouth drops and I start laughing because, of course, nothing about this angel of a woman has ever been ordinary. She laughs, too.

"I think we're in for the adventure of our lives."

"Me too."

"Come here." I reach for her, pulling her closer until she's flush against my chest.

It always felt like my life didn't really begin until I rescued her from that county jail in Massachusetts.

The two of us went on one wild ride where we needed each other to keep going on the journey.

We're still on that journey.

It's the kind that never ends.

It only keeps getting better and better.

ABOUT THE AUTHOR

Faith Summers is the Dark Contemporary Romance pen name of *USA Today* Bestselling Author, Khardine Gray.

Warning !! Expect wild romance stories of the scorching hot variety and deliciously dark romance with the kind of alpha male bad boys best reserved for your fantasies.

Made in the USA
Las Vegas, NV
11 February 2025